IRON CROWNE

IRON CROWNE

CD REISS

Copyright 2019 – Flip City Media

All rights reserved

This is a work of purest fiction.

Any similarities to persons living or dead is not only a coincidence, it says volumes about who you associate with.

CHAPTER 1

OLIVIA

The first time I met Byron Crowne, he was breaking ground on the most disgusting, showy, look-how-big-my-dick-is spec house ever conceived. Ninety thousand square feet. Five pools. Thirty bathrooms. A moat. A literal moat. All of it was perched on the only Bel-Air hilltop with 360-degree views.

He was known throughout Los Angeles as the King of the Spec. He bought premium property, tore down whatever was on it, and immediately petitioned city councils for environmental abatement so he didn't have to do impact studies. He promised jobs, community input, and the actual moon. Then he did what every spec developer did—turned it around to sell at a huge markup.

He was one of the scions of the Crowne Petroleum dynasty, but everyone said it wasn't the money that got him past all the rules. It was his charm and cunning. Which was really about money because charm and cunning weren't free.

I'd never counted on how handsome he was.

Dressed for a demolition site in boots and jeans, Mitch and I approached a group of people looking at plans on the hood of a truck.

"Mr. Crowne," I said over the roar of the yellow bulldozer pushing the detritus of the old house. The structure had been a scrapper from the minute it was listed, but that wasn't the point. The offense came from what Crowne was trying to replace it with.

Byron Crowne looked up, and the second his eyes locked on mine, I slowed my stride. Even in the rugged setting, his shirt was crisp and his tie was centered. He towered over the men he spoke with, commanding and confident, copper-highlighted brown hair flicking in the breeze. He was thirty-five, six-three, and broad-shouldered with green eyes that seemed slightly larger than expected. They gave the illusion of sincerity and trustworthiness, contrasted by the snide curve of his mouth. He was a mixed message. A loophole in a rock-solid contract. The coexistence of lies and truths.

He was terrible. I knew that. But he'd cast a spell over me without saying a word.

"Yes?" he said, glancing at Mitch, who stood behind me. The woman and two men he was speaking to parted like the Sea of Reeds.

"My name is Olivia Monroe," I said. "And I'm from the Environmental Protection Fund."

His eyebrows were full and manly, low over his eyes, and when one arched, the jade in his eyes shot from the shadows. His mouth crooked on the left when he smiled.

"Nice to meet you." He didn't mean it.

"It's come to our attention that the northwest corner of your proposed structure encroaches on the proposed boundary of the Stone Canyon Creek Preserve."

"Creek?" He looked down the hill.

The drought had left a dry ditch where the creek had been, but he didn't comment on that. He didn't need to.

"Stone Canyon Creek is coming under review for wildlife protection by the Board of Supervisors. You can't build on it without impact statements. Your permits are illegal."

"You're a lawyer?"

"Yes, and I—"

"They're making them more attractive every year, aren't they?"

He was trying to disarm me, and it would have worked on anyone else. I'd been brought up to take a compliment separate from inappropriate context.

"We're filing a temporary restraining order on your permits, and we'll get it," I said, chin high. "If you stop construction now, revise the footprint, and file the correct impact reports, you can avoid years in court, and you can still pitch it as bordering the preserve."

"I'll have an expedited review through in a week."

"And I'll stop it."

He laughed to himself and stepped closer to me. "Olivia Monroe. You're related to Rhonda Monroe?"

"She's my mother."

"You have her eyes."

My mother had been a model, so the compliment wasn't lost on me. No. The only thing lost was my senses. They were melting like an ice cube in the July sun, dripping into the well of my pelvis, where he was causing an inexplicable, unwanted arousal.

"And you have the inappropriate sense of entitlement of every man who ever tried to stop me."

"Mister Crowne," Mitch cut in, "we're here to give you notice—"

"Why *are* you here?" he asked, looking at me.

The air between us warmed, expanding until it pressed against my chest.

"To save both of us trouble."

"You're clocking billable hours to protect a creek that doesn't exist anymore. That flavor of trouble is pretty profitable for you."

"I'm not in it for the money, Mr. Crowne." Somehow, I'd been cornered into defending myself when he was the one who should have been offering apologies and promising to rectify his wrongs.

"I'm sure," he said. "File your complaint. We'll find out who should be issuing warnings."

Any response I made would have cemented my position as the underdog. The likely casualty of his dominance. David to his Goliath. I discarded them all and nodded once. "This courtesy won't be repeated."

"'Courtesy is only a thin veneer on the general selfishness.'" He quoted Balzac, looking me up and down.

Even though the sun was hot, my skin felt chilled and exposed. People were looking, and I felt as if he'd stripped me bare with a few words.

"Good day, Mr. Crowne."

"Ms. Monroe."

How could I walk away when I was locked in place by the way his attention made my mouth dry and my panties wet?

A pressure on my elbow pulled me out of the moment. Mitch, letting me know it was time to go. I spun on the heel of my boot and walked back to the car. When I opened the door to get in, I saw Byron Crowne standing in the same spot with the sky as a background, watching me go.

* * *

"'COURTESY IS ONLY a thin veneer on the general selfishness,'" I said. "Does he even know what that means? And the way he questioned whether I was in it for the money. Ugh."

"Guys like him…" Brown coils of hair danced across Emilio's forehead when he shook his head. He kept his blue eyes on the roux, his thin face turned down, tapered fingers handling the wooden spoon the way a conductor handles his baton. "They can't understand that some things aren't about money."

We were in his little one-bedroom bungalow in West Hollywood.

His family had come from Naples two generations before. They spoke Italian in their house in Long Beach and kept up Catholic traditions. Yet they'd realized he was gay from a young age, embraced his boyfriends, and made no bones about loving him. Their only complaint was his lack of children.

"He has more than he can spend," I said. "It's about power. Dominance. Leaving his mark on the entire city."

The idea of it was ugly. Gross. Animalistic. Shameful.

Emilio and I had met eight years before, when I was interning for the City of Los Angeles and his first restaurant had come under environmental scrutiny. He'd been more affable about it than Crowne. After he complied, he invited me in for a private dinner. That was when he discovered my special talent. I could taste what was hidden to most people.

"And what are you in it for?" He scraped the roux into a saucepot.

"The environment," I said.

"You'd do more for the environment if you took the bus to work," he said.

He was right. I cared about the environment, but I fought for it because it was where I'd landed and I was good at it. Passion was optional.

"I recycle."

"Alert the media. We have an activist here."

"Are we arguing? Because I'm hungry enough to take your balls off."

His second restaurant was named after his grandmother, Amelia. It was opening soon. Most nights, he was there, perfecting the menu, and when he wasn't, he cooked things for me to try. I loved it because my "supertasting" was unrelated to anything else in my life.

"You need my balls." He put down the pan and stirred what was in the pot. "Speaking of... how did it go this morning?"

Emilio's DNA had been in a syringe a nurse named Luciana had inserted between my legs earlier that day. He was going to be the biological father of my child. Our agreement was cast in legalese and notarizations. He wasn't interested in fatherhood any more than I was interested in having a partner in parenthood. He'd demanded unclehood, and that was something I could give him.

"Uncomfortable, but…" I twisted two fingers and held them up. "Fingers crossed."

"Fingers crossed he looks like you."

"He?"

"I'm avoiding saying 'it.' Can you grab me the cheese?"

I slid off the barstool and got him the bowl of shredded cheese.

"He thinks he's unstoppable," I said.

"The baby? That's a good sign, no?"

"Crowne. The retrofit in Culver City was a joke, and the Board of Supervisors signed off on it like nothing mattered. So, Byron Crowne's ego is propped up with another win."

"Ah," Emilio said, stirring in the cheese. "It's the winning."

"Yeah. He won because I wasn't on the other side of the table. Again. It's a sickening habit I'm going to break."

"You sure you're not punching above your weight?"

"You really don't like your balls."

"I don't want to see you get hurt."

"You won't."

I'd never lost a case, and I was sure Byron Crowne wouldn't be any different.

But at night, under the covers, I let him win.

In the dim zone between reality and dreams, where no one could see, I let him into a fantasy.

I sat at a bar in a short silk dress I had in my closet. It was navy blue with cap sleeves and hugged my body just enough to confuse business and pleasure. I wore it to official functions with pearls and my red-soled stilettos, letting one dangle off my toes when I crossed my legs.

Fantasy Byron sat on the next stool. Boldly, he put his hand on my knee, uncrossed it, and pushed my legs open. The shoe fell off. I tried to close my legs, but he was strong, and when he forced them open anyway, a shot of pleasure ran through my body. I let him push his hand under my skirt to my soaked panties and press his thumb against my clit as he said, "Courtesy once is courtesy enough."

CHAPTER 2

OLIVIA

"Hold please," my legal assistant, Amara, said into the phone as I approached her desk.

"Good morning, Amara."

"Byron Crowne on four."

My fingers tingled to pick it up. Almost two weeks after our restraining order was filed, his dirt-moving machines were quiet. Our respective teams had motions flying back and forth. He had no reason to call me.

"He wouldn't say what it was about," Amara added. "Should I tell him to call back?"

"No. I'll take it now."

I went into my tiny office and closed the door. My hand hovered over the flashing light for line four. I was still gripping my mail in the other hand as I breathed in confidence and exhaled the worry that he'd disarm me again.

"Stop," I whispered to myself, forcing the first nonsexual thing I could think of into my mind. The beach. The desk blotter. Cheese sauce. Sperm-filled syringes. I hit the button and picked up the receiver.

"Ms. Monroe," he said before I could utter a greeting.

I'd expected his secretary, and his voice stunned me into silence. Without the background noise of the wind and the bulldozer, the sound of his voice was calibrated to cut right into the more guarded parts of me.

"Ms. Monroe?"

"Mr. Crowne," I said with a tone so icy I sounded angry. I wasn't. I was situated exactly between excitement and shock, with enough control to suppress both into clipped syllables.

"I want to meet with you."

Not a question. A honey-dipped statement of desire meant to be immediately satisfied.

"You have lawyers. Talk to them about the motion I just filed. Meeting with opposing counsel is completely inappropriate."

"Eight at the M Hotel bar."

As if he hadn't even heard me. Not that I'd denied him. I needed to lead with something more definite. "Meeting you is inappropriate as I'm currently litigating against you."

Not to mention having to explain why I was out with such a despicable man. But there was no reason to get personal. Not yet.

"And you can leave the lackey at the office." He acted as if I hadn't refused him.

"Mitch Rowland?"

"Whatever his name is." In my mind, I could see him wave away the detail.

In four lines, I'd exasperated him. He hadn't counted on this phone call taking so long. I kind of enjoyed irritating him.

"We have nothing to discuss in a hotel bar, Mr. Crowne."

"Ms. Monroe, you're thirty-two years old. Now might be a good time to get over yourself."

His words snapped me out of the soft, lavender fog he'd led me into where my body tingled and my attention swirled around his voice even as I denied him what he wanted.

"I'll work on that."

I hung up before he could say another word.

That felt good. Really good.

Still standing at my desk, I pulled out the chair to start my day. The intercom beeped.

"Yes, Amara?"

"Mr. Crowne's on three."

"Tell him I'm out."

"We're in the conference room at eight thirty."

"On it."

I gathered my things and left my office before I surrendered to my weakness and picked up Byron Crowne's call.

* * *

"What did he want exactly?" Mitch asked, tapping the eraser side of his pencil on his legal pad. We were early for the meeting, so I'd told him about the call.

"To meet me at a hotel bar."

"You're joking."

"Do I joke?"

"You do not." He balanced the eraser on the yellow pad, slid his fingers down the pencil, and pivoted it at the end, then pressed the point to the paper, slid his fingers down the shaft, pivoted, and started the process over.

"I have no clue what he wanted."

"At a hotel bar?" He tossed the pencil. "He wants to seduce you so he can build that monstrosity."

"I don't think he's that simple."

"You're giving him a lot of credit."

"It's a mistake to underestimate your opponent."

He nodded. That had been his handicap as a litigator. Losing his need to fight before he'd won. I fought to the end, never assuming the opposition was dead until I had their beating heart in my hand.

"I should go with you," Mitch said.

"I didn't say I was going." I checked my watch. "He'll tell me what he wants before it gets that far."

"You need to tell Kimberly. His attorneys. Everyone."

"I will."

"You should meet him. Let him make his move."

Our other lawyers filed in for the morning meeting. The conversation with Mitch was over for now.

Entrapping Crowne wasn't how I wanted to play it. I won by playing fair, and I won with my pride intact. If I met him in a hotel bar, I couldn't guarantee I'd leave without doing something I'd regret the next morning.

ONE LINE, like a pink middle finger in a sea of urine, telling me to fuck off.

I put the piss stick in the garbage and got off the toilet.

Dr. Galang would want a blood test, but it didn't matter. One line was one line. The third time wasn't the charm. It was just the third failure.

I knew what I wanted, what I didn't want, and what I needed.

Babies had always melted my heart, but it wasn't until my younger sister, Isabelle, had her first daughter that my confidence that it would happen for me eventually turned into a sense of urgency. I chalked it up to some biological affliction I should ignore, but when Shane and I had broken up, I couldn't pretend it was just hormones anymore. My boyfriend of three years went off with an older woman, and I didn't care. Not about him, his companionship, or the mere adequacy of his dick. I wasn't disappointed that I wouldn't have to listen to him snore for the rest of my life. I was crushed that I'd have to start over at thirty-one with a shrinking window of fertility.

I didn't need a man to love me, and I didn't want a partner. My mother had done it alone, and I could too. I wanted a baby. Hopefully two. I wanted to love them with everything I had, raise them carefully. Give them tools to build their own lives. I wanted to keep them safe for as long as I could, then stand back to watch who they became.

But. Again. One line.

I knew this didn't make me a failure as a woman. I was feminine and strong. Repeating that truth in my head over and over did nothing to shake the feeling that I was broken. Perfectly healthy by all medical measures but somehow malfunctioning in my most delicate places. I'd cast those places in iron to get through law school, through the assumptions that a woman wasn't the right person to stand up against the powerful, through years of demeaning comments and sexual harassment.

I'd locked my womanhood away. Now nothing gentle or vulnerable could get through.

None of that was true, but it was, because when I tried to cry about it, I couldn't.

CHAPTER 3

OLIVIA

"I'm sorry I'm late," Isabelle said when I saw her in the lobby of the Stock Hotel. "Leo couldn't get Sarah down, and I had to jump in."

"It's not a problem." Wearing my navy silk dress and black stilettos as if I'd dressed for a fantasy that wouldn't come true, we entered the elevator.

"Do I look all right?" She had our father's thick, dark hair and deep-set brown eyes and our mother's long limbs. The plain, black dress and heels were fine, but her hair was falling out of her twist. She had on too much eyeshadow and not enough blush, as if she'd lost her sense of what she should look like when she went out.

"You look great."

"It's nice to get out."

"Mom does sponsorship to get you out of the house once a year."

The doors opened to the rooftop bar of the Stock Hotel, a showcase of colorful cushions, endangered wood, and conversation-appropriate music. I gave our names to the woman with the clipboard for the Mothers Against Gun Violence event.

"How is Leo?" I refused a glass of champagne from a waiter's tray. "Did he take his test yet?"

Her husband was an interior decorator and studying for his architectural licensure test.

"December. He studies all night. I figure I won't get laid again until the night of the test."

"The Monroe beauties!" a man in his sixties said, holding his hand out to us.

"Mr. Jebbet!" Isabelle cried.

"Drake, please." He kissed her cheek. "You're not sixteen anymore."

Drake Jebbet had been a top photographer when our mother was working. He'd taken black-and-white pictures of us that still hung on Mom's walls.

As Isabelle answered questions about her children with delight, I happened to look over her shoulder at the bar.

He was there.

Byron Crowne. Alone in a custom-tailored tuxedo that he wore as if it wasn't formal at all. He was looking at me while he tipped his scotch.

Should I have acted surprised to see him? Or was he surprised to see me?

"Can I get you a drink?" I asked Jebbet and Isabelle.

He held up his Old Fashioned. "I'm good."

"I'm driving," Isabelle replied.

"Back in a bit."

Jebbet offered his arm to Isabelle. "Do you remember Veronica Bash? From Vogue?"

I let him take my sister to have her own good time while I headed for Crowne, keeping my composure despite a banging heart and knees that suddenly had a hard time balancing on my heels.

Deliberate steps. One foot in front of the other. Pearls rolling against my neck, silk swishing against my curves. Every place his eyes touched came awake under the heat of his attention.

"Hello," he said when I got there and leaned my hip against the stool next to him. "Have a seat."

"You always get your way, don't you?"

He smirked, leaning an elbow on the bar. "Not always."

"Really?" I hadn't expected him to ever admit losing.

"For instance, you're still standing."

Without thinking, I slid onto the seat. Did I do it because I didn't want to disappoint him or because I wanted to be right about him getting his way? Could both be true?

"Don't ask me for any specifics about the case," I said, crossing my legs. "I can talk to you in public, but I'm not tanking my career for you."

"Fair enough. What would you like to talk about?"

"What brings you to an event for a cause you don't give a damn about?"

"I could ask you the same question, or I could ask you what you're drinking."

Admitting he didn't give a damn was fair. Implying I didn't was less so. Asking what I wanted to drink in the same sentence was just plain impressive.

"Ginger ale with lime, please."

With barely a gesture, he called for the bartender, who bent across the bar to hear him because Byron Crowne didn't raise his voice or lean over for any man. Only when I got my drink did he sit, and when I arched my foot to give him another inch of room, the heel of my shoe slid off and dangled from my toes.

The fantasy began here, with his hand on my knee, uncrossing my legs and pushing them open so he could get his hand up my skirt to touch panties so wet I was sure they'd soaked through the silk of my dress.

I didn't know if I was fantasizing or playing out a scene that had already started.

"This is an auspicious meeting," he said, laying his right hand on my heel with tenderness, care, and even respect. My heart jumped when he touched me, but my arousal had a life of its own, demanding I stay still for him. "I owe you an explanation in person."

With a gentleness I never would have attributed to Byron Crowne, he took the heel of my shoe in his left hand and, with his right hand on the bridge, pushed my shoe back onto my foot with quiet strength and reverential confidence.

"For what?" I asked, both shoes on and his hand still resting on my foot.

His gaze met mine. Coupled with his strong hand lingering on my stockings, the entire fantasy played itself out with a new beginning.

I added to the question to define the reality before me. "What do you owe me an explanation for?"

His hands. He had to move them off my ankle before I exploded, but I didn't want him to. Ever. And his eyes. He had to look away—but when he did, I would be utterly unmoored.

"I owe you an explanation for what I'm going to have to do if you pursue this." He leaned back, sliding his hands away, and reality reentered my consciousness like the curling smoke of an incoming cloud. "When you came to the job site to challenge me, I was glad. I don't like things to be too easy. I work best in a fight. But see, the problem for the enemy—and I hate to think of such a beautiful creature as an enemy—the problem is…I always win. And not just win."

A battlefield burned in his eyes. It was terrifying.

He was terrible. Everyone knew it. People knew who he was. I could be seen with him. He'd touched me. They'd seen, and they'd think I was weak and awestruck. They'd tsk and shake their heads.

He'd drawn me in like a fish on a hook.

Finally, he looked away to arc his fingers over his short glass of amber whiskey. The spell moved from his eyes to the articulation of his strong hands. I wanted to tear myself away so I'd know if anyone saw us. I could do damage control, except I couldn't control myself. His hands were works of art as the fingers pivoted on the glass and lifted it to his face.

"I will ruin you, Ms. Monroe." He sipped, green eyes watching me over the rim, then placed the drink back on the bar in a languid arch. "I don't want to, so since you gave me the courtesy of a warning, I'll do the same for you."

"I thought courtesy was a thin veneer on selfishness."

"It is. If you don't want to be destroyed, you'll remove the obstacles to me developing the Bel-Air property."

The fantasy I'd built snapped like a twig underfoot. With each word he spoke, a sapling of rage grew in its place. "Is that a threat?"

"The stock answer is that it's a fact. Maybe it's that. But it's more. It's a warning and also..." He took a chest-expanding breath with a look of regret and even powerlessness over who he was. It was the most tangible expression of his humanity I'd seen, and though my fury was still growing, I let him finish out of respect for it. "I have to offer a profound apology now, when I'm inclined to make it and you're most likely to hear it."

I uncrossed my legs and pressed my knees together, leaning toward him so I didn't have to raise my voice. "You've lost your mind if you think this will be that easy."

"That's the point."

"That you've lost your mind?"

"That I don't like it easy." He locked eyes with me again, but his gaze went deeper. He didn't look *at* me but *into* me. "I understand now. You need the fight too."

I did. And it needed to be seen so there were no misunderstandings.

"Let me warn you," I said before taking a sip of my ginger ale. It chilled the heat in my chest. "As a courtesy. The EPF had a shit record before I came on. But now? Every arrogant asshole developer like you asks for permission, not forgiveness, because you won't get it. They all thought they could buy a workaround, and every single one of them was forced, by me, to comply with the law. Sheikhs and Chinese businessmen. Corporations who tried to buy us off. And you? You'll comply. Because I'm going to make your life a hell of lawsuits and neighborhood pushback. You're going to be labeled a criminal and a failure. When I'm done with you, you'll need my permission to dig a hole in your own backyard."

The winner walked away first, leaving their opponent staring at an empty chair, but his smirk held me there because it was the smile of a man who'd won. If I walked on that note, I'd be running away.

"So, you're in," he said. "Despite what I just told you."

"Yes."

"I already knew you were worthy." He tipped back the last of his drink before placing his glass exactly in the wet ring it had left on the bar. "You're tough. Persistent. Smart. A little cunning."

"And you know this how?"

"I did my homework. Have you done yours?"

He pushed his glass across the bar, tracing a track of condensation, before leaving me there, staring at his empty barstool like a loser.

CHAPTER 4

OLIVIA

Linda Lee wasn't a bullshitter, but she had a gift for coming at people sideways, fooling them with direct talk and short sentences that gave them the impression that she didn't have underlying motivations. She made and maintained relationships with people who knew people who knew people in an asymmetrical web of connections she kept in her head.

This talent made her an excellent investigator. She worked mostly for journalists, cross-checking assumption against fact. I'd met her four years before, when she'd asked for a sit-down about the Gold Line extension impact statements, and I wound up telling her about the dynamics of my family. She countered with her own.

We sat on a planter ledge outside my office building. We'd ordered from different food trucks. I had a Southern fried chicken salad, and she had a sausage on a stick. Her glasses were oversized black frames around prescription lenses that reduced the disarming sharpness of her brown eyes. Straight, black hair cascaded over each shoulder. She wore no makeup except carefully applied bright-red lipstick.

"One hundred twenty-two properties in LA County alone," Linda said, flipping through the notebook she'd laid between us. "No liens. No safety issues. Every complaint rectified on time. No debt he can't manage. I mean, the Crownes, right?" She bit the tip of her sausage while holding a napkin against her chest to protect her black sweater.

"Right. I know all that."

We spoke softly in the shade of an old ficus. The street was crowded with tourists and strangers, but you never knew who was around.

"Engaged once. Samantha Bettencourt of the Grosse Pointe Bettencourts. The party was on the family yacht. It was insane. Justin Beckett and Brad Sinclair had a fistfight"

"That party was five years ago."

"Six." She blew on the sausage. "She died fourteen months after the announcement."

"How?"

"Broken light in the pool. Electrocuted."

"Yikes."

"He hasn't dated anyone since she died. Every socialite and actress in LA is trying to pin him down. But nothing. He's seen alone or brings his sister to events."

"He's been celibate for five years and change?"

"Didn't say that." In three bites, she exposed half the stick, chewing with her hand over her mouth. I waited until she'd swallowed and touched the corners of her lips with her napkin. "He's got a thing for normals."

"Normals?" I asked. She did have a way with words.

"Women with regular jobs. Regular families. Not like him. Not even like you."

"Like me?"

"You're half in, half out. No?"

She was right. Because of my mother, I knew plenty of people in what could have been called high society, but I didn't really travel in those circles. Even in my private schools, the kids with Crowne-sized wealth usually hadn't socialized with kids without it.

So, I wasn't his type. Good. That was actually helpful. Now maybe my desire would obey the scolding of my common sense.

"Where does he meet the normals?"

"He has a little house in Silver Lake. On Edgecliff Street. He goes to bars on the East Side... uses his real name but doesn't say anything about his money. He spends a few weeks fucking them, and they go their separate ways. I found one woman in Frogtown. Waitress. Said it was the best week of her life but had no idea he wasn't just a handsome stranger who didn't want a commitment."

My brain lit up with an image. I was on my hands and knees, and he was behind me, shoving his cock in while yanking back my hair, growling, *You want it like this.*

I had to take a breath and look away as a bolt of liquid heat shot from my spine to the throb between my legs. I stabbed my salad and ate it, chewing slowly.

"So," I said after swallowing, "these women are the only thing he doesn't completely own or completely destroy."

My body wanted me to be one of those women. It wanted his fist closing around my hair and his hands moving it like a doll's. It wanted him to helm the best week of its life, then walk away undestroyed and unowned.

Linda slid the last of her sausage off the stick with her fingers and popped it in her mouth.

"Point is," she said as she pinched her napkin, "he's completely undistracted from work. He's got nothing else to do but fight you."

"And he loves a fight."

"Yes."

"Is that all you have?"

"For now." She closed her notebook. "Am I off the clock?"

"Yes. How are you feeling?"

"Only a tiny bit stressed that there might be sausage on my face."

I looked at her closely, already aware there wasn't a speck of food on her cheek or lips, but she needed to know I wasn't being casual about it. "You're clean."

Until her shoulders relaxed and her chest expanded with a full, deep breath, I wouldn't have noticed how tense she was. Her OCD might never be under control completely, but she managed her outward appearance beautifully.

"Thank you." She took off her glasses. "So… how bad do you want him?"

"Who?" I knew exactly who she meant.

"When I started talking about who Byron Crowne took home, you went blank."

I'd sent her to find out about his personal life, so she'd expected me to press for details and ask questions. Instead, I'd let my mind wander to places and pass locked gates I rarely opened in public. "I was paying attention."

I'd decided to deflect, but Linda Lee wasn't the kind of conversationalist who got slapped off course. "You looked like you were watching a porno in your head."

Facts were facts.

"He's a nice-looking guy, and it's been a while." I snapped the top of my salad closed. "Which means nothing. I don't need the complications."

"Okay." She said it as if she wanted to believe me.

She should have because I wasn't lying. I was getting pregnant, and I didn't need to start a thing with a guy who'd want to be the father. Especially not a guy who saw me as a conquest.

You're tough. Persistent. Smart. A little cunning.

"How's the babymaking going?" she asked, fishing a bottle of sanitizer out of her bag.

"Nothing. Not this month."

"Ah, sorry about that."

"Linda," I said.

She squeezed a lump of gel into her palm. "Yeah?"

"Byron said he'd done his homework on me. If you did research on me, what would you find?"

She rubbed her hands together. "I don't do opposition research on friends."

"Is that a policy?"

"It's the first time anyone's asked. I don't want it to be weird."

It was weird. It was weird to ask her, and it was weird to care what the subject of one of the many lawsuits I was heading knew about me.

"Yeah. Never mind."

The EPF had already background-checked me. I was clean. What else mattered?

I already knew you were worthy.

Byron hadn't said that as if my worthiness was based in my lawfulness. He'd sounded as if he'd noticed something no one else had. Something that made me less than clean yet more appealing. He could have been acting that way to scare me, or maybe dirtiness was what he enjoyed in an opponent.

Maybe that was something Linda wouldn't understand. Maybe it was something only a man like Byron could see.

Standing on Wilshire Boulevard in a lunchtime crowd, waiting for Linda to touch everything in her bag to make sure it was there, I remembered his eyes seeing inside me, his gaze a physical presence. I heard his voice in my head.

I see you.

You are worthy.

I will destroy you.

My little two-bedroom house at the base of the Runyon Canyon was squeezed between apartment buildings, which made it cheap to buy and hard to sell. But I hadn't bought it just to sell it. It was central to everything in the city, close to my mother, and it was all mine.

Once the sun went down and the air cooled off, Runyon Canyon was the perfect place for a jog. The iron-gated trailhead with its blond stone pillars was only two blocks from my house. The hills were challenging but not brutal, and the streets were wide enough to avoid getting sideswiped around blind turns. The slivers of scenery were like little rewards for a jog well taken.

I was the only jogger heading up toward Fire Road when a man blew past me on the left. With my earbuds in, I couldn't hear the crickets or owls, and if there had been other runners that night, I wouldn't have heard them coming up behind me. So, he took me by surprise.

Using his speed as a benchmark, I picked up the pace, closing the gap between us. He was fast. I was faster, and if I wasn't, I would be before we hit Clouds Rest.

He was fit and had longer legs. His wet T-shirt stuck to the bulging muscles of his back as I came within reach. As if he could feel me behind him, he pumped faster. I chased, sweat pouring off me, using the energy I needed to complete the run.

The dirt trail narrowed, twisting up the mountain. He was too far ahead to catch at this pace.

I sprinted up the hill. The music in my earbuds couldn't get past the whoosh of breath in my ears and the pounding of my heart.

I had him. I could practically smell his sweat and adrenaline. He might keep running, but if I pushed, I'd beat him to the bench at Clouds Rest.

"On your left," I gasped when we were almost shoulder to shoulder, and I passed on the last few steps.

I didn't have to look at him as we reached the crest of the hill at the same time, because it didn't matter who he was. It only mattered that I'd caught him.

With his hand on the single lamppost, he looked at me and he barked out a laugh.

After that, it mattered who he was, and the photo finish became wholly inadequate.

With nothing left, I stopped at the top, pulling out my earbuds before leaning on the back of a wood plank bench with my hands on my knees, gulping breaths like a drowning woman.

Byron's tightly muscled legs were all I could see from my crouch. He was standing upright with his foot on a stone as if he'd been taking a moonlight stroll.

"Fuck you," I gasped.

"Is that an invitation?"

God damn his perfect body. He wasn't even out of breath.

Well, then I wasn't either.

I stood up and tried to get control of my body. Though I could slow the hard, fast gulps my lungs needed, my chest still heaved with the effort. The movement wasn't lost on him. His gaze went to my breasts for a moment before finding my eyes again. Obviously he had his own control issues. Noted.

"Are you all right?" he asked.

"What are you doing here?"

"Having a run."

"You live in Holmby Hills."

He shrugged. "I live lots of places," he said, indicating the stretch of the Los Angeles Basin beneath us. "I like the view here."

The sun had just set, leaving an orange glow at the horizon. A net of crisscrossing lines of light sectioned off the dark city. He stood in front of the bench with his hands on his hips. With no guardrail between the drop and the view, he looked like a sovereign lord surveying his kingdom. There was no question of his dominance over the city. No doubt in his stance that if he could see something, it could be his. He wasn't defiant or insolent. His power was as much a fact as the radiance of the setting sun.

I loathed his assumptions. I hated his unquestioning expectations. I despised the authority he carried. Was it his confidence that turned me on? Or the fact that I couldn't stand him for it?

"I'll see you at the injunction hearing," I said, turning to go down the hill.

"Where are you going?"

"To finish my run."

"Live a little, Olivia." He crossed his arms and regarded my heaving chest once more. The moon and light pollution made the appreciation in his eyes just visible. "You beat me. You deserve the breather."

My bearing changed. I went from "jog down the hill" to "hear him out" with his simple false acquiescence. "It was a tie."

"Did you know they curved the 101 Freeway around Hollywood Presbyterian? They changed the whole route to avoid a church."

I stood next to him so I wouldn't have to look at him. At five-ten, I usually felt tall enough to go toe-to-toe with any man, but Byron was six-three if he was an inch and I felt overwhelmed by the extra height.

"And they bulldozed right through neighborhoods. Which cut them off and demolished millions in wealth equity."

"Tell me something," he said. "What made the daughter of a model care about the environment so much?"

"Children of models can't care about the world?"

"To be honest? They can, but it's unusual when they could be modeling themselves."

I shouldn't have been talking to him, much less allowing compliments, but there was no harm in a personal fact. Knowing my motivations changed nothing about the case.

I stood next to him with my arms crossed, looking over the city. "You building that monstrosity in Bel-Air? I know what that's about."

"Really?"

"You want to make a mark on the world. Do something that no one's done and slap your name on it. It'll be there long after you're dead. It'll be the biggest, most expensive single-family house in the city for a long time."

"True." He agreed as if he hadn't considered his legacy before.

"I want to make my mark by taking on guys like you. Every inch of land I save from you has my name on it."

"And you get a charge out of taking my name off it." His eyes drifted to my shoulder.

"You think it's about you?"

Just then, I felt a tickle on my arm. It wasn't the breeze or a leaf blowing by. When I looked down to confirm, I saw huge spider legs and froze. I could identify a black widow, but this one was striped, brown, massive. My fear centers lit up, thoughtlessly releasing adrenaline that demanded I fight or run, and in the moment of decision between the two, I went as dead as a possum.

Byron took the entire spider in his hand and casually threw it over the bluff.

"Oh my God," I gasped. "Thank you."

"You all right?" He laid his palm on the place where the spider had been.

"Yeah. It was probably nothing, but—"

"It was a recluse."

"It was huge."

He laughed. "No, it wasn't."

His thumb stroked the skin of my arm. He shouldn't have been doing that, but my body wasn't interested in the shoulds and shouldn'ts of his touch.

"It just surprised me."

"Some things are surprising to me too." Pensively, he ran his fingertips over my bare arm.

All I had to do was pull away, but his fingers were magnets pulling all my arousal to the trails of his skin on mine.

"I can't imagine you surprised by anything," I said.

"I bet you have some surprises in you."

His fingers drifted across my forearm, awakening new nerve endings. My eyelids fluttered involuntarily.

He smirked, dropping his hand. With the connection broken, I snapped out of the trance and into shame for allowing him to touch me in the first place. My face got hot, and my chest thrummed with anxiety.

"We shouldn't be talking," I said.

"We're in public," he said, indicating the breadth of the city and its millions of inhabitants with one sweep of his arm. "We're not talking specifics in your case against me."

The particularities of the moment were irrelevant.

"I'm not going to be seduced," I snapped, ready to leave it there until his smug look destroyed my common sense. "I'm not some Frogtown waitress."

He seemed unruffled by what I knew even as I wanted to swallow back the words.

"No," he said. "You're not. I bet you come like one though." In my shock, he had a moment to lean toward me, into the light where his eyes blazed green and his jaw looked sharp enough to cut deep. "I bet I can make you beg for it like a starving animal."

My mouth opened to respond, and the words on the tip of my tongue were, "Prove it."

No. I couldn't. With his smirk and his arched brow, he was too powerful a temptation. I pressed the tip of my tongue to the back of my teeth and held the words there, squashing them between my pride and my professionalism. Nothing could come out. Neither a lie of denial nor an invitation I'd regret.

The words were held back, but the force of the rejection was too strong for my will. It yanked me toward him as he thrust forward, smashing us together in a kiss that pushed and pulled at the same time. Fresh sweat and hot breaths, tongues that stabbed and twisted, hands clutching hair and fistfuls of damp cotton. He gripped my hip and hair, and I dug my fingers into the hard muscles of his arm as if I wanted to rip off his skin. We tore each other apart with that kiss, mindlessly surrendering to an embrace that shattered boundaries and drove a stake through the heart of caution.

He shoved me away, leaving me gasping for that moment again.

"I was right about you," he said as if he'd bet I'd be compliant and was deciding on whether or not to take the prize.

I couldn't sign off on that, but with his taste on my tongue, I couldn't deny it any more than I could resist him.

There was only one thing to do.

I turned tail and ran down the hill, yearning for him to follow and hoping he didn't. I didn't slow down to a jog until I realized he wasn't behind me.

When I closed my front door, I leaned against it as if blocking a savage army on the other side. But it was too late. His taste was still on my tongue, and the feel of his body was still in my grip. I'd let the savage in with me.

I stripped down, exposing still-hard nipples and leaving soaked panties on the floor.

Everything about that encounter had been inappropriate, especially the swollen throb of my clit and the dense lubrication of the tender flesh between my legs. I set the shower to cold and got in, but I didn't make it two minutes with the washcloth over my breasts. I pinched a nipple through the rough fabric.

...beg for it like a starving animal.

As I pushed the washcloth inside my thighs and up to my pussy, I tried to imagine another man. An actor. A model. The guy who'd fixed my sink last week. But the harder I rubbed, the more they all had Byron's face, and when they spoke—

...beg for it.

—they sounded like him as they hurt me and pleasured me with the ferocity of our kiss, stabbing me with their cocks as I begged for it harder. I surrendered to the force of my orgasm, dropping to my knees with Byron's face and voice in my head.

Breathless, I got a fresh washcloth and washed the fantasy off my body, convincing myself I didn't want what Byron seemed to offer. I was a thirty-two-year-old woman. I'd had good sex my whole adult life without any of that nonsense. Shane and I had been together three years, and it was fine. Greg had been a little more experimental during the two years we dated. Also fine. More of that would be okay, and I didn't need to lust after a man I despised to get it.

I couldn't run into him again. We couldn't exchange words, personal or otherwise. The state bar had a grievance committee that existed to disbar lawyers like me for bullshit like this.

Byron Crowne was an arrogant asshole. A manipulative creep with a mile-wide sense of entitlement. He was doing this on purpose.

I wouldn't give him the satisfaction of a single flirtation, much less another kiss. It had taken him fifteen minutes to overstep in a dozen ways and for me to invite him to do more.

He was an awful human. Period. I was better than this.

That was his appeal and the reason to resist him.

Somehow, I had to win this lawsuit without having sex with Byron Crowne.

CHAPTER 5

OLIVIA

If Dr. Galang had a desk, I'd never spoken to him across it. He met with patients in a small room with a single window. It had two comfortable chairs and a couch with matching damask upholstery, warm lighting from a tall lamp in the corner, landscape paintings, and plants everywhere. A table under the window had rows of pictures of him, his wife, and his four children. The room smelled of lavender and happiness.

He was from Manila originally, but his accent had been rubbed away from decades in Cambridge and Los Angeles. In spite of his bald head and reading glasses, his age was impossible to assume, but I had to guess he was in his fifties or sixties. Old enough to be the best.

He placed my file on the wooden table but didn't open it. "So, no luck this month."

"No. I've been doing everything. Eating right. Exercising."

My legs were crossed, and my pump hung from the foot that dangled.

Bad habit.

I pushed the shoe back on, knowing I'd wiggle out of it when I wasn't paying attention.

"How are the fertility drugs affecting you?" he asked.

"They're fine."

"Mood swings? Cramps?"

"Nothing. I mean, I'm always moody."

He chuckled. "This is the point where hope starts losing to frustration. It's time for me to ask if you want to continue this journey."

"I do."

"Good. Good. Do you want to talk next steps?"

"Yes."

"So." He laid his hands on his knees. "It's too soon to say the IUI isn't working. I think two more rounds before IVF is the next option. You weren't keen on it when we spoke last."

At the beginning, the idea of extracting an egg, mixing it with Emilio's sperm in a petri dish, and implanting it seemed a bridge too far, but then I'd been full of hope that the simpler techniques would work. Before I'd invested so heavily in failing completely.

"Is it me?" I asked. "Are my tubes bad? Is it my eggs?"

"Your eggs are fine. And it's too soon to start treating infertility. What I have seen..." He held up his finger. "As someone who's been doing this a long time, sometimes the potential mother's mindset is crucial."

"My mindset?"

"Ms. Monroe," he said with a voice of serious, personal compassion, "what do you do for fun?"

"Fun? Like what?"

"Do you have friends you see? A romantic partner in your life?"

"I have friends."

"Is there any chance you could maybe take a vacation with them? Relax for a couple of weeks?"

I hadn't had a vacation in two years. I'd taken time off from work but usually spent it catching up on papers and amicus briefs I didn't otherwise have time to go over. I considered it quite relaxing, but I knew Dr. Galang had something else in mind.

"I have a lot going on," I said.

"In my experience, the body operates best when it's given the message that there's space in one's life for a baby. We're just animals. We're descended from hunter-gatherers who spent all day worrying about food and shelter. Pregnancy and childbirth were life-threatening processes. If you keep telling your body that you're busy, it's going to react by making sure you survive."

"I'm not quitting my job."

He laughed. "Don't do that, no, no. Just… whenever you can take it easy, take it easy. See your friends. If you can work less, work less. Have you tried meditation?"

"It stresses me out."

He smiled as if he'd met women like me and he knew all the excuses. I felt like a hot cookie on a tray being slid onto a plate of dozens that looked and tasted exactly the same.

"How do they do?" I asked him as if he could read my mind, then realized he couldn't. "Women doing IUI who get stressed out doing meditation? How often do they get pregnant?"

"I don't have hard data. Anecdotally? We're successful at about the same rate, but it takes longer."

"I'm patient," I said, trying to convince myself as much as him.

"Good. I want you to stay upbeat."

"I'll try."

"And relax."

"I'll relax like it's my job."

* * *

EMILIO TOOK another sip of espresso.

"I have never had coffee this good," he said.

"Told you." Linda had traded her thick, black frames for thin wire ones and braided her hair. Her father's Koreatown coffee shop was hidden in the corner of a strip mall. Linda had convinced Emilio to sample it for the new restaurant. It was the best coffee in Los Angeles and had such a crowd we three had to sit at the bar at seven in the morning.

"Amelia needs it." He often referred to his new restaurant as if it was actually his grandmother.

"The trick to working with my dad is you wait a long time for him to come out of the back, then you let him do the talking."

"Got it." He looked over the menu. "I want to try this Honduran pour-over."

"Me too," I said.

"I thought you were on one cup a day," he said, ordering two from the barista.

"The doctor said I should relax." I shrugged. "This is me relaxing."

"You should take a jog instead. Make-out sessions are like opium."

"Uncle Daddy can shut up now," I said, wishing I hadn't told them about Byron and me kissing on Runyon Canyon.

"He's kind of right," Linda added. "Sex releases all the good baby hormones."

"Stop."

They were making me think about him. The way he'd touched me as if he could—and would—tear me apart like a savage. The way I kept fantasizing about exactly that kind of scary, furious sex with him.

"She's just saying what the doctor wouldn't," Emilio said. "Sex is nature's Disneyland, and damn I wish I had the time for it."

"I hate him." They hadn't said I should have sex with Byron in particular, but I was talking back the thoughts that considered it. "I'm sure he didn't show up for a jog by chance. He thinks he's so charming I'll loosen my grip on his balls."

"Maybe he wants your grip on his balls." Emilio nodded to the waiter when he delivered the pour-overs. "Not figuratively."

"Not interested."

"You kissed him last night because you weren't interested?"

"You want Byron Crowne," Linda sang into her cup. She held a napkin against the bottom of it in case it dripped.

"I do not." The lady doth protest too much. Even when the lady was me. "That kiss could get me disbarred as it is. I'd be a laughingstock, and he'd be..." I paused, looking for the right insult.

"...better than Tiny Tim?" Emilio finished.

"He wasn't tiny."

"Better than Pete the Screamer."

"Definitely better than Pete the Screamer." I shuddered as I named him.

They were harping on my few short-term boyfriends because they knew Crowne wouldn't be any more than that.

"Dad alert," Linda said, pointing at her father emerging from the back.

Brian Lee wore a straw fedora and horn-rimmed glasses. His tan from his trip to Guatemala was just fading. When he saw us, he made a beeline with one hand out. He laid it on Linda's back and kissed her cheek.

"Hello, sweetheart." He reached out to hug me. "And Olivia. Nice to see you here."

"Where else would I go for the best?"

"Nowhere! Best in town. You must be Emilio?" They shook hands. "Let me show you this Arabica I just brought back from Atitlan."

When they were out of earshot, Linda pushed away her mug. "I found out something else about Byron."

"What?" The hair on the back of my neck prickled.

"I was doing some oppo for a client, and he came up. It wasn't relevant to the job, so it's not a breach, but as a friend..." She glanced at her dad and Emilio, then the door, and cleared her throat.

"Tell me," I begged.

"His fiancée? Samantha Bettencourt?"

"You told me what happened."

"She wasn't wearing her engagement ring when she went swimming in the middle of the night. No one knew where it was. Turns out, the plumber found it in the drain catch under the house and hocked it. Three carats. Showed up in a pawn shop in Whittier. Hush-hush."

"So... they broke up before? And she didn't tell anyone?"

"No one told anyone. It would look bad. You know how those people are. They hire PR firms to manage their kids' images the day they're born. I mean, bad enough there was a broken light in a billionaire's pool. But she was swimming at three in the morning, fully dressed."

"He killed her? Are you saying—?"

"No, no. No evidence of that." She wiped a brown ring off the counter with a napkin. "But it does raise questions. Don't you think?"

* * *

SAMANTHA BETTENCOURT HAD THROWN her ring down the toilet. Maybe it had slipped off her finger, but what were the odds? Slim. Real slim.

If the PR was to be believed, she and Byron were the "perfect couple." There had been no indication that they'd broken up prior to her death, but that didn't mean anything. Linda was right. Families like the Bettencourts and Crownes tightly controlled their image. Nothing was reported that the family didn't want everyone to know.

The breakup would have made waves. Every woman in socialite circles would have gone on full alert if the oldest Crowne brother had become available.

Which one had done the breaking up?

I walked into my office, imagining scenarios. Infidelity. Commitment-phobia. Stupid, arrogant behavior on Byron's part.

By the time I got to Amara's desk, I'd decided it was his fault because he was the most awful man ever to walk the earth. Then as I saw the vase of roses on her desk, I had to wonder why it mattered.

"Who's the lucky guy?" I said, indicating the two dozen roses. They weren't a single color, but a motley selection of pink, red, white, and yellow.

"You," Amara said. "So. Who's the lucky guy?"

"No clue," I lied, plucking the card from the clip. I had a clue.

"Whoever he is, he's indecisive."

"Not my type, then." I slid the handwritten card out of the envelope.

Dear Ms. Monroe,

I hope you can accept my apology for last night. I was out of line.
  (I wasn't sure of your favorite color, so I got all of them.)

Byron

Not exactly indecisive, but covering his bases.

I bet I can make you beg for it like a starving animal.

Out of line didn't even begin to describe what had happened. Now there were witnesses and a paper trail. I was as responsible for the kiss as he was, but before that, he'd been disrespectful. Disgusting. Insolent. Egocentric. He'd treated me like a hill he wanted to climb, and I was no man's mountain.

I lifted the roses from the vase and dropped them in the garbage.

"Well, then," Amara said.

"We'll keep the vase." The note went into the blue recycling bin.

"You got it," she replied as she picked up the phone. "Olivia Monroe's desk."

I strode into my office. Forgiveness wasn't my forte. Offering it would have given him an opening to shove the door open further, and he'd have taken it as a sign to stroll right in.

"Olivia," Amara called, "it's Crowne."

Of course it was. He wasn't going to give up. I should have known that.

I stormed into my office and snapped up the phone, leaving the door open. "You're fucking kid—"

"Hold for Mr. Crowne," a young woman's voice said before the click.

Crap. I'd cursed at his secretary. As much as I'd been righteous in my rage, I shouldn't have directed it at her. By the time he picked up, I was cowed by my own behavior, which made me hate him even more.

"Ms. Monroe," he said. That voice. It existed on a dozen resonant wavelengths.

"What do you want?" Still sharp. At least I wasn't cursing.

"I want to know if you read the note before you threw it out."

It was almost as if he knew me.

"I did." I held back a thank-you or offer of forgiveness.

"Should I hang up?"

Was he retreating? That wouldn't do. I didn't want him to run. I wanted him to fight until the bell rang even if I didn't want him to get what he was fighting for.

"Why?" I asked. "You'll only stay on if I accept your apology?"

He breathed a laugh. Either he thought I was funny, or he really expected forgiveness. "Which color rose do you prefer?"

"What's the difference?" I dropped into my chair.

"So I know what to send next time."

"There's not going to be a next time."

I could practically hear him smile in the pause that followed.

"What did you do when you got home?" he asked as if he knew I'd abused a washcloth.

"Went to bed."

"Do you want to know what I did? It made a mess."

"Let me ask you something. Do you do this shit to all the women lawyers you're up against?"

"Let me ask you something. Do your hands shake and does your breath get all heavy for every man you take to court?"

"Only the ones I want to destroy."

"Good," he said as if we'd decided something. "I only say this shit to women I want to destroy. But I don't think we mean the same thing."

I knew what he meant. It was perfectly clear to my body, which redirected all its fluids to my panties.

"Meet me tonight," he said.

"For what?"

"Business."

"What business?"

"You know exactly what business."

"You're trying to get me disbarred because you're scared of me."

He laughed. "I don't want to talk about the case. I couldn't care less about it."

"We have nothing else to discuss."

"The address is on the back of the card."

He did what I should have done the minute the conversation went off the rails.

He hung up.

CHAPTER 6

OLIVIA

The fake-apology note I fished out of the recycling bin had a Silver Lake address on the back.

Shocker.

Obviously, I wasn't going over there. I was going to stay home and work. Go over a Ninth-Circuit decision on the Endangered Species Act that had nothing to do with me. Maybe have a glass of wine before bed.

I was home, in yoga pants and a beat-up T-shirt, with the court's opinion spread out on the kitchen counter because though Dr. Galang had told me to relax, he hadn't dictated how. As I read the last of it, I considered going up to Silver Lake.

Byron wanted something I was itching to deliver, and he knew I wanted him. I'd blown it, and I had to get control back. Avoiding him would make it worse. Getting in his face and telling him to suck a bag of dicks would put a stake in this once and for all.

I went to the bedroom to change when I saw myself in the closet mirror.

My blond hair was up in a sloppy ponytail, and the T-shirt was shapeless and unflattering. With my makeup washed away, I looked unremarkable. Maybe I didn't have to change my clothes at all. The yoga pants would send the right signal—not interested in sex and not concerned with my business impression.

I could have probably driven there, but parking in Silver Lake was a nightmare, so I called a car.

In the back of the Uber, a block away from his little sex pad, I wavered.

"Can you wait for me?" I asked the driver when she stopped on the quiet street.

"I have another call," she said, meeting my eyes in the mirror. "You going to be all right?"

She was concerned in the way women are for other women.

"I'm fine. I'll just call another if I need it."

"Should I wait for you to get in?"

The lights were on, and a black BMW was in the driveway. He was there. I wouldn't be left alone on the porch.

"It's okay," I said. "Get your next ride."

Once I was past the front gate, she drove away. I was left with me and my stupid, reckless, hormone-driven choices.

Don't you dare blame the fertility drugs.

The quaint little house, with its disarmingly soft lights and rosebushes, was designed to seem anodyne. As if nothing bad could happen there. A perfect property to bring strange women to. It worked like a charm on me, draining my resolve to tell him to fuck off face-to-face.

My better self tried to get a foothold on my will. As I opened the front gate and stepped onto the front walk of the little house, my choice was made and my illusions fell away.

Before I was all the way onto the porch, he opened the door. A short glass of scotch in each hand. A full day's shadow on his cheeks.

Suit trousers. Light blue shirt with two open buttons at the top, revealing just enough hair to make me imagine the rest of his body.

I already knew he was gorgeous and erotically powerful, but it was the vulnerability of his bare feet that did me in. I felt too safe, and knowing that did nothing to rouse my defenses.

"A peace offering," he said as I approached, handing me a glass of scotch. "It's a single malt from Japan."

I took it. "I don't drink on school nights."

"Just a taste." He held up his glass, and I clinked it.

I took the tiniest of sips. Just a taste. To do otherwise would have appeared weak.

He looked me up and down, from my Keds to my mess of a ponytail, with a slow deliberation that made me as self-conscious of the shoddiness of my outfit as the hungering of the body under it.

"Problem?" I asked.

"There's a poetic symmetry to what you're wearing."

He stepped out of the doorway to let me in.

I made a quick inventory of the front room. Original art but no one flashy or famous. Expensive but nondescript furniture. A grand piano without personal photos on it. Understated for a man known to be showy with his wealth.

"You play piano?" I asked after he closed the door behind me.

"Yes." He went to the sidebar to refill his drink. "But not in a long time. Here." He held out his hand for my glass. "What did you think of it?"

"A little charcoal. Sweet on the back. Hints of bell turmeric and cinnamon."

"That all?" He took my glass, brushing his finger against my thumb, leaving a trail of sensation on my skin like a boat leaving a flared wake in still water.

"It tasted like a drive up Mulholland with the top down."

He stood there with his two glasses, silently waiting for me to explain what the hell I was talking about.

I decided to elaborate instead. "At two in the morning on the Sunday of a holiday weekend, in November when the palm trees drop their seeds and one hits you in the cheek. It hurts, but you laugh anyway because everything is just fine and Tom Petty's on the radio."

He smirked and laid my glass on a silver tray. "I'm glad you liked it."

"What did you mean about poetic symmetry?" I asked.

"You were similarly dressed last night."

"I didn't come here to kiss you."

He swirled his scotch. "Didn't you?" He drained his glass and put it next to mine.

"I didn't."

"You came to tell me that in person?"

"You didn't seem to believe me over the phone."

He put his hands in his pockets, drawing my eyes to his belt and the tightness of his waist. I looked away too quickly.

"What I believe is complicated," he said. "Because you're complicated."

"Flattery is such a blunt tool, Mr. Crowne."

"Call me Byron. Please."

"You can call me Ms. Monroe."

"See? Complicated. You come here looking like you rolled out of bed, then demand formality. It's enticing. And that's not flattery. It's fact. So." He crossed his arms and leaned on the piano. "Be here."

He turned and walked to the back of the house, flicking on a light to reveal an open kitchen so immaculate and free of pots or canisters I couldn't imagine anything had been cooked in it.

"Have you ever had snow tea?" he asked, pulling out a barstool from under the matte-black-topped island.

"Yes." I sat, and he navigated around the island. "That's not a rhetorical question, right? You have some?"

Snow tea was white lichen from tiny high-elevation regions in China. It had a light taste of grass and meadows that was more grounding than calming. Linda's father had procured some for me, and I drank it at night when I couldn't sleep.

"If you want it," he said, turning on the burner under the chrome teapot, "I'm making it."

"I'd love that."

How did he know?

Of all the things to have in a kitchen that has so little.

Careful.

The package he pulled from the cabinet was half empty, suggesting he drank it here often.

Or he could have dumped it.

"What got you into snow tea?" I asked.

"I did some overland travel in China."

"First class, I assume."

"You assume incorrectly, but we toss lowest and highest scores. I graduated from college without a plan, so my parents sent me to work in the Crowne office in Beijing. Took me a week to realize I didn't know people and I never would from inside those walls. So, I loaded up a backpack with forty pounds of stuff, which I dumped thirty pounds of anyway. Took the busses and trains. Learned a little of the language. Tried not to get killed."

"How long did that last?"

"Six months. Then I went back to all this."

The only red flag was how believable the story was.

"Did you invite me here to impress me with your hot drink selection?"

"You're impressed? That was easy."

I neither confirmed nor denied to him what I could not confirm or deny to myself. I was firmly planted in the gray area between what I should and shouldn't do.

"We should talk," he said. "Like adults."

"About?"

"Are you always this coy?" He laid both hands on the counter, rugged fingers splayed to a size that could fist my biceps. "Or do you think the one who gets to the point first loses?"

"Maybe." I folded my fingers together like a good student.

"Lawyers." He shook his head. "My tongue can still taste the back of your throat. Do you want me to describe it?"

"No."

"It tastes like a run up a mountain on a cool night to a view you can't see in the dark but you know it's there. All the way to the ocean. So close you can smell it and so far it's silent."

The teapot hissed, shielding my reaction. He shut off the burner and reached up into a cabinet, then pulled down two identical glass mugs. The kitchen was more functional than it appeared.

"You want to address what happened on Runyon," I guessed.

"Don't you?"

He laid the identical cups side by side and put equal amounts of tea powder in each while I tried to ignore the thrum of my heart.

Ethically, I was supposed to disclose any personal relationship with a client or opposing counsel that might color my advocacy. But this incident with Byron Crowne? A man I professed was the gold standard in assholery? It was nothing. It had to be. I'd never be that much of a doormat.

"And that brings us here," he said, pouring hot water into the cups. "Not to what's in the past, but what's in the future."

He retrieved a silver spoon. I'd never thought stirring two mugs of tea could be manly, but his quick, decisive spins and single taps on the rims were utterly masculine. The way he picked up the cup by doming his hand over the top and pressing his fingertips to the hot glass so that I could take the handle suggested dominance over pain and control over the elements.

"Thank you." The burning sensation in the backs of my fingers confirmed the cup was scalding. I put it down slowly, trying to match his forbearance and barely succeeding.

When I looked at him, he was watching me so closely I knew we were playing the same game.

"The future," I said, cupping my hand around the glass, ignoring the scorch on my palm.

"Any time after this moment." He took a big sip of tea. If the heat didn't peel off the roof of his mouth, I'd eat my damn shoe. And yet he didn't just take it as if it was lukewarm…he took another without even blowing on the top.

"What do you have in mind?" I gripped the handle and took a sip. I could do this.

"Fucking you."

I nearly spit the tea before it scalded me, but I held it, letting it blister the roof of my mouth as if he and I were being scored on our ability to hide pain.

Of course, he hadn't played fair. Dropping that bomb as I drank was cheating.

I put down the cup, done with the pain game. "What?"

"Did I misread you last night?"

By all measures, he was asking me what I thought, but he was really telling me what he knew.

"You're not misreading."

He came around the island and sat on the stool next to me, legs spread as if he needed to take up as much space as possible. "Good."

"We kissed. We're both adults. Of course you'd think that meant fucking was in the future."

"It's not?" His eyebrows twitched upward in bemusement.

"I hadn't planned on it."

"Change the plan."

I had jurisdiction over my body. He was reminding me of that at the same time as he called me to be ruled by my basest desires.

But he wasn't reminding me. His tone wasn't a gentle prod. It was a command, and I didn't take orders.

Usually.

Especially from men.

Generally.

Because none of the men I'd known issued an order the way he did. His words were saturated with the historically proven knowledge that obedience followed them.

"Why should I?"

He considered his cup as if committing to his goal, then studied the way my finger tapped the counter as if choosing a strategy, then pondered my face as he decided on his tactic.

"Because you're wet already," he said with a deep knowledge of what aroused women looked like. "Because you want what I can give you. Your head hasn't even acknowledged it, but your body knows."

"That's…" I was going to end with a denial, but my nipples were hard. "Not relevant. You and I don't make sense."

"That's correct." He gulped tea. I left my cup on the counter, refusing the challenge. "We are a disaster. You despise me too much to want a relationship and just enough to turn you on. And from what I can tell, you don't want to get involved enough to force an ethical quandary. So, if you agree in principle, I have a proposal."

Agreeing in principle meant revealing how badly my body ached for him.

Disagreeing meant never satisfying that ache.

"I agree in principle."

"My proposal is one night. One full night…"

I could commit to that, and I was about to when he continued.

"Where I own your body."

"Wait."

"You let me own you when we fuck. You come when I say. You obey me without hesitating. That's what you want, and you know it."

My cheeks prickled, radiating the heat of my shame. "No, then." I pushed my cup away. "It's never been like that. I've had three long relationships and a couple of flings but never—"

"Really enjoyed it."

I couldn't hear another word out of him. It was all lies. Lies and stories to make himself feel powerful and me feel vulnerable.

You mean turned on.

"Be honest with me." He abandoned his cup and stood. "Be honest with yourself. I'm not the only man you could fuck at any given moment. You could have your pick. So, why did you come here?"

"I wanted to see the look on your face when I told you to fuck off."

"I'm right here." He held out his arms as if asking for a blow to the chest. "Tell me."

As with his bare feet, the vulnerability of his posture drew me in. I obeyed him and did what I came to do at the same time.

"Fuck off."

"Is that it?"

"No."

"Give it to me, then."

Was he really asking for the depth of my disdain? To what end? His play didn't matter. There was nothing more important in that moment than wiping that gorgeous grin off his perfect face.

"You're a scumbag from a family of scumbags. You think you can walk all over everything and everyone to get any trinket you want. You're a selfish, egotistical, arrogant, worthless human being."

"You done?"

"You're manipulative, calculating, and foul. And you don't even care. You lean into it because you have no moral compass."

"Ouch."

"Don't pretend anything hurts you."

"Stop pretending everything you hate isn't everything you want."

My answers fell somewhere between "wrong" and "I know you are, but what am I?" They were inadequate, and they were lies.

Byron reached for me slowly, laying his hand on the back of my neck. I couldn't breathe through the thrum of my veins.

"You're nothing but hunger," he said. "Every time you talk. Every move. Every decision you make. Your need soaks through you. You think you have it under control, but all I see is how much you want everything you hate."

His hand tightened on the back of my neck. He was six inches away, and I wanted him. I'd told myself we wouldn't talk specifics. That I'd stay inside ethical lines I thought were elastic but weren't.

I'd gotten in that Uber to have him.

No. That was too simple. I'd come to give myself to him, but I couldn't admit it.

"You're wrong," I hissed, leaning into his body.

"Want me to prove it?"

"Do it." I laid my hands on his chest and tightened my fingers on his shirt. "I dare you."

Our mouths crashed together, and he pushed me against the counter. My legs wrapped around him as he ground the shape of his hard cock against me. I pushed forward as if I could get him inside me through our clothes.

He grabbed my ponytail and yanked it back, exposing my throat. "You want to fuck?"

"Yes," I squeaked.

"You need the fight." He lunged hard against me while pulling my hair. "You are a self-righteous." He shoved harder with every pause. "Naïve. Little. Girl. And you're out. Of. Your. Depth."

I was too close to orgasm to be angry at his words or to react with anything but a hard groan. My hands pulled apart, ripping his shirt open, reaching into the gap to feel his body in its raw humanness.

"What do you want?" he growled.

I feared I'd gone too far and put everything I'd ever wanted in danger. I had to seize enough control to draw a line. "I need..."

"What?"

"I need a condom."

He pulled my hair harder, pinning me as his other hand slid under my shirt and bra for a bare nipple. I put my hands behind me to keep from falling, leveraging myself against the countertop.

"Beg for my cock, and I'll wrap it before I fuck you." He squeezed hard enough to hurt, and my hips bucked with pleasure.

"Please," I obeyed without thinking.

He angled my head so I was looking right into his cold, green eyes. I didn't care if he was a controlling asshole who got off on me begging.

"Please. I want your cock in me so bad. Please."

He twisted my nipple and sucked a breath in when I moaned. "See how sweet you are now? How nice you beg?"

"Please."

He picked up my mug. "Finish the tea."

The shape of his cock still rigid against the damp crotch of my sweatpants, he laid his hand on my throat and put the cup to my lips. When he tipped it into my mouth, it was cool enough to drink without burning my tongue.

"Drink," he whispered. "I want to feel you swallow."

The weight of his palm lay on my undulating throat, over the flow of sweet, tangy tea.

"Aren't you sexy?" He pressed his erection between my legs and poured tea into my mouth. "Aren't you a good girl?"

Involuntarily, I made a purring *mmm* in response, then gulped hard to be an even better girl. He was in command. Ten feet tall. King of Mount Olivia.

"Your throat's going to feel so tight around my cock." He tightened his hand slightly. "Do you swallow, Olivia?" I couldn't answer while he was pouring tea into me, but he didn't want me to. "You will. You'll take every drop in your throat. Every inch in your cunt. You'll take my cock anywhere I put it, and you'll come when I allow it. You'll scream in pleasure, then beg for more."

He took his hand off my throat and put the empty cup to the side. Every moment was tightly controlled and deliberately paced to heighten my anticipation.

But we needed to get one thing out of the way. I couldn't relax until that was done.

"I have a condom," I said.

He reacted by not reacting. When he was in control, nothing could surprise him.

"We won't need them." He ran a finger along my collarbone, watching it trace a line across my skin.

"That's not negotiable."

His eyes met mine.

"I'm not negotiating that."

Before I could push him off me or unwrap my legs from his waist, he pinned me to the counter.

"We agreed to one night." He gripped under my knees and lowered my feet to the floor. "Tonight's half over."

He got back on the barstool. Even after I pulled my shirt down, I felt naked. Worse. He saw the throb between my legs, the untended ache he'd left me with in an act of cruel control.

"This was a mistake."

"Olivia," he whispered, offering nothing after except an expression that spoke volumes. He didn't want me to leave, but no matter the reason, no was no.

"You had consent," I said. "Past that, I have nothing to offer you or your ego. I don't come when called."

I brushed past him, through the living room, into the dark street where I didn't have a car.

Crap.

I took my phone from my pocket, but as soon as it lit up, he was on the porch.

"Let me call you a car," he said as he came down the walk with shoes on his feet and his trousers tight at the crotch. The rod of his erection was clearly outlined when he was in the light.

I couldn't bear the sight of him or his lack of shame. He was a reminder of my weakness, the orgasm I'd begged for, the passion he'd cut off as if it was just another night in Silver Lake.

"I have it." I started walking.

Across the street, a handful of young, bearded hipsters were hanging out on a porch, laughing and talking, while behind me, his gate clacked shut and his footsteps hurried to me.

"This isn't Bel-Air," he said as he caught up.

"I live in Hollywood, thank you."

"It's not safe."

I stopped, spinning to face him. "No. Just no."

"Let me walk you to Sunset."

"Fuck off, Byron. I mean it."

"Hey!" a man's voice came from across the street.

We both turned. Two of the bearded hipsters were at the edge of their yard.

"Dude!" said the taller one with a beard down to his chest. "Leave her alone."

"You need to mind your business," Byron called, using the words of every abuser to ever live.

"That's not going help," I said softly, then more loudly, "It's okay. I'm fine."

The shorter guy, a Latino who was stocky with neglected muscle, handed his beer to Long Beard and crossed the street.

"Ma'am," he said when he was close, "I'm sorry, but that's what my mom said for twenty years, and she wasn't. So that's on me." He addressed Byron. "But this is on you. The lady told you to fuck off."

Byron seemed to assess the situation better after a moment of thought. He put his hands in his pockets. "I'll be happy to fuck off once she's safe in a car, not roaming the streets in a huff."

Stocky looked back at his friends, who had crossed to the curb, then at me. "Tell you what," he said to me. "You call an Uber right here, and I'll wait with you."

"And who are you?" Byron asked. "Who made you safe?"

Stocky reached into his pocket and pulled out a silver badge. His name was Carlos Hernandez. Officer Carlos Hernandez.

"The City of Los Angeles says I'm safe. So, I'll tell you what." He slid the badge back into his pants. "I'll stand with her and wait. You sit right there on your porch and watch. And from now on…" He pointed at the house he'd come from and Byron's modest sex pad. "I'll be watching you. And you don't want that."

Byron's pause was loaded with the potential for a blowup. This house on Edgecliff wasn't his primary residence. He had the money and power to take it or leave it. Or he could throw his weight around, which would turn me off more than any house he built.

I found myself hoping he wouldn't.

"Of course not," Byron replied.

I expected a thinly veiled threat to follow. Some power play. A promise to throw some Crowne influence into the mix. But that was it. He didn't play for a win. The hands in his pockets weren't to give Officer Hernandez a false sense of security.

I realized in the next second that his neighbors didn't know he was a real-estate magnate from one of the richest families in the world and it was important to him that it stay that way.

"You know what?" I said, opening my phone. "I'm going to call an Uber, and you guys can figure it out."

"Cool." Hernandez crossed his thick arms and widened his stance. "You wanna step away please, sir?"

The cop wasn't messing around. He didn't care that he'd taken as much of a win as Byron could offer. I glanced at the man whose fingers had just gauged the movement of my throat and saw a lion in a trap. Such a small thing, and he was struggling to keep his temper under wraps.

"Two minutes," I said, holding up the phone. "A red Kia. I'd like to be alone, if possible."

"You heard the lady."

"Thank you, officer," I said. "But I'm feeling a little encroached right now. I'll be right here until the car comes, but would you mind? Both of you? Just kinda going back into your corners?"

Hernandez nodded first, taking a step back into the street.

"I'll be right on the porch," Byron said.

"Thank you," I replied with a little smile meant to soothe him.

"Good," the cop said.

"Thank you, officer. I was okay, but thank you for standing up for me."

"Cool."

Neither of them moved first. Jesus Christ. Men.

"Okay," I said. "On three. you both go. One-two-three-go."

They did. Byron went behind his front gate but didn't get on the porch. Hernandez joined his buddies on the opposite curb. The car arrived ninety seconds later.

Once I got in, I breathed.

I'd seen Byron lose. I didn't expect to ever see it again.

At least I knew what was important to him. He'd take a defeat to protect his privacy.

But as the car pulled up to my building, it occurred to me that Byron played the long game.

Would he hold a grudge against his neighbor or let it go?

The same could be asked of what had happened between him and me.

Was his pursuit over?

Or had it just begun?

CHAPTER 7

OLIVIA

The next morning, my pussy still screamed with dissatisfaction my fingers couldn't cure. Not even twice. I blamed the fertility meds, the year-plus without sex, the time of the month. All of it was to block out the fact that I hadn't felt so swollen with lust before I met Byron.

I tried to concentrate on my work, but even as I worked my way through the third motion to compel some basic chain of title documents, the truth kept pushing through.

My mother called. Perfect opportunity to think about anything else.

"Hey," I said. "How's it going?"

"Fine. I just had a guy come to look at the foundation." She'd bought a house in the Hollywood Hills at the height of her career and hadn't updated it since.

"How much?"

"Nothing I can't handle, so I appreciate the offer you're about to make, but I have it."

"Can you live there while they fix it?"

"Not if I get the roof done at the same time. Isabelle already offered."

"Or you can stay with me."

"Thank you. I raised my daughters right. I'll let you know, okay?"

"Okay."

"The Eclipse event is Sunday night," she said. The show at the LA Mod happened once a year during a total solar eclipse somewhere in the world. It showcased new and emerging artists to the people who could afford to invest in them. People like the Crownes. "I can't go, and it's a lot of fun. Maybe you'll see someone you know there?"

The emotional openness that made her a terrific model made her terrible at dropping hints.

"Who's going that you want me to see?"

I knew her as well as I knew myself. She was glad I'd asked.

"Alan Barton," she said as if she was dangling a carrot in front of a show horse. "Unless you bring a date, in which case—"

"I haven't had a crush on Alan since eleventh grade."

We weren't Crowne rich. We weren't even Barton rich. But my mother had managed her career and investments well, sending us to private schools so we'd learn to walk comfortably in the halls of power.

"He just got divorced." More lilting carrot voice.

"That's too bad," I said. "She seemed all right."

"She is truly lovely." Mom sighed. "But she couldn't handle it."

Alan had ignored every high-society imperative and married a Nordstrom's salesgirl from the shoe department. They'd seemed perfect, but the pressures and expectations of society life must have been a shock. Money cured a lot…but not everything.

"Well," I said, "that sucks."

"Will you go? I have to RSVP. It could be fun."

Relaxing was turning into a full-time job.

"I'll think about it. Maybe Isabelle can get away."

"Leo has study group that night."

"Ah."

"So. How are the treatments coming?" The question had a candy coating of upbeat life coach over a chewy, tiptoe-tentative core.

"Trying again next week. I'll call you when it sticks."

"You know what's going to happen? You're going to get pregnant the regular way. You're going to meet a nice man and—"

"Those are in short supply."

"Alan's nice."

I sighed, trying to see the love and concern in her words instead of the overbearing prompts. She meant well. She'd had a lot of professional success and personal disappointment in her life, and she wanted an easier path for me. So did I, but I didn't have any idea how to get there.

* * *

THE GUESTS at the Eclipse worked hard to be photographed on their best sides while the art worked harder to be cutting edge. The black-tie guests discussed canvasses draped with black garbage bags and gray stucco (a statement about the environmental impact of housing), a molded Styrofoam tower shaped like a tree trunk (permanence and impermanence), a red room with shiny plastic orbs hanging from the ceiling (the bloodstream of consciousness), and a dark room showing a video of a man setting houses on fire.

"You okay if I go talk to someone?" Linda whispered. "For work."

"Text me."

She moved away, revealing the tall, beautiful man in the dimness, and I froze. The proportions of his face and form electrified every nerve in my body, grabbing my attention with a reminder of his hand on my throat. My second reaction was fury. He had to be stalking me.

Why else would he show up here? My next reaction was curiosity. Why?

A moment after, my brain caught up to my body, pulling it back by the shirt before I flung questions and accusations at him.

It wasn't Byron.

It was his brother Logan, the quiet Crowne who wasn't photographed. He had a subtle power that echoed Byron's, and I understood why rumor in social circles was that he was being groomed to take over the Crowne fortune.

Note taken: Byron was brash and savage. Logan was understated but no less formidable. The sight of him gave me the same feeling of awe without the sexual arousal.

I walked into the main gallery.

"Olivia Monroe!" Alan Barton called as soon as my eyes adjusted.

"Hey," I said before kissing each of his cheeks. He was wearing a traditional tuxedo that made him seem taller than his five foot nine. But I was in heels, so the poor guy was stuck looking up at me.

"You look amazing," he said.

"You too."

His dark-brown hair was brushed back, and his cheeks were shaved clean. He had the dimpled smile of an approachable heartthrob. Exactly the kind of sweet, unthreatening man I dated, back when I dated.

"I haven't seen you since... when?" he said, taking stock of me.

"Three years ago, I think." His wedding.

He laughed, and I was reminded of the charm of his smile. "Right. That."

"How's the world of international financial instruments?"

"Full of scrappers and sharks. But I'm used to it." He offered me his arm, and I took it. "Win some, lose some. We come out ahead in either case."

"Good attitude."

"I'm getting out of this birdcage," he murmured as he guided me across the room for no real reason, then smiled at Lisa Guggenheim before keeping us moving. That was the trick to having a conversation. "Everyone's in my business. Ruined my marriage."

"I heard," I whispered. "I'm so sorry."

"Me too. I'm taking a spot on the London exchange." He took a champagne flute from a waiter's tray and handed it to me.

"It's ten times worse there."

"If you're British," Alan said, taking a glass for himself. "I'm just an American." He held up his flute. "To social expectations."

I clicked and pretended to drink to that.

"Fuck them all," he said, waving his arm at the black-tie crowd.

"When did you get so crude?" I nudged him.

"Does it not work for me?"

"Depends who you're trying to work."

"What if I'm trying to work you?"

In the moment he took to consider the effect of his admission and I took to ask myself if I wanted to be seduced, a flash went off. We both turned. An event photographer in a cheap tux jacket, black skirt, and pink bangs waved at us.

"Sneaky," Alan said to her, wagging his finger. "Take it properly."

He put his arm around me, and we faced the camera. The flash went off again, and she thanked us.

The bell rang for the start of a performance piece in the west gallery.

"I promised I'd see this," Alan said. "Come with?"

"I have to use the ladies'."

"All right. Find me though. I want to curse at you some more."

"Good. You need the practice."

I was looking at my phone on the way to the bathroom, which was why I crashed into a wall of tuxedo. "Excuse—"

The suit was stuffed with sex and topped with emerald eyes that burned through me. Why did he always look so angry? And why did that turn me on? His gaze was unequivocal, unyielding, branding me with fury, and I met it with my own intensity. If he was the unstoppable force, I would be an unmovable object.

"Me," I finished but without apology. When he didn't move, I repeated myself. "Excuse. Me."

"I wouldn't have touched you if I knew you were looking for a man you could crush."

"Are we having the same conversation?"

"Alan Barton is a weakling," he said.

My brow furrowed. What did he think he knew? And did he expect me to defend myself against it? I didn't owe him an explanation. Not a word.

He took out his phone and, with a single swipe, opened it to the event's private website, where the subjects of the pictures had approval. Alan and I were smiling together in the moments after he'd admitted he was trying to charm me. We weren't touching, but there was an intimacy that came with mutual vulnerability.

"You've lost your mind," I said.

"Yes. I have," he growled. "You want me to fight for you. That's your game."

"Me? Mr. Not Now? Everything's a game to…" I caught myself, glancing around to make sure no one could hear.

The valets were gathered by the podium, and the concierge was behind the counter. The personal drivers in their black jackets huddled around an ashtray by their Bentleys and Rolls-Royces. The acoustics were too unpredictable.

Reading my mind, Byron took my arm and pulled me back around the corner.

"You're impatient," he hissed.

"You can say no any time." I jerked my arm from his grasp. "So can I."

"What about now?"

"Now wha—"

He cut me off with a kiss. A smashing, brutal, demanding kiss that I surrendered to as soon as I realized it was happening. He tasted of seltzer and lime and smelled of leather and fire. The heat melted my irritation into a gum-sized black spot in the floor. He held me up with his embrace, and I let him.

A man can say a lot with a kiss, but the tongue twisting against mine and lips that locked on my mouth couldn't explain why he hadn't fucked me when I'd asked or why he came to the Eclipse show at all.

"Tell me there's not another man between us tonight," he said between kisses.

"There isn't." He sucked away the rest with his lips. I couldn't leave it there. I had no idea what I was promising him. I pushed him away just hard enough to break the kiss without leaving his embrace. "Byron. There isn't anyone. There isn't an us either."

He closed his eyes for a moment, tightening his jaw. "I can't stop thinking about having you. You're burning a path through my mind. Ever since I had you in the palm of my hand, it's been you. I need to have a night with you before it's all ash."

"I'm just a mountain you want to climb."

He kissed my neck, gently running his teeth along sensitive skin. I groaned with pleasure, clutching the shoulders of his jacket.

"Let me climb it. Let me conquer you."

"We shouldn't," I said, but what I meant was, *Give me a reason to say yes.*

"I keep a room at the Waldorf. Let me take you there. One night is tonight. Let me hear you come. Let me feel your legs around me. I want to see your eyes roll back with pleasure. I'll kiss the rug burns on your knees. I'll feed you strawberries and champagne after I fuck you, then I'll fuck you again. I want to mark you with my teeth. I want to make your ass red and your cunt so sore you can't walk without thinking of me. And then…"

When he pulled back to look in my eyes, I was breathless and soaking wet.

"Then when the soreness wears off, you forget. We both forget. We can hate each other again. We can be mortal enemies the rest of our lives. We'll fight for what we want, and one of us will win."

His eyes were so close I saw through the arrogance to the rawest of human needs. Or maybe they were mirrors and I saw my own. He hadn't given me a practical reason to say yes, but he'd given me plenty to agree to.

"I'm confirming about the condoms," I said. "I have them. You wear them. The second you argue about it, we're done."

"Agreed."

"Good."

"Anything else?"

"No."

"So, it's a yes?"

"Yes," I said.

He failed to hide his surprise. That was gratifying.

"Let's go now."

I texted Linda to let her know I was leaving.

I shut the phone before she could ask for an explanation.

* * *

DISCERNMENT IS the enemy of delight. Pleasure and its pursuit take the shortcut around logic. Knowing better didn't mean we did better.

His driver was a ruddy-cheeked Asian man at least as tall as Byron, and he opened the back of the Bentley without judgment. Why I was expecting judgment was a mystery that could wait.

"Thank you, Yusup." Byron let me in the back first, then he spoke to Yusup for a moment before sliding in across from me.

The door closed. The heavily tinted windows shrouded the night. We didn't say a word as the car exited the lot. He set his feet wide and laid his hands on his knees, regarding every part of my body with utter seriousness. That was my moment to back out. Go back to the party.

When the car made it to the street and the stern ardor of his face was lit in the intermittent pattern of the streetlights, I checked in with myself. I could stop it. I could still go back and make small talk with old friends. I could, but I didn't want to. At all.

"You ready?" he asked from the shadows.

"Yes."

"I'm in charge. I think you'll like it that way."

"I'll let you know if I don't."

"Open your legs."

His low, commanding voice wedged itself between my knees and pushed them apart as far as the skirt allowed.

"Wider."

No one had ever spoken to me with the assumption that I'd obey. Especially not a lover, and I knew I didn't want to ever live without it again.

I pulled the skirt over the tops of my stockings and opened up until the air conditioning hit the wet crotch of my panties.

"Good girl," he said, making me gasp at the thought he was pleased. He smiled, leaning forward, and ran his hands inside the bare tops of my thighs. "What do you want tonight?"

"Your cock."

"You sure?" He drew the backs of his fingers along the fabric of my lace underwear.

"Yes. Please yes."

"Pick your butt up a little."

I did, and he hooked his fingers on the waistband of my

underwear, pulling them down a few inches above midthigh. My open legs stretched the elastic lace to near breaking.

"You want to come," he said, laying his thumb on my clit.

"Yes."

He pushed two fingers inside me and increased the pressure on my nub. "I want to possess you completely. For this night, I own your orgasms. You come when I say. You ask. You beg to give them to me."

"One night." I managed to breathe out some sense as he rotated his thumb.

"That's all."

"Yes. Okay."

"You are so sexy. Your nipples are hard. Your breaths are coming with the same rhythm as my hand on your cunt. I could do whatever I wanted to you, and you'd beg me to keep going."

His attentions went from turn-on to tease, keeping me on one side of release.

"Do it. Do whatever you want."

Leaving my panties stretched between them, he pushed my legs up and kneeled on the floor between them. He bit the tender insides of my thighs, sucking through his teeth until I gasped with pain.

"Stop?" he asked, looking up at me.

"No." I surprised myself. He'd come close to breaking the skin. I shouldn't have wanted more this badly. "Keep going."

He moved to the other thigh, biting and sucking one painful spot that was now connected to my pleasure by a thick electrical cable.

"You like that," he said.

"Yes."

"I hope that's not your first pleasant surprise."

Before I could reply, he ran his tongue along my seam, tickling the tip of my clit. The bite marks throbbed in a complementary pulse, rising to meet the arousal of my pussy as he gently wedged his fingers inside me.

My hands gripping the back of his head, he spread my lips apart and flicked my nub, then sucked gently, before flicking again, playing my body like a game he'd mastered.

I groaned, jerking into him. So close, I was so close. What was stopping me?

"Count down from five," Byron said from the other side of my closed eyelids. "On one, you may come."

He went down again, flicking and sucking in the same rhythm as if he didn't need to wait for me to agree to his game.

I might as well play.

"Five."

Three fingers inside me.

"Four."

His thumb, slick with my juices, slid to my asshole.

"Three."

All sucking now.

"Two."

Thumb pressed to my ass but not entering. The tingling sensation. The anticipation of a violation.

"Oneeeeeee…" I exploded in a long *nnn*, body left behind as my consciousness disappeared into an ecstasy Byron elongated with the precise manipulation of his tongue.

When I came around, I was gripping his scalp as if I wanted to take out the hair.

"Sorry." I let go.

"Taste yourself." He kissed me deeply, filling my mouth with the salty tartness of my pussy. The flavor was layered with brine and bitters and lost to the elusive mint taste of his tongue as it wore off.

"Now you." I reached for his belt.

"No time," he said without looking up to see where we were. "We're here."

The car stopped under the warm lights of the Waldorf as if Byron had a direct line to his exact placement on the earth.

I reached for my panties, but he stayed my hand. "Keep them down under the skirt."

He closed my knees and pulled my dress down with a smirk of delicious mischief as he sat back in his seat. I didn't have a moment to object before the doorman opened the car. Byron got out, holding his hand to me to help me out of the back seat. Behind him, men in red jackets whistled for cabs, tourists milled about, and a klatch of girls looked at the city through their phones.

Suddenly, the world had gone from deep shadows and dark, secret places to brightly lit and very public. I'd be seen pulling up my underwear.

"Come," Byron said.

I took his hand and stood on the pavement. "This isn't what we agreed to."

I struggled to mount the steps with my underwear sliding down to where my garters met the tops of my stockings. They wouldn't fall farther, but they were restrictive and admittedly wet.

"It was implied." With my hand in his crooked arm, we walked the length of the crowded lobby. "And your hot little cunt needs some freedom, don't you think?"

Without the protection of the fabric, every step rubbed my legs against my swollen clit, and his expression told me he knew it.

A red jacket opened the brass door of the private elevator. "Penthouse, Mr. Crowne?"

"Please."

"The service you ordered is ready in your room."

"Good."

We got into the elevator, and the attendant pressed the button, staying in the car with us.

"This isn't making me not hate you," I whispered.

"But it's making you want me."

"Fuck you," I murmured.

"It'll be my pleasure."

The doors opened, and I had to take three little steps out. Byron opened the only door and guided me in, closing and locking it behind him. We stood on the marble, looking at each other, me with my panties down, him in a tuxedo. He opened his jacket button, exposing the enormous shape of his erection.

Seeing other people had woken me from my sexual haze. I still wanted this, whatever this was, but being in public had shone light on the stretch of my life, and it didn't include Byron Crowne.

"Just one night," I said.

He yanked open his bowtie. "That's all we need." He shrugged out of his jacket. "Don't you agree?"

"I do."

He came behind me and methodically unhooked the fastening of my dress, then he pulled the zipper down, letting his fingers graze the length of my spine. He unhooked my bra. Slowly, he brushed the dress and bra off my shoulders and let it drop to the floor.

"Look at yourself," he said into my ear, reaching around me to turn my chin slightly, making me face a foyer mirror over a table.

His gorgeous face was over my bare shoulder, my breasts were high and tight, and my thighs were still restricted. He unpinned my hair, letting it fall down my neck.

"You're so beautiful." Wrapping his arms around me to cup my breasts from behind, he said, "Watching that beauty collapse when you come..." He closed his fingers on my nipples and pinched them. I leaned back into him, throwing my head against his shoulder in pleasure when his fingers were tight enough to hurt me. "It's all I can think about. That moment when you go from beautiful to transcendent."

"Take it," I groaned. "Take that moment. It's yours."

In the mirror, I watched as his right hand released my breast and moved up under my chin, holding my jaw steady while his left slid down my torso to where my lowered panties exposed me. I edged my body upward and parted my legs so he could maneuver, and maneuver he did, pressing hard against my clit before flicking it.

I uttered a long *nnn* between my teeth.

"Open your eyes," he said softly. "Watch yourself giving it to me."

I hadn't even realized they were closed. His face was next to mine in the mirror, watching my reaction as he worked me, going from soft to hard and back again, taking the stimulation away long enough to make my brows knot with hunger.

"Do you want to come?"

"Yes."

"How badly?"

In the mirror, with my body melting in his embrace, he wasn't the man I wanted to destroy. He was the man who held my catharsis in his hands.

"Bad. Please."

"Come for me."

Without stopping or teasing, he gave me my orgasm, holding me up when my knees buckled, keeping my face on his when my neck wanted to arch upward. His grip was a rein on the wild horse of my pleasure, and with that boundary secured, the release expanded in every other direction.

When I was no more than twitching flesh, he let me lean on the hall table, head down, his arms around my waist. He kissed my back.

"You're so beautiful," he said.

I was brought back to the reality of who he was, what he'd done, and what I'd just allowed. More importantly, I realized what I was going to continue allowing for the rest of the night, and a part of me shrank back in stunned wonder. I overrode it and turned to face him.

"Thank you," I said.

In response, he knelt in front of me and slid down my underpants and stockings. I leaned on the table when he reached my feet so I could step out of my shoes.

"Don't thank me until we're done," he said, standing in front of me.

My eyes traced down the line of his jaw to his chin, then halfway down his chest where my view of his skin was cut off by a closed button.

"Why am I naked and you're not?" I asked, running my hand along the path of my gaze and pinching open his shirt buttons.

"Are you always so impatient?" He opened his belt, then his pants.

My touch followed down to the warm front of his briefs. "Only to pay a debt."

"Get on your knees and open your mouth."

I wanted to worship at his feet. Give myself to him. Fight as if I was yet to be conquered. Offer my body like a spoil of war.

Kneeling before him, I stroked the enormous rod under the last piece of his clothing. He took out his cock, fisting it below the liquid-tipped crimson head, dark and swollen. It was a club. A cudgel. He was going to kill me with it, and I was going to surrender to it. I wanted to taste it on the broken battlefield of my will, subjugated and defiled like captured territory.

He put his free hand on my jaw and forced my mouth open, looking down into me as if he could see the bottom of my soul. "I said to open your mouth."

"Sorry," I said around his pressing fingers.

"You want to taste forgiveness?" he said.

"Yes."

I stuck out my tongue, and he laid the tip on it. He tasted of dried plums, salt, and fresh linen.

"Take it," he said, putting a hand behind my head. "All of it."

When he pushed me into him, I opened my throat and took him to where my tongue tasted bitter melon, breathing through my nose as he jerked forward harder on the next thrusts.

"Jesus, Olivia." He stopped and looked down at me.

I pulled my mouth off him. "What?"

"Fuck. How far can you take it?"

"You said all of it." I laid my hands on his thighs. "When I want to get good at something, I get good at it. You're welcome, asshole."

Before he could reply, I took him all the way, leaving my nose pressed to his stomach because I had something to prove.

So did he apparently. He jerked out with a gasp, eyes squeezed shut.

"Come on," I said. "Let me finish."

In his own way, he surrendered, letting me take him even as he set the rhythm, holding my head when he came down my throat. Forgiveness tasted like Callery blossoms, pennies, and bleach. It tasted like a sweet seed in a bitter fruit.

When he was done, he helped me up.

"Now," I said after I'd swallowed everything, "you get to taste."

I jammed my tongue in his mouth before he could refuse and was pleasantly surprised at his acceptance.

"I could fall asleep right now," I said, so relaxed my eyes were drooping.

"The penthouse has a perfectly serviceable bed."

He scooped me up under my shoulders and knees as if I were a bag of feathers and crossed the front room.

He pushed the door open with his shoulder. The bright, moving lights of the city disappeared into the dark splotch of Bel-Air. By the bed, a champagne bucket and a bowl of fiercely red strawberries sat on a service cart. He laid me on the duvet and stood at the foot of the bed.

"Olivia the Righteous. Champion of champions. Vanquisher of my resistance. Tell me what you want."

Vanquisher of my resistance.

I got up on my elbows. I'd been so focused on my fight to refuse him that I hadn't considered that he'd spent a moment struggling with his desires. More than the knowledge that he'd lost the same battle I had, the admission itself made me want him.

"I want to fuck."

"Do you?"

"Don't make me fight for it, because I will."

He smiled and took off his shirt, throwing it on the floor.

"I know." He got a condom out of his pocket before tossing his pants over a chair. He stood at the bed's edge with his enormous dick sheathed in a condom, ready for me.

When he crawled onto the mattress, I opened for him with renewed hunger. We kissed, savoring every taste, every touch, until I reached between us for his cock and pushed my hips into it.

"Please," I whispered.

"Please what?"

"Please fuck me."

He groaned, and his hand joined mine, lining himself up and looking into my eyes.

"Now." The word was an impatient gasp.

He entered me, stretching unused muscles and stimulating pleasure centers left unsatisfied in the front hall. With a grunt, he pushed himself deep and paused.

"Yes," I cried, clawing his back.

He took me then, letting go of whatever had stayed him before. His release was like the detonation of a concrete wall, as if he'd been holding a grenade in his fist. His thrusts were powerful, unrestrained, unyielding. He took the soft parts of my body in his control with the ferocity of an animal. The power of him inside me accepted no less than utter surrender, and I gave it, letting pleasure wash over me with each drive forward.

"By-Byron," I squeaked. "I—"

The rest was lost clamping down on a flood.

"Come," he said, pushing deep. "Give it to me."

I let go before he finished his sentence, giving him my howl of ecstasy, grasping the skin and muscle of his back. His balls pulsed against me as he came with a last thrust that was so deep it hurt, but so precise it caused a new wave of delirium.

His lips were in the crook under my jaw when I opened my eyes, and the champagne and strawberries were in my view.

"You killed me," I said, turning back to him. "I'm fully dead. You can't feed strawberries and champagne to a dead woman."

I expected a smile or a laugh. Maybe a promise that the right proportion of berries and bubbly, administered by an expert such as himself, was known to revive the deadest of the dead. But that was not what happened. His face went dark, rebuilding the concrete wall I'd imagined blowing a hole through.

"Are you okay?" I asked when he got off me.

"I'm fine." He rubbed his face and stepped off the bed. "You can have some." He pointed at the strawberries and champagne. "They're for you. Obviously. I'm going to the bathroom for a second."

He closed the door behind him.

You killed me. I'm fully dead.

Well, that hadn't been the right thing to say, and it was obvious I'd reminded him of Samantha at the wrong time.

Partly, that was my fault. But not really. Because if he was still too raw about her, he had no business having sex with me or anyone.

Or was I making up what had just happened? Overthinking it? Was I weaving a story that would make it easier to go back to hating him tomorrow?

The shower went on.

I got up and laid my hand on the bathroom door's brass lever.

Had he locked it?

Did I want to know?

What I wanted was irrelevant. What I needed was to know where I stood with him.

Gently, I pushed down on the lever, and it stopped before the latch opened.

It was locked.

I was alone, on the other side of a locked door, naked from toes to tits with no armor but my ravaged skin. Exposed to the despicable man whose stabbing cock had broken down my defenses and made my pussy sore. I'd thought I had the upper hand, but that was a fool's assumption. He'd been better positioned from the moment I got into his car.

I found the second bathroom and cleaned up between my legs. My mascara was smudged, and my hair was a nest. As I rubbed under my eyes in an attempt to make myself presentable, the shower on the other side of the wall was turned off.

I looked at myself in the mirror one last time.

With furling nipples, my body said yes to the possibility of his hands and his cock. Just a few more times, maybe. Then Byron Crowne and Olivia Monroe would be back on opposite sides of the table, where we belonged.

I could wait, just to see if I'd misinterpreted his coldness. Maybe his reaction wasn't about Samantha, and maybe it wasn't what had set him off. Or maybe he hadn't been set off at all. Maybe we were good for another turn or two before the sun came up. We'd agreed to an entire night, not a fuck and a dodge out the door. There were so many things we hadn't explored yet, and we had hours.

And then, like a slow, thick leak, a trickle of fluid dropped inside my thigh.

That shouldn't be. I reached down and took some on my finger and recognized the texture and smell of it.

It wasn't my body's response to the sex. It wasn't mine at all.

Still naked, I stormed to the other bathroom and pounded on the door. "Byron!"

He opened the door, towel around his waist, hair and skin wet, eyes scanning my body as if he was considering another go at it.

"The condom broke?"

"It did. I was—"

"What the *fuck*?"

"Going to tell you as soon as I got out."

"*What the fuck?*" I didn't realize I was shouting until I saw his reaction.

"I didn't realize until—"

"I'm on fertility drugs! You piece of shit. I'm ovulating, and I'm on—"

"Wait," he barked. "You're what?"

I stormed to the outer room where the floor was littered with my clothes. I slid my dress over my head as I gave him an explanation I didn't owe him. "I'm trying to have a baby. I'm getting intrauterine insemination, and the next one is tomorrow morning."

"Why did you insist on a condom then?"

"I want a baby. But not yours." I stuffed my hairpins and stockings in my bag. "Not some random guy I fucked for—"

"I'm a *random guy*?"

"Shut up. Just shut your fucking mouth. This isn't a game. This is my life, and I don't want you in it."

Period. Bottom line. Nonnegotiable.

And now?

Now I might be stuck with him forever. The thought of it opened my adrenal floodgates, giving me two options: fight or fly.

Choosing flight, I opened the door and rushed into the little hallway. He followed in his towel.

"Can you wait a second?" he said.

I pushed the button. "No."

Then I waited. It wouldn't be long. The elevator was exclusive to the penthouse, but I was stuck there. Every second would be torment while the DNA inside me would probably fight like hell to get to its destination.

"Let me get this straight," he said as if he could decorate the hallway with his perfect body until the towel dried and fell off. "You're paying a doctor to put some stranger's sperm in you."

"He's not a stranger. Not that it's your business. But it's my friend, Emilio." I pressed the button again, but it didn't glow any brighter. "He's just helping me out. He doesn't want to raise a baby any more than I want a partner."

He scoffed. "I bet he wants to try the old-fashioned way."

"He's gay," I punched the button again. "So, you can put your jealousy, or whatever that is, back in the box it came in."

"Olivia," he said with the tone of a hostage negotiator, "can you slow down for a minute?"

"No. I feel trapped. So just back up."

He surprised me and backed up. The distance brought down the heat in my blood.

"What are you going to do now?"

He didn't demand an answer or bark at me. It was just a question, and it was totally my decision. I hadn't thought about it past getting away from him.

The elevator doors slid open, revealing the same operator who had brought us up.

"Going down, Mr. Crowne?"

"I don't know," Byron said, looking at me.

"Can you come back in two minutes?" I answered.

"Of course."

The doors closed. Byron leaned on the penthouse's open doorjamb, towel drooping below the groove of his Adonis belt.

"I have options," I said.

"What are they?"

"They're not actually your concern."

"Agreed. But tell me anyway."

I sighed, looking at the space above where the picture railing met the wallpaper. There was an uneven notch on the wood. It had gotten brushed over when the molding was painted. Even here, in a hallway seen by the wealthiest guests of the Waldorf Astoria Hotel in Beverly Hills, imperfections had to be made right.

"One, I call off tomorrow's insemination, spend two weeks praying I'm not having your baby."

He nodded, wearing an iron mask over his opinions.

"Two," I continued. "Go into Dr. Galang tomorrow. Get inseminated as usual. Wait until I know if I'm carrying one of two men's babies, then spend nine months in misery, praying it's not yours. Have a DNA test to find out if my prayers were answered."

"Which one is better?" he asked, jumping the gun.

"Three. Call off tomorrow's insemination and get Plan B. Morning-after pills. That'll cut the whole thing off before it has a chance to fertilize. Start over next month."

"Wait." He pushed himself off the jamb with his shoulder.

"Byron." I held out my hands to ward him off. Not just his physical presence, but his voice and his command. He'd soften me into considering what he wanted. I'd be lost.

"Just…" he started as if he knew bossing me around would shut me down. "Please just—"

"No. This is my life. Do you understand? *My life.*"

The elevator opened.

"Ma'am?" the operator asked.

"Thank you." I stepped inside, and Byron came to the edge of the doors.

"Can you let me know?" he asked. "Can you just tell me what you do?"

"Yes. I will."

The doors closed.

CHAPTER 8

OLIVIA

The drug store was big into tinctures and herbal remedies. The pharmacy in the back had a PA on staff who listened to my story and disappeared to get my pills. While I waited, I browsed homeopathic stress reducers and vitamins that promised peace. Turning the corner, I landed in a section that smelled of sweet powder and actually did offer a slice of harmony. On the bottom shelf, a box of breast pump attachments had a picture of a porcelain-skinned woman with a baby. The design was soothing shades of green and lavender. On the other side of the box, an African-American woman gazed down at her infant with a blaze of love in her eyes.

Me, me.

That could be me. I could direct all that love at my baby.

"Ms. Monroe?" the pharmacist called from three rows away, her youthful voice reaching the right pitch to find me without shouting.

I put the box back and went to the window. "That's me."

"Have you used this medication before?" Her nametag said Jun.

"Yeah. Long time ago."

After a breakup with my first college boyfriend, I got drunk and screwed a man whose name I couldn't remember in a frat-house bathroom. The girls in my house said it would be a great rebound. It sucked. I didn't have to do it twice to prove it.

"So, you may experience some side effects," Jun said, holding a lavender-and-green box with fine type printed all over. "Nausea, vomiting, headache. Menstrual bleeding may be accompanied by cramping."

My phone buzzed. Byron was texting while Jun explained the circumstances that should lead me to call my doctor.

"Okay." I held my hand out for the box.

"Do you need a cup of water?"

"Yes, please."

—*What did you decide?*—

I read, then ignored Byron's text until I'd finished signing the screen and paying.

—*Can't talk. At the pharmacist*—

I sat on the chairs set up for customers waiting for their medicine and put my water cup on the table. I opened the box and slid out a tiny white pill encased in a plastic blister seal.

—*Did you take it?*—

—*Can we talk before you do?*—

Though it was perfectly expected for a man to minimize what getting pregnant meant to a woman and suddenly, desperately, want whatever baby he'd seeded, I was shocked at his hesitancy. Two simple questions illustrated how powerless he felt.

—*It's not going to change anything*—

—*I know*—

—*Can I call you?*—

I called him instead.

"Hello," I said, my voice low in the small space.

"Where are you?"

"The pharmacy."

"Did you...?"

"Not yet."

I could hear him swallow but not much else. Outside the window, people hustled to work with their phones at their ears and coffee in their hands.

"Can you talk me through this?" he asked finally.

"What do you want me to say?"

"What happens?"

"I'm going to go to work feeling like shit, and I'm going to feel shitty all day."

"Not that."

"Thanks for your concern."

"That's not what I meant."

"You want me to assure you of something?" I sniped. "You want to feel better? Like, that the egg isn't fertilized and I'm not killing a precious Crowne embryo?"

"No. I want you to tell me if this is going to keep you from succeeding next month."

Why should he care? It wasn't his business. Not even a little.

Not unless he actually cared about me, which was a possibility I hadn't considered until that moment, and as much as I tried to dismiss it, I didn't want to. If I chose to accept his care, I had to accept the fact that it comforted me.

"Really?" I could barely hide my suspicion. "That's what you need to talk about?"

"Do I want you to do this? No, Olivia, I don't. I could sit here and promise to send you all the money in the world and never get in the way, but that's not going to move you, and to be frank, I'd never trust you again."

He was the most infuriating, inconsistent, contradictory man I'd ever met.

"You'd never trust *me*?"

"I'd never trust you are who you are. You don't give up that easily. So, I'm not going to try to convince you. You want to go it alone, fine. Go it alone. What's really bothering me is that you distrust me enough to not get what you want out of your own life."

A dust bunny was caught between the chair leg and the linoleum floor. It wasn't until he was done that I realized I was staring at it with my hand over my mouth.

"Olivia?"

I was snapped from my reverie. "Yes."

"Yes, what? Is this going to keep you from having a baby later?"

"I talked to my doctor. It's fine. It'll mess up this cycle. Maybe the next one. Not more."

"Okay."

"Okay," I repeated.

"You left your underwear."

He wasn't trying to be sexy, but the information was so small compared to the magnitude of what was going on that I wanted to choke him.

"Is there something else we need to talk about?" I asked.

"No," he said. "Business as usual, then?"

"Business as usual."

We hung up. I could hate him again. Go full fire-of-a-thousand-suns, et cetera, et cetera.

No problem.

The box had a window. The pills were blister-packed inside like babies in glass blankets.

All I had to do was take them.

Now.

Before it was too late.

Jun was at her computer. I put the box on the counter and reached across for the cup of water, tossing it back as if it was the last tequila shot before the bar closed.

I'd made a decision, but I didn't know why.

* * *

"I THOUGHT you had a doctor's appointment?" Amara asked as the elevator doors closed. We'd gotten on together, holding our coffee cups and staring at the lighted numbers.

"Change of plans."

"Saw the pictures of the Eclipse thing though. Who's the hot number?"

The thought that somehow she'd found out about Byron stopped every mental process. I had to force myself not to freeze in my tracks.

She couldn't know. We hadn't been photographed. And she knew what Byron looked like. She wouldn't have to ask who he was.

"Alan Barton?" I asked. The doors opened, and we stepped into the hall.

"That's the one."

My relief was deeply felt, but I watched it flood me as if I was standing outside myself with my arms crossed, shaking my head in disapproval. *Why did you do something you don't want anyone to know about?*

Guilt flooded where relief had been. Not that I'd hurt anyone, but that I'd put myself in a position where I could be hurt. The night with him needed to be secret or, as a matter of ethics, it needed to be disclosed to my team and the judge who got the case.

"Conference room in five," Martin said as he approached. "With Kimberly."

"Do you know what it's about?"

"Bel-Air, I think," he replied.

"I'll grab your notes," Amara said, dashing away.

Martin and I walked down the hall.

"We tried to call you last night," he said as we entered the conference room. "Where were you?"

"Sorry. I shut off the phone."

"Do you have a fever?" he asked as we sat. "Your face is red."

"Hello, hello!" Kimberly blew in like a plastic bag in a windstorm, wearing a suit jacket, matching trousers, and a blue tie. Though Kimberly was a feminine name, my boss preferred gender neutral pronouns. It had taken me a week to get used to it, but now I couldn't think of them any other way.

"You're back just in time, Monroe." They threw themselves into the chair at the head of the table. "Guess who I ran into at the gym this morning? Don't bother. Betty Bellini, the Bellini side of Bellini and Jonson. Architects to the rich and environmentally careless. We were chatting in spin class, if you can call trying to talk while barely breathing a 'chat,' and she mentioned she was tired from spending all night at plan check. So, me, being curious but not wanting to alarm the woman during her cardio workout, I called my buddy Jason the building inspector, and guess who pulled new permits late yesterday and, color me shocked, got rush approval on a damn Sunday night? Don't answer. Let me just bask in how impressed you are for a moment."

They could bask all they wanted. I knew the answer. Mitch and I were in the middle of litigating two dozen cases, but the timing of the revision was too much of a coincidence.

"What were the changes?" I asked.

"Placement of the electrical box and a one-foot shift on the west side of the footprint. And since the judge put a stay on the permit, not the property, he thinks he bought a one-way ticket to Doing-Whatever-the-Fuck-He-Wants-ville."

"We'll file another injunction before he breaks ground," I said.

"Ground's broken," Kimberly said. "They started moving dirt this morning at 7:31, apparently."

I bolted upright as if my chair had caught fire. "I'm going over there."

Kimberly leaned back with fingers laced together over their abdomen. "Nope. I filed for an inspection confirming compliance, and Crowne filed for an independent auditor to monitor the site on his dime, which the judge won't approve. Yes, it happened that fast." Kimberly stood. "He's not going to move a shoebox of dirt off that property without a proper accounting."

Kimberly was in a state of self-awe, and I should have been as well, but now there would be no hearing. We'd have to go to a full-blown trial.

He'd made all these moves while holing me up in a hotel room. He must have had the revised plans already and probably had an independent auditor set up beforehand. All he had to do was show up at the Eclipse event and promise me a night of pleasure.

I'd been played. I should have known better.

Knowing what he was, I'd begged for it like a dog in heat.

Begged.

I was a loser. A lightweight.

Chump. Patsy. Dupe. Stooge.

Never again.

Now this was war.

CHAPTER 9

OLIVIA

I'd managed to get through the day without eating my own liver in rage. We did all the things we were supposed to do to get Byron to halt construction. None of them needed my anger, and none would work quickly enough. The permit signoff wasn't a big deal. He didn't know I'd undone those before, but he was about to find out.

I could scrape out a win, as always, but I couldn't shake my emotional uneasiness.

The night was a lie. The gloaming at the horizon, the cooling fall air, the mating call of the crickets as I pulled up my street. All of it was a lie of peace and contentment.

Byron Crowne playing me like a fiddle had been eating me hollow all day, and on what should have been a lovely drive home with the car top down, it got worse. Without the constant noise of tasks to do and people to talk to, that bitter, sticky rage and shame got bigger.

My house didn't have a gate in front. The front yard had a path right up to the front door, and the driveway was open to the usually quiet street. The apartment buildings on either side weren't noisy most nights, and the busiest boulevard was two blocks away.

I pulled in, put the convertible top up, and walked up to my front porch with my keyring on my finger, figuring I'd stew until I was too exhausted to sleep. I was so focused on my bitterness I didn't see Byron on the porch swing until I turned the key.

Then I gasped, dropped my bag and held my hands out to defend myself.

"Whoa," he said with a chuckle, as if I couldn't hurt him.

"What the fuck are you doing here?"

"I wanted to see if you were all right." His tie was loosened, and his top shirt button undone, leading me to imagine the body underneath. The hardness under my fingers, the undulating muscles under the skin.

"I'm fine." I pushed the door open.

"Were you sick today?"

"Why?" I stopped myself. He didn't know I hadn't taken the pills. I didn't want to tell him. He didn't need another win over Team Olivia. "Why do you care?"

"I don't know." He was serious. He didn't know why he cared. What a dick.

"I'm not sick," I said. "So, you can go before I call the cops."

I waited at the door while he stood, buttoned his jacket, looked across the street as if he needed a moment to think, then looked back at me.

"You look like you had a bad day."

"Yeah," I said, dropping my bag inside the house while I still had a foot on the porch. "Today, I found out you distracted me while your people got a late-night signoff on new plans that are half a percent different. Nice play, Mr. Crowne."

He nodded. All the confirmation I needed was in that motion.

"I enjoyed it very much," he said, stepping forward, closer to both the stairs and me. He could have turned either way, but his body language committed to neither. "You did too."

"And now you're on my porch." I put both feet inside the house and crossed my arms. "What's going on behind my back now?"

"Nothing. I swear. This is strictly a personal visit."

"Pure concern for my health and well-being," I scoffed.

"You don't believe me?"

"Why should I?"

He faced fully in my direction. "I meant it when I said I couldn't stop thinking about you. All day, I had to stop myself from calling to see how you were."

"That doesn't make me like you."

"Believe me." He came closer, leaving his toes on the porch side of the door. He looked down at me with a heat that burned through my clothes and snaked its way between my legs like a long, sparking fuse. "This obsession I have doesn't mean I like you either."

"We agree, then."

"Oh, this? On this we are in total agreement. You're an annoying, yipping little dog in a pen of Rottweilers."

His words were insulting, but his expression confirmed his metaphor. He looked at me like a starving animal, and under it, I shook with anticipation and loathing.

"You going to fuck me or not?" I spat.

"Can you?"

"Can I?"

He thought I'd taken the pills and had no idea what the effect was. Right.

"You could," I said. "Nothing stopping us. But last night's over. We agreed."

"You trusted me to keep a promise?" he growled.

I lost a piece of my mind, putting one hand on his chest and gripping a handful of jacket. "No. I didn't."

In a heartbeat, we were kissing in my dark living room, door slamming behind us. He pushed me back, jamming his hand up my shirt as I slammed into a side table, knocking down a vase. I shoved him into the wall, rattling the picture over him, and yanked his belt out of the loops.

"You got something planned while you fuck me this time?" I pulled the belt free of the buckle and landed a punishing kiss.

"No." He bit my lower lip and pulled my skirt up over my ass. "But you do."

He spun us around and back, tripping us both onto the couch, where he held me down with his hand on my chest. I grappled for his clothes with a violence I didn't know I had in me. His jacket button broke away and clicked to the floor.

"Maybe I do," I said as if it mattered. As if I cared about anything but getting his cock inside me.

He pushed my knees apart and grabbed the fabric of my pantyhose, shredding them. Without preamble or a shred of human decency, he shoved two fingers inside me, and I nearly came from the roughness of his touch, crying out with my eyes closed and my back arched. He took them out before the orgasm fully blossomed so he could take out his erection.

Fisting it with his right hand, he leaned down and laid his left hand under my jaw, putting enough pressure on it to keep me from moving. "I'm going to wrap this up, and I'm going to fuck the yipping dog right out of you."

"No."

He froze, lessening the pressure on my throat.

"You don't have what it takes," I added.

Kneeling straight, he got a condom out of his jacket pocket before ripping off the jacket. He wrapped his cock, then pulled my legs up so I was bent at the waist with my underwear and shredded stockings stretched tight between my legs.

"Take it, then." In one hard thrust, he was inside me. In two, he was buried to the base.

I twisted in pleasure, and he took me sideways, one leg over his hip and one under, ramming deep and hard as if he wanted to kill me with his cock.

"That's all you have?" I gasped.

He growled, ripping my stockings apart, then my underwear, allowing him to spread my legs apart and push so deep his body rubbed my clit.

"This better?" His question was a challenge. "Or like this?"

He slammed in deeper than I thought possible, shifting against my throbbing core as if he was in a contest to get me off.

"Should I let you come?"

"I come when I want." I reached between my legs, but he took my wrists and held them over my head.

"What now, huh?" He gyrated deeply, gripping my wrists so hard the pain of my helplessness was exquisite. "What are you going to do now?"

"Come when I… oh God. Faster."

He didn't go faster. He didn't slow down either. "Tell me how much you like it."

"Faster, asshole."

"How bad do you want me to make you come?"

"Fuck you." I wanted to slap him, but his hold on my hands was too strong. "Fuck you. I want to come. I need to. Make me come, you fuck. Give it to me harder. Make me come."

He leaned down and pushed my bra aside with his chin, then he put his mouth on the pliable flesh at the top of my breast. "You're not ready."

"I am!"

He sucked the skin of my breast, fucking harder as he sucked me into his teeth into a painful, delicious, agonizing bite that left no room for any other thoughts or sensations.

As I came, he groaned through his teeth, sucking flesh as he exploded into me. My orgasm went on and on, taking hold of my thrashing body, which was held down by the wrist and tit.

When he let go, the darkness in the room swam, and my anchor to the earth was my gulped breath and his softening cock inside me.

"Olivia, one." He kissed the spot he'd wounded with tenderness I hadn't known he was capable of. "Pills, zero."

"I hate this," I said.

"You seemed to like it."

"Not that."

"What, then?"

"I didn't take the pills."

"You…" He straightened his arms, his face high enough to be illuminated by the streetlight through the window. "You what?"

"I'm sorry."

"So, what does that mean exactly?"

"I'm not trying to trap you. It's not that. I won't—"

"But you could get pregnant?"

"From last night. Yes."

He stood up in the blue light of the night, dick hanging out, shirt half-undone and wrinkled at the tail.

"And you want it?" He said it as if he couldn't believe it. As if the whole conversation in the pharmacy hadn't happened.

"Well, yes. I mean, I'm pissed that it's yours. Obviously."

"So, you didn't get the IUI this morning?"

"No. I was busy dealing with your backstabbing bullshit." I sat up straight on the couch, naked in front of him, sore and messy, and regarded him standing there with his dick hanging out.

His smirk and his regal bearing didn't seem cultivated to intimidate, but as much a part of him as his green eyes.

"But I wouldn't have gone anyway," I continued. "This way, if I am, then I know whose it is and how it happened. I don't need the stress of waiting for the DNA."

He hadn't moved since he stood, half-silhouetted in the darkness, the details of his face in blue shadow. He wasn't sincere or trustworthy. Some manipulation was probably behind trying to convince me not to take the morning-after pills.

"Did you change your mind?" I asked.

"No."

"So, why are you standing there like you're shocked?"

"How long before you know?"

"I usually take an early test, then the doctor confirms."

"I need a date."

Quelling enough annoyance to throw a shoe at him, I sucked in a breath so hard it was audible halfway across the room.

"Please," he added.

"Two weeks. Next Sunday, earliest."

"I want to be there."

"Where? In the toilet when I piss on a stick?"

He sat next to me in the dark, hands folded in his lap. The bite on my breast was throbbing, and my clothes were situated uncomfortably, but I didn't move.

"I know you hate me," he said. "I know I stand for everything you despise in a person."

"What was the hint?"

"But if we share a child…" He turned to face me, one green eye catching the light. "I don't want you to feel that way."

"You promised you'd leave me alone."

"I will. If that's what you want, I'll disappear. You'll never see me again. But what if you wanted me around for him? Wouldn't that be better?"

"What if the moon was made of green cheese?"

"The bottom would fall out of the dairy market, and a child would have a father. Preferable, no?"

I faced forward with a sigh. I didn't want Byron to feel trapped, and he wasn't. I was the one hemmed in on all sides.

"What are you trying to manipulate me into?" I asked. "This isn't some play to build that house, is it? Because if it is—"

"My God, you think I'm some kind of monster?"

"I'm not sure what I think right now." Somewhere on the block, a car alarm showed off seven ways to shriek. "Have you heard of Francois Hollande?"

"The director? French, right?"

"He's my father. If you were into obscure foreign films, you'd be oohing and aahing over what a 'genius auteur' he is. And even if you only cared about American movies, you'd be asking what he did after *City in Thunder,* but thankfully, you're neither. Bursting people's bubble is a pain in the ass."

The alarm died, and a mockingbird took up the call, whistling in seven melodies.

"When he met my mother," I continued, "she was a model, and of course she wanted to get into acting. I mean, she was twenty-three and not getting any younger. So, she meets my dad, and he's famous in France. He was trying to get something going here that might make him some money. She auditions, and he gives her the lead in *City in Thunder,* to which you're saying, 'That was Ursula Rozen, who isn't your mother,' right?"

"Right."

"Well, so of course they start sleeping together, and three months before shooting, he knocks her up with my sister. She can't play the part pregnant. To which you're saying, 'It takes two,' or 'Why didn't she use birth control?' or some garbage I'm going to stop you from saying right now. Because when I asked my mother that, she shrugged and said they were out of condoms and he was really insistent. *Insistent.* Don't speak. I don't want you to tell me what that means to you, but it means something very definite to me. She lost the part, and more importantly, she stayed with him. She married him. Even after she found out he'd recast with Ursula Rozen weeks before he was 'insistent.' She still married him, and she stayed married when he knocked her up again with me two years later. This way, he didn't have to cast her in *Eastern Wind*... which you never saw because by then my mother finally got smart. She hired a private investigator, found out he was fucking the wife of the studio head, and that finished him. Fatal blow. No movie. No friends. Done."

"What did he do?"

"Slunk back to France. We haven't heard from him since."

The mockingbird gave up and tweeted another melody.

"How old were you?"

I shrugged. My flashes of memory of the gray-haired man who talked funny: him standing over the stove with his hand over mine so he could guide the spoon around the corners of the pan, or reading a script by a window, or asking me to say the word *squirrel* over and over with his eyes on my mouth to figure out how the hell I made those sounds... None of that mattered.

"So." I stood so I could pull up my underwear and pull down my skirt. "I know what my mother put herself through when she should have known better. I'm not doing that. You might be manipulating me for some kind of financial gain, or you might not. The point isn't that I don't trust you, because that's obvious. The point is that really..." Clothes back where they belonged, I crossed my arms. "Really... I don't trust me."

CHAPTER 10

BYRON

I'd met a lot of women in my life, but none who shapeshifted like Olivia Monroe. She'd started as a pawn in a game, shifted into a worthy opponent, then the object of my desire, and in the past few hours, between telling me she was trying to get pregnant and the moment she explained the holes in her trust, she'd become someone I wanted to care for.

Now, standing before me in a dark room with her arms crossed, she'd shifted into a woman too complex to fathom. If there had been straight lines between what I wanted and what she wanted, I'd have known the play, but they were curved around themselves like a gold chain in the bottom of a drawer. I could easily discern the unknotted lengths of chain where I wanted to fuck her. But the rest was hopelessly tangled, and yanking too hard would break the whole thing.

"I have an idea," I said, giving myself a moment to change my mind by putting my dick back in my pants. "It's the worst idea I ever had." I zipped up.

She reached under the table lamp to click it on, and I could finally see our surroundings.

"Let's hear it." She sat on a white chair with blue flowers upholstered into the fabric. I recognized the pattern as a custom weave from Surya, and it didn't match the couch, which looked as if it came from a dorm. The rug was a floral IKEA job, and the side table was a thirty-year-old rosewood Niemeyer. If the lamp was brighter, I'd probably see the same mix of high and low. Nonetheless, her cool beauty and the glow of her skin elevated everything in the room.

"You don't trust yourself with me."

"I'm not trying to stroke your ego."

"As a tactic, flattery is beneath you."

"But it's not beneath you," she said, acknowledging that I'd flattered her and that nothing I said would make her believe it wasn't a tactic.

"In the end, either you're pregnant, or you aren't. If you are, I'm going to keep my promise and leave you alone. But I don't want to. I want to take care of it, and you, and be as much of a father as you'll let me be. Which I understand you don't want. You have a career; you have enough money to get by. You think I'm more trouble than I'm worth. I want to convince you otherwise. I'm not..." I held my hand up to stop her train of thought. "*Not* interviewing for the job of husband. That's not in the cards. But I want you to see me as a father. I want you, in the ledger of your life, to see I can be in the plus column."

"What's your deal?"

"My deal?"

She crossed her legs and leaned her elbow on the arm of the chair that was closer to me. "Why are you so intent on this?"

That was as good a time as any to tell her the hard truth. It would make things easier later.

"The odds of me ever loving a woman are nil," I said. "Getting married is less than nil. I'm not husband material. However, that doesn't mean I don't want children. A family of my own."

"And I can give you a child without the hassle?"

"The same thing you want."

She nodded with a cock to her head as if she might actually believe me. "We've fucked twice already, and this time, just now, it wasn't carefully thought out. It was… I mean, for me it…" She held her tongue and looked down. Her eyelashes cast long shadows on her cheeks. "I don't have great control around you, and I already said I don't trust myself."

"I have control."

"You can't control me." Her blue eyes blazed as if she'd forgotten who called the shots when her legs were spread. The thought gave my balls a twinge.

"Everything you hate about me as a partner isn't going to change."

"But I'm supposed to embrace you as a family man?"

"I think it's worth a try. Listen, it's Labor Day weekend. My family has a place up in Santa Barbara. Come up. We have a house. It's—"

"What are you going to tell them? I'm an egg bank, and you have a deposit maturing?"

"There are enough bedrooms for me to bring a friend."

She scoffed and sat back in her chair with her face turned to the ceiling. "You don't know people at all."

"It's not about what they think. It's about what you think."

"I think you've got some kind of hard-on for me and it's scrambling your brain."

I laughed. She was right. She was a cord of desire running between my head and my dick. I'd never felt such a strong pull from a woman. Her scent, a soft lavender that sneaked up on the edges of my consciousness, was a narcotic lulling me into a haze of sexual need.

But for all that, she knew the lesser truth. I wouldn't confuse desire for love. Ever.

Neither would she.

"I have a hard-on for you," I admitted. "Your body, your voice, the way you walk into a room makes me want to fuck you. But I'm not scrambled. I can't love you or anyone. That's not in the cards for me, and as far as I go, it's not in the cards for you either. You won't ever cross that line, because you despise me. You know I'm wrong for you. That's why I trust you."

She regarded me, tenting her fingertips and tapping them as if giving rhythm to her thoughts. "This might work. Except the jealousy over Alan."

"I wanted you, and he was an unexpected obstacle."

"Will every man I meet be an obstacle?"

She was thinking into the future, and she was right to. If there was a baby between us, we needed utter clarity for the long term.

"As long as you and I are fucking, I offer exclusivity. And we'll fuck until we're bored. No hard feelings."

"Do you have any actual emotions?"

"Not anymore. No."

She laughed and slid down in her seat. We had a deal, and with it, the possibility of her spreading her legs before dawn.

But not quite.

"I need to ask you something you're sensitive about," she said.

"I know what this is."

There weren't too many things anyone would suspect me of being sensitive about.

"Samantha," she confirmed. "Was it suicide?"

I'd expected questions about my feelings, which ones had died and which were still hanging around. The death was a death, and few people asked anything past what had been announced. Years of walls built around the truth set my jaw against an answer.

"Is this line of questioning a deal-breaker?" I asked.

"You've delineated the exact ways I trust you and the exact ways I don't," she said. "But I have no idea of the lines around where you trust me."

I sat in a chair across from her shadowed shape, settling in. I had nothing to prove to her or anyone, but I wanted to fuck her more than I wanted to keep a secret. Or maybe I was a fool.

Both could be true.

"Early in the morning," I said, "when everyone was asleep, she used a crowbar to break the pool light. Then she jumped in wearing her pajamas. She didn't drown. It was electrocution."

"I'm so sorry."

"Faster that way actually. Her parents didn't want anyone to know. I honored their wishes and trust you will too."

With that, for reasons I couldn't define, I'd widened the lines of trust by a mile and a half. Sam's suicide was a source of shame for me, and this woman wasn't close enough to me to know it. I waited to feel a stab of regret but didn't.

"I will," she said with an emotionally flat seriousness that only increased the trust by another half a mile.

"Thank you."

"Do you have any idea why she did it?"

I knew I couldn't tell her, but at the same time... I was compelled to.

"We had a fight." I tapped my knee. No more. We'd hit the line. "So. There you have it. Is that all?"

"Are you okay about it?"

"Am I fucked up if I say yes?"

"You're fucked up," she said. "You are one fucked up son of a bitch. You're hard as iron. Sometimes you're hot. Sometimes you're cold. But still cast iron through and through."

I stood, and she looked up at me with her legs crossed and her posture relaxed as if she had the upper hand.

She did. She'd earned it, and if we were doing this thing, I needed to let her have moments of victory. I'd made the mistake of being too hard with a woman already, and I wouldn't do it again.

"You understand me, then."

"No." Pushing herself up on the arms of the chair, she stood nose to nose with me, our bodies barely brushing against each other. The sharp smell of sex came from her. When she spoke, her breath fell on my lips, and I wanted to feel her from the inside one more time. "I don't understand you. But I don't need to."

"This, Olivia." I kissed her. "This is why I trust you."

We were kissing again, and I was getting hard under the pants I'd just zipped up when she gently pushed me back.

"Go," she said. "Before we're up all night."

With a little effort, I could have taken her. I could have persuaded her the orgasms would be worth the lost sleep, but I needed to convince her she could trust me.

I plucked my jacket off the floor and got into it while she opened the front door.

We kissed one last time, and I left.

EARLY THE NEXT MORNING, surrounded by the humble silence of big, yellow earth-moving machines, I stood on what was truly the most perfect piece of land in Los Angeles. Ocean view to one side. City views in every other direction. On a clear day, you could see the future, and the sun was rising without a drop of marine layer between me and what I'd been convinced I'd never have.

A spit-shined black Suburban crunched rocks and dirt under its tires as it rolled onto the lot. By the time I got close enough to hear the engine, it was turned off and Logan got out in a suit, tie, and shoes made for the office.

"I told you to wear boots," I said after a quick hug and a back slap.

"I'm not staying long enough to step on a nail."

"It's your foot."

"So," he said, turning to catch all of the view. "This is it?"

"This is it."

"Your choice for the One Big Thing."

"It is."

Until both our parents died, which wasn't happening any time soon, each of us could request a family investment in what we called the One Big Thing. After that, we were limited by trust funds, which were ample enough to keep us in gold-plated dinnerware, golf club memberships, and my string of spec houses, but not nearly enough to fund a project of this size. It was planned that way to make sure we learned how to raise our own capital, avoid waste, and prioritize investments over wanton spending.

"You had some environmentalists on you over the footprint?"

"Fixed. We're solid."

"Thank God," Logan said. "Dad has regrets over Colton's OBT."

"I'm not Colton."

Of the six of us, only my younger brother Colton had called in the OBT so far, taking it in cash when he turned twenty-one. He blew it in two years, setting the bad example we all strove to avoid.

"No, you're not. But when you decided not to run Crowne Industries, he got a little worried."

"Too much responsibility," I replied. "Too many eyeballs in my business. You can have it."

Over the ridge, a cloud of dust was kicked up by the arriving crew.

"Your loss," Logan said. "It's fun, you know."

"Sure. While we're on the subject of fun…"

"Were we?"

"Labor Day weekend. Crownestead. You going?"

When Mom's hands had started tremoring constantly, our parents moved up to our summer house in Santa Barbara to live full-time.

"Dad considers that a working holiday, so yes. Lyric will bring a dozen annoying friends; Colton may show up. Dante's who knows where."

"And Liam?"

"Playing daddy at Malin's parents'."

"Ah."

"Why? No one to torment?"

"Counting bedrooms." A handful of trucks pulled in, and men in work clothes spilled out. "I'm bringing someone."

Logan was easy to read, and for him, I was too. The less I tried to say, the more information he'd get out of me.

"What's her name?" he asked.

"Olivia. She's a friend."

Logan could have said plenty. He could have teased or prodded, and after half a lifetime of living with him, I knew he wanted to. But he didn't. He hadn't given me a hard time about women since Samantha died.

"You'd better get to work," he said. "See you in Santa Barbara."

CHAPTER 11

OLIVIA

After work, I went to Amelia's to help Emilio with the menu. The construction team was putting up the custom lighting and art deco brass finishings when I arrived. An array of small plates was lined up along the bar.

"What's this one?" I asked as Emilio held up a wedge of bread with a clear gelatin wiggling on the edge.

"Bone marrow with raspberry reduction."

He fed it to me. I chewed slowly.

"Salty. Maybe too salty?"

"More raspberry." He made a note in a little book.

"I wanted to tell you something," I said.

"You hate it? Just say so."

"No. Not that. About the IUI."

"Did my virility finally show up?"

"No, I mean, I don't know. I skipped this month."

"Second thoughts? Giving it a rest? Manuel!" he interrupted himself, shouting to the construction supervisor before rattling something off in Spanish.

Manuel agreed, but *si* was all I understood.

"Sorry." He forked a ball of gnocchi. "Tell me if this is too meaty."

He fed it to me, and I took my time chewing.

"Not. It's good. Cloves?"

"Yep." Another note in his book. "Russel's telling me I need a hamburger. I'm like, Jesus Christ, can we be the one place in LA without a twenty-two-dollar ground beef sandwich on the menu?"

"About the baby thing?"

"Yep." He shifted the plates around.

"Someone else…"

He froze with a dish in each hand.

"This cycle… someone else got in, I guess you'd say. It was the night before the IUI appointment, so I was ovulating. I didn't want any confusion. So."

He put down the food. "Don't tell me who."

"I can neither confirm nor deny."

"It was Byron Crowne," he guessed as if he was stating a fact.

"Confirmed."

"Girl." Hector, the sous chef, delivered two steaming plates into Emilio's hands and cleared the dirties. "You hate him."

"I do, but I think that kind of works in bed. It's…"

"Hot." He put the new dishes on the bar in front of me.

"So hot the condom broke. Are you mad? You can still be the world's best uncle."

"It's your body, baby. What did you tell him?"

"Everything. I had to. Right? I mean, fair is fair. Then I was going to take the morning-after pill and call it a wash, but I couldn't. I just… I want this too badly."

"And what about him?"

I sighed. It was a short, complicated story he deserved to hear. "He's down for it, but he wants to be *involved*."

"Uh-oh."

"He invited me to a family weekend in Santa Barbara. He thinks spending time with him will prove he'd be a decent father. This guy. Do you know what he was doing while we were in bed the other night?"

"Hopefully not sleeping."

"He was backstabbing me. And I'm supposed to believe he'll be Mr. Honesty from now on? How is a weekend at the beach going to change that?"

"I hear his parents are nice."

"You hear..."

His parents. He wanted me to meet his parents.

"Olivia? What's going on in your head?"

"He's so fucked up and so transparent. He's trying to demonstrate that whatever I think of him, I'll like his family."

"You might." He pushed a glass of lemon water to me. "Cleanse your palette. The *coniglio* is subtle, and I don't want you to miss the surprise."

I drank the cold, acidic water to prepare my palette for the rabbit stew.

If I was ready to like his family, I was ready for just about anything.

* * *

A BENTLEY CAME for me on Friday evening. He wasn't in it. His driver, Yusup, whom I remembered from the Eclipse show, handed me a soft, white card in an envelope. "Byron Crowne" was embossed on the back flap. I opened it while he loaded my bag into the trunk.

DEAR OLIVIA,

. . .

I'm sorry I can't join you for the ride. I had to come up early to take care of some business. Yusup will do whatever you need to make your trip comfortable.

I decided not to tell anyone in my family about the possible pregnancy. I don't want them to get their hopes up. Hope you agree.

—Byron

I AGREED. For two people who couldn't stand each other, we saw eye-to-eye on a lot of things.

"Ms. Monroe." Yusup stood by the open door. "Do we need to stop anywhere before we go?"

"No." I got in, and he closed the door. The inside smelled of new leather and luxury.

When he was settled in the driver's seat, he turned to me. "There's a window between us. Would you like some privacy?"

"No, I'm good."

He nodded and pulled away. "There's a console to your left if you want to listen to music or the news, water in the pouch in front. You can charge your phone if you like."

"What kind of music do you like?" I asked.

"I'm a classic rock guy myself."

That sounded good. I scrolled through the stations until I found one playing Led Zeppelin.

"What does Byron listen to?" I asked.

"News, mostly. Stock tickers. Music tends to more lady rock."

"Excuse me?"

"Songwriters and their guitars. Liz Phair. Amy Winehouse. That kind of thing."

Surprising. I could barely imagine Byron enjoying music at all, much less songs with metaphor-heavy lyrics.

"How long have you worked for Byron?"

The car got on the 101 and sped up without a rumble or a change in the engine noise.

"Going on six years. I sold him his first Bentley, then he hired me. He said he could tell I was ready to leave the dealership. Man oh man, he was right. And couldn't beat the pay."

The tinted windows dimmed the passing night.

"Did you know his fiancée?" I asked.

"Nice lady. Terrible what happened."

"Yeah."

"He was busted up about it."

What did "busted up" mean for a man like Byron Crowne? Was he snippy? Angry? More stoic than ever?

"I bet," I said. "He's a sensitive guy."

"Sure was."

Past tense? *Was* sensitive? Was the chauffeur referring to a specific incident in the past or his boss as he used to be? Before I could weasel my way into clarification, Yusup changed the subject.

"You're going to love the house," he said. "Great pool. Right on the beach. They have a stable of rescued thoroughbred runts. Do you ride?"

"A little in high school, but not competitively."

"Maybe he won't try to race you, then."

I laughed. Even Byron's driver knew he wanted to win at everything.

* * *

Yusup and I braved the Friday night traffic with small talk and only one bathroom stop. His parents were Muslim Uighurs from Western

China, and they had brought him and his sister to the United States when they were small. He wasn't eager to tell me about the Chinese government's unwanted attention to his people, but I pressed him. By the time we got to the Santa Barbara coast at nine thirty that night, I knew enough to be angry on his behalf.

"The Crownes have done everything they could to get my grandmother over here," Yusup said as the car turned up a small street dotted with houses set far behind wrought iron fences. "But China isn't impressed with money or lawyers."

"What are they impressed with?"

"Nothing. Absolutely nothing, man. Ted Crowne had a refinery in Ningbo province. He threatened to close it unless China issued visas to her and anyone she wanted to bring. They called his bluff."

"So, he didn't close it?" We drove up into the hills, through an iron gate with a crown in the center that opened as the car approached.

"No, he closed it. China took it over like that." He snapped his fingers. "They don't like to lose. Not for one grandma or a hundred. But the Crownes are honorable. They're people of their word. Ted apologized to me like he hadn't lost millions on that refinery."

Yusup stopped the car at the top of the circular drive. The Spanish-style house looked modest from the front, lush with crawling, flowering vines and old trees that, come morning, would cast the yard in shade.

Yusup turned to make eye contact as he put the car in park. "I hope I didn't bring you down."

"Not at all. You made a boring ride very interesting."

Byron came out the front door wearing jeans and a deep-green, unbuttoned polo. He opened the back door for me while Yusup got my bag from the trunk.

"How was your ride?" Byron asked, offering his hand. I took it and let him lift me out.

"Fine. Yusup's a great conversationalist."

"It's the car salesman in him," he announced as if it was a running joke between him and his driver. "Careful or he'll sell you a Rolls."

"It's the superior drive, if you ask me." Yusup slammed the trunk closed. "Can I take this upstairs?"

"I have it." Byron took the bag. "Thank you."

"Thank you!" I called.

Yusup waved and drove the car around the side of the house.

"You tired?" Byron asked, leading me to the front door, then into a large entryway with warm stone floors and high ceilings with exposed beams.

"Not really."

"Good. Everyone's at the pool."

"A swim sounds nice."

"You can change in your room." He held out his hand but dropped it before I could take it, as if thinking better of holding my hand. I'd never seen him so unsure of himself.

I'd have to take it easy on him.

He led me through a living room with a crackling fireplace and huge, open sliding doors that led to a patio, up a flight of wood stairs, looking back at me to talk. "My mother put you in the room over the pool. If Lyric and her friends stay up late back there, we can switch."

"I'm sure it's fine."

The upper floor had two short hallways. Byron led me left and into my room, where he placed my bag on a bench at the foot of the bed. The doors opened onto a balcony with two chairs and a table with fresh flowers in the center. The bed was frothy with pure-white linens, the woods were stained clean gray, and the air was thick with ocean salt.

I heard splashing and talking from below. In the moments of silence, the sound of crashing waves came through.

He put his hands behind his back. "Will this be all right?"

"It's gorgeous."

"Good. Good. Bathroom through here." He reached through an ajar door and flicked a switch, lighting up the pure-white porcelain of the sink. His biceps tensed as if it took all his strength to keep his hands behind him.

"I should change," I said.

"My room is across the hall," he said.

"Is that a hint for later?"

He smirked, and a touch of cockiness came back. "I don't want to embarrass my family." He let his hands drop to his sides.

"Me neither."

"So, if I bend you over the bed right now, I can hold my hand over your mouth so they won't hear you scream."

A vision of him holding me down and stifling my screams of pleasure shredded my maturity. I was ready to bend myself over the bed when a peal of young female laughter came from downstairs, saving me from temptation.

"Byron?"

"Olivia?" His voice was rough with desire.

"Get out."

Judging from the tightness of his mouth, it took all his strength to leave.

* * *

THE BIKINI FIT PERFECTLY. If I was pregnant, it was too soon to start showing, but I still checked myself in the mirror to make sure, and I was still disappointed there was no change. I put on a robe and went downstairs, navigating poorly through a library and two living rooms before I found my way around to the back of the house.

"You must be Olivia," a woman in her sixties, with a short, gray pixie cut and a sheer robe over her bathing suit, called from the kitchen. She was pouring white wine into two glasses set on the stainless countertop. "I'm Doreen Crowne."

"Hi, Mrs.—"

"Doreen, please." She jammed the bottle into a bucket of ice to open her arms for me. The embrace was warm but not overly familiar.

"Nice to meet you, Doreen."

"I hope you like Chablis." She handed me a glass. "Kind of old school, but on a hot night, it's perfect."

A potentially pregnant woman shouldn't drink. I took the glass anyway. "Thank you."

"Come," she said as she slid open the back door. "Everyone's so excited to meet you!"

I followed her out, hoping she was exaggerating.

The turquoise pool was shaped like a bitmapped comma with a hot tub at the narrowest end. Two men sat at a table by themselves, speaking earnestly and quietly under an overhang of grape vine. The middle-aged man had to be Ted Crowne. Byron had his lips and his intensity. The younger man I recognized as Logan from the Eclipse show. On the left of the pool were empty banks of private couches. To the right were sun chairs occupied by four women in their twenties, huddling together over the glow of their phones. Directly forward there was nothing but blackness on the horizon, but in the morning, there would be an unobstructed view of the ocean.

There were flowers and plants everywhere. Every corner had a potted mini-tree. Vines wound through the overhung eaves. As I let myself relax into the intimacy and warmth of the foliage and soft lighting, my eyes fell on the reason I was there.

Byron stood at the edge of the pool, still fully dressed except for his bare toes curling around the curve of the tile. The underwater lights shimmered from beneath him, turning his expression from friendly, to lustful, to powerful, and back again.

Which one was really him? Or had the rippling water exposed a complex reality?

"You must be Olivia." A man's voice came from my right, but Byron's lips hadn't moved.

"Yes," I said in that general direction.

Ted was standing to greet me, and Doreen led me over. A heat lamp flamed above us.

"Olivia, this is Ted, Byron's father."

We shook hands over the table, which was covered in papers and folders.

"This is such a beautiful house," I said.

"Thank you," he said. "When I inherited this place, it was falling down. Doreen brought it back to life." He nodded to his wife with deep admiration.

"Want to buy it?" Logan asked, closing his laptop before standing.

"Logan," Doreen scolded.

"It's a ridiculous expense." He shook my hand. "Except when we have such lovely guests."

"We talked about this." Byron's voice was right behind me. He'd approached so quickly and quietly I jumped a little.

"Did we?" Logan smirked, sitting and opening his laptop.

"My brother's a world-class flirt. Ignore him."

Byron eyed my wine glass suspiciously. I held onto it. He wasn't the boss of me, and I didn't have to prove I was keeping healthy. Not to him.

"He was being friendly," Doreen objected. "Which he should keep doing."

Doreen pushed the laptop closed.

"Yeah," Lyric said, walking over in a bikini top and a towel around her waist. Her damp hair hung loose to her waist, curling slightly as it dried. "Put that shit away, dude." She rolled her eyes. "I'm Lyric. Nice to meet you."

Her hand was cool and damp from a recent swim.

"Nice to meet you."

She pointed at her friends. "That's Corinne, Kristy, and Karla."

Two of the three waved. The third didn't look up from her phone.

"I'm going in to get some chips. Want anything?" she asked me.

"I'm fine, thank you."

"Refill me, would you?" Logan pushed a short glass with ice on the bottom toward her. "The Macallan. Thanks."

"Basics get their own." She strutted into the house with a defiant sway to her hips.

"They wanted a girl," Byron muttered.

"You boys needed a sister," Ted replied, then looked at his wife with a smirk that must have been patented for the Crowne gene pool. He pulled out a chair. "Sit, Olivia."

"I was thinking of jumping in first." I put down my glass.

"Go on," Doreen said, sitting. "It's perfect."

The diving board was on the side with the couch banks, and Byron followed me there.

"Sorry about them," he said.

"Who?"

"My family. We have a habit of inter-sibling harassment."

"I think it's cute." I slid out of the robe and dropped it on a lounger.

"You're trying to kill me in that bikini," he murmured.

I stepped up onto the diving board. "Death is too good for you."

Without hesitation, I dove headfirst into the cool shock of the water, letting the loud whoosh and gurgle turn into placid white noise. I let my mind relax and let my body go limp and passive so the air in my lungs and buoyancy could carry it to the surface. Thoughts floated away, and for a single moment, I didn't want anything but the caress of the water.

An underwater eruption yanked me out of my reverie, then hard hands gripped my arms and I was pulled upward, gasping for air not because I was out of breath, but because I was too stunned to hold it.

"You're okay?" Byron held me tightly, as if I'd sink like a stone without him. His brown hair was black with water and flattened to his face, and his lashes were stuck together. The polo was stuck to his chest, and water dripped from his lips. He was struggling to tread water.

"Me? You could drown wearing jeans in the pool."

"Just… don't do that." He let go, looking away from me.

"Do what?"

I followed his gaze. Doreen was standing. Lyric was at the door with a bowl of chips in her hand. All her friends were on the edges of their chairs, ignoring their phones to stare at us. Logan remained seated, but Ted was on his feet.

"You guys," I said. "Really. I'm a California state bronze medalist. Freestyle."

Logan laughed and came to the edge closest to me, holding out his hand. The stairs were only halfway across the pool, but Logan's intention was clear: prove competence. I swam toward him, leaving Byron behind.

"It's not you," Logan said. "They're worried Byron's going to sink."

I locked wrists with him, and he pulled me out. Doreen brought me a huge striped towel and insisted on wrapping it around my shoulders.

"He's jumpy," she said under her breath.

Lyric brought the chips to her cohort, and they went back to their phones.

Byron sloshed up the stairs, taking a few gallons in the heavy weaves of his clothes.

"You're a hero looking for a crisis," Logan said, handing him a towel.

"You're the crisis." Byron grabbed the towel, but Logan didn't let it go.

A tug-of-war ensued so quickly I almost missed Logan pulling the towel and ducking to get Byron over his shoulders to throw him back in. But Byron recovered enough to pull Logan in with him, and both of them landed in the water fully clothed.

I laughed, and Byron seemed to forget himself long enough to lean on his brother's shoulders to dunk him. Logan got out from under and tried to return the favor. They smiled and splashed, wrestling for dominance like two kittens in the same litter.

Next to me, Doreen sighed. "They've been like that since they were kids."

"They're cute."

"You haven't touched your wine. Do you want to try another bottle?"

"It's late, and I think the long drive dehydrated me. I don't want to get a headache."

"I have just the thing."

The pool's surface slapped and swayed. Byron got out from under Logan and flipped his wet hair out of his eyes to look at me with a grin that was only possible on a face that was relaxed with a heart that was happy. I'd never seen him like that, and I took a moment to file the memory of it before following Doreen into the kitchen.

"One of our cooks made us a lemonade," she said, taking a glass pitcher from the huge refrigerator. When it closed, it looked like another cabinet. "Do you like ginger? She shaves a little in with lime zest, and it's wonderful."

"Sure."

"So, you're a swimmer?"

"High school, so not really anymore. I just wanted Byron to stop thinking I'd drown."

She poured plopped ice from the bucket into two tall glasses. "He's usually fine, but after he found Samantha…" She cringed. "Did he tell you that?"

"I'm glad you did."

"I shouldn't have."

"Now I know not to play dead in the pool."

She poured the lemonade pensively. "It changed him."

"How?"

I didn't expect her to answer, but she must have made up her mind to do so in the time it took her to put the pitcher away.

"He's been a bit closed off since then. Tightly wound, if you know what I mean."

"I sure do."

"When I heard you were coming," she handed me a glass, "I was so happy. He hasn't mentioned a woman in five years."

"It's not all that serious." *You might have a grandchild though.*

"Well, he brought you here. He must think very highly of you."

We can't stand each other.

She was prodding me because her son must have told her next to nothing about me or why I was there. I didn't want to lie to such a kind, cordial person, but I couldn't tell her the truth either.

"Lemonade toast." I lifted my glass. "To people we think highly of."

She clicked with me just as Lyric and all her friends came in, chatting and giggling. Behind them, the two sodden brothers talked at the edge of the pool with their father. Across the patio, Byron's eyes met mine. Though he may have thought highly of me, he had raw, carnal hunger on his mind. He stripped me naked without laying a finger on me, and for the first time since we met, I forgot I hated him.

* * *

Was it the magic of a healthy family that turned down the heat of my loathing? Over the kitchen counters and enough lemonade to send me to the bathroom twice, Doreen and Ted asked me about my life, my childhood, and my famous mother while Byron sat quietly. He interjected to wisecrack or ask a clarifying question he usually knew the answer to, but otherwise he left it to his parents to charm me until close to midnight, when Doreen rubbed her neck as if it ached.

"Cinderella didn't actually turn into a pumpkin at midnight," Ted said, holding his hand out to his wife.

"Her dress disappeared," I added.

"Well, I'd better get my wife to bed before then."

Doreen took his hand and stood. "Dancing with a prince can take it out of you." With Ted helping her keep her balance, she leaned over to plant a kiss on my cheek. "It was great to meet you. Nellie will be here bright and early to make us breakfast."

"Thank you," I said.

"Good night," Ted said, leading Doreen out of the room slowly, as if she needed him to help her get there.

I caught sight of Byron watching them go, and for the second time that night, I felt as though I was seeing a wistful expression I wasn't meant to.

"Is she all right?" I asked.

"The Parkinson's gets worse when she's tired."

So many questions rushed to get through, and my manners were such a well-trained bodyguard that I froze with my lips parted.

"Not hereditary," Byron said as if he knew the most pressing question. "Not her case at least. We've all been checked out. My mother is the victim of a random environmental mutation."

"I'm sorry," I said. "That's terrible."

"It is, but the medication helps, and she has my father, so it's tolerable."

The sentiment behind his statement was the last thing I'd expected from Byron Crowne. He was a man who powered through life, not one who believed two people could find comfort in each other's arms.

"I'm wiped out." I took my glass to the sink and turned on the faucet.

"We have a staff to take care of that."

"My mother didn't raise me to leave dishes."

From behind me, he turned off the water and took the glass from my hand. "Your mother raised you well. But our dirty dishes support a dozen people. Let them do their jobs."

I faced him, and he put his hands on the counter on either side of me. His hair had dried, but when I laid my hands on his waist, his shirt was damp and cool.

"Fine," I said. "You win."

"Get used to it." He ran his nose along my cheek.

"I'm really tired."

"How tired?"

"Too tired for a visit tonight."

He pulled away just enough to let me see the flecks of his eyes. They weren't green but a mix of blue and light brown. How had I not seen that before?

"Is that your final word?"

"Yes."

His eyes grew more distant as he leaned away. "Let me walk you up, then."

As he led me through the formal dining room, I stopped at a large painting. It was square, four feet by four feet, probably oil, rendered with traditional strokes. The scene was outdoors, bordered by large desert palms with a floor of California poppies. The eight members of the Crowne family sat on a blue checkered blanket facing the viewer. Ted and Doreen on either side but leaning toward each other. Doreen had a book on one knee and her arm around a toddler in a pink dress. A tear ran down the little girl's cheek as if she'd just gotten over a tantrum. One boy of about seven or so had his hand on her shoulder, comforting her. Another boy, close in age, sat with his knees up, facing away from the rest of his family. I recognized green-eyed, early-teen Byron in his jeans and polo, but his hair was a mess and he was making rabbit ears behind his serious brother Logan's back with one hand. With the other, it looked as though they were having a tug-of-war over a Lego build.

"I almost didn't recognize you with the smile," I said.

He scoffed. "The artist spent a month with us. She's supposedly famous for capturing relationships. Personalities. That kind of thing."

"Who's this?" I pointed at a stern-looking boy of about seven years standing behind Ted.

"Liam. And this is Colton." The boy had on a bright, mismatched outfit and held a donut in his hand. The other was behind his back. "He was about nine."

"Liked donuts, did he?"

"He likes pleasure and detests hard work."

"A bacchanalian."

"She got him right. The rest of us, I don't know."

Maybe he didn't know. Maybe he was in denial or making sure he kept his mask on straight. I thought the artist had been onto something Byron didn't want me to see.

"Ready?" Byron said, heading for the stairs.

I followed him to my bedroom door. "This is fun," I said with my hand on the knob. "Thank you for inviting me."

"Good night." He laid his hand on the doorknob to his room.

"Good night."

We paused, and I considered a visit across the hall. But he broke the spell, opening his door first as if he was determined to respect my wish to sleep. I turned the knob. We went into our rooms at the same time.

CHAPTER 12

OLIVIA

I left the curtains open, thinking they faced west and I'd be greeted by soft morning light. But they were south-facing enough to let the full blast of the sun edge onto my sleeping face.

When I got out of the shower, I heard women talking and the sound of a broom on the hall floor. Outside, a man skimmed the pool, and another pruned the grape leaves.

Lured by the smell of bacon, I went to the kitchen. A woman with a short, tight afro and navy apron had four pans going. Bacon, sausage, eggs, ham. She was shucking a watermelon that had given its life to participate in a bowl of fruit salad.

"Hi," I said. "You must be Nellie?"

She glanced up from scooping poached eggs for only a moment. "I am." Her accent had a Louisiana patois. "Can I make you an omlette?"

"I can wait for the poached, if you don't mind."

"I'll make you some. Coffee's up on the patio. The orange juice is fresh."

"Thank you."

A sideboard of food had been set up on the deck on the other side of the doors. No one seemed to be up except Logan, who scrolled through an iPad screen with a notebook in front of him. I got myself coffee and a croissant, then sat silently at the table so he could finish writing his notes.

"Good morning," he said. "Sleep all right?"

"I did. Thank you."

He laid his pencil to the side, closed the book, and turned the iPad facedown. "So. Olivia Monroe. You look like your mother."

"That's what I'm told."

"Have you done any modeling?"

"My mother taught me that's not a long-term plan."

A woman came out with a plate of poached eggs and toast, setting it before Logan. Another refilled his coffee.

"Thank you," he said to her before addressing me. "So, you went to Loyola Law. Why not Princeton?"

Telling me what I already knew about myself must have been his way of telling me he'd looked into my background deeply enough to know which schools I'd turned down. If that was his game, I could play. I had nothing to hide.

"They made me an offer I couldn't refuse." I took a sip of coffee, but it was too hot, and I cringed.

He slashed an egg with the side of his fork, letting the yolk drip over his toast. "There's a saying: if you want to know a woman, don't look at what she accepts. Look at what she rejects."

"You can say the same for men."

He gave a short nod. "Maybe." He put a piece of egg and toast in his mouth and paused to chew. "So, it was money?"

"It gets cold in New Jersey," I said. "I'm a thin-blooded California girl. And also, yes. Money. Loyola picking up the tab in a temperate climate was better than freezing my ass off for half tuition."

"Smart."

"You have me at a disadvantage," I said. "I have no idea where you went."

"Stanford. Two years. Then I dropped out."

"Why?"

The woman who had brought Logan's eggs brought me a similar plate. I thanked her, and when she left, he answered.

"There was only one thing in the world I ever wanted, and staying wasn't going to get me any closer to it."

"Let me guess. The flying trapeze."

He laughed. "Not exactly. I wanted to run Crowne Industries, but my brother had three years on me. If I was going to catch up, I couldn't waste any time learning the business. I figured he'd fight to the death for it."

"You won, I guess?"

He shook his head and sliced his egg with a casual confidence. "He gave it up to do his own thing. The spec houses."

"He's making a real success of it. This one he has going now is huge."

"And you're invested in stopping him." He isolated one piece and stabbed it. "You might win too." He scraped the fork on his teeth.

"I will win."

"Here's the thing." Logan laid down his fork. "You seem all right. But you have a conflict here. This friendship, or whatever you're calling it, with my brother will get complicated no matter who wins. And my investment…*our* investment in Byron's success is more than financial."

He left it there as if he'd given me enough information to infer where his interests and his brother's parted ways. I picked up my coffee. It was cool enough to drink. I took a big swallow.

"If he fails," I said after my cup clicked in the porcelain saucer, "you're back to competing for your job."

"Not much of a competition, but sure." He gave a cocky shrug.

Chatter and dishes clacking rose from the kitchen. "Let's say... sure. I'm not in the mood to win a succession fight. The point is I don't want to see him hurt by that or anything. Now, I'm not one to get between my brothers and the women they bring home, but in this case, I want you to know I'm not going to sit by and watch this turn ugly."

I couldn't help but smile. What was in the water in the Crowne household that made these boys so primed for battle?

"What turn ugly?" Byron's voice came from the doorway to the kitchen. He wore running shoes and a sweaty T-shirt. He pulled it up, exposing his washboard stomach, and wiped his face with the hem.

"Your fucking face," Logan said.

Byron didn't believe him. I could read it like a well-lit billboard in the middle of the night.

"Logan thinks the environmental lawsuit isn't going away. He wants me to play nice."

Byron scoffed and poured a cup of coffee. "You don't know her." He sat next to me, stretching out as if the chair was a couch. "She plays to win."

"I play fair." I pressed my fork into an egg until it bled onto the toast.

"That's good to know," Logan said.

"Do you ride?" Byron asked me. "Horses."

"When I was younger."

"We have a stable down the hill. I can have someone tack up for you. We can ride the trail to Royal Ridge and be back before it gets too hot."

"Sounds great." I finally took a bite of my breakfast. It was delicious.

When I glanced at Byron, he was gazing at me with a distrust I hadn't seen since the day we met.

CHAPTER 13

BYRON

Logan wasn't to be trusted with Olivia. He wouldn't try to fuck her, but he'd make it a point to work the angles so I'd be fucked. I was the only other man in the world who could run Crowne Industries, so I was the only one who put the fear of God into him. Fear was a bad decision-maker.

"What the hell was that?" After a shower, I found him exactly where I expected. Working in the office, banging at his laptop as if he was pissing on his territory.

"What was what?"

I came around to his side of the desk and slapped his laptop closed. "I heard the whole thing."

"Why didn't you say so?" He leaned back and looked at me as if we were having a casual conversation. "Oh, wait. You wanted to see what she'd say. Am I right?"

"I'm not discussing Olivia."

"Did her answer satisfy you?"

The problem with my brother in any position of power was that he was too aboveboard for his own good. If he didn't tell the full truth in words, I could easily read the entirety of his scheme on his face.

"Leave her alone," I said. "She's not that important."

"Our mother thinks it's serious with you two. Said she had the tingle as soon as she saw her."

"Jesus." I fell into a chair.

He'd taken the wind right out of me. My mother's foolproof way of discerning a couple's longevity struck the back of her neck. It hadn't been wrong yet.

"Yeah," Logan said. "She even waved her fingers that way she does."

"I'll talk to her."

"Good idea. She's so excited she practically did a step dance. She thought, after Samantha, you'd never bring anyone around. But you go ahead and ruin her week. Tell her the tingle's wrong. Promise her you're going to mope around the rest of your life."

"Excuse me?" I snapped, and he swallowed hard, knowing he'd overstepped.

"I'm sorry. That wasn't fair."

"You've never lost anyone. I'd never wish it on you."

"I know. But—"

"But?"

"But it's possible you've started to come out of grieving. It's possible you're vulnerable to a woman who's looking to give herself an edge."

I laughed. I had to.

He was right.

If anyone would go to extraordinary lengths to gain an advantage, it was Olivia Monroe.

And if there was any woman I trusted wasn't doing exactly that, it was her.

* * *

I FOUND Olivia sitting on the couch with my mother, looking at photo albums. They were cooing at a picture of me at five wearing a Superman costume to the kindergarten Halloween party.

"You were so cute!" Olivia exclaimed when she saw me.

This whole huddled meetup... brought to you by the fucking tingle.

"We should go."

"Wait!" Mom held up one hand and flipped through pages with the other. "This was the year after! He wouldn't let us buy him a new one! And look how happy he was."

I knew the picture. Bigger me in the same costume. Belt too small. Little red underwear sagging at the crotch because I'd pulled at them all day, blissed out on being the same guy I'd been the year before. If I could have worn it a third year, I would have.

"Do you still have it?" Olivia asked Mom.

"I do."

"Okay," I snapped. "Let's not. Shall we?"

"He wasn't always such a stick in the mud," my mother murmured to Olivia.

"Courtney's got the horses tacked," I said.

"Are you going to Dead Man's Grove?" Mom closed the album. "Nellie can pack you a lunch."

"Oh, that name sounds..." Olivia didn't finish the sentence. Her expression said it all.

I explained. "If we'd ride down too close to dinner, our father would tell us if we didn't get back in time, we were dead men. So."

"He never killed them, but there was this one time—"

"We should go," I interrupted my mother more sternly than intended. "Please."

"I'll tell you later," Mom whispered. "Funny story."

Olivia came toward me, and Mom tucked away the album with a satisfied smile.

* * *

THE TRAIL to Dead Man's Grove narrowed as it turned down the ridge, and I pulled Keats to a stop so Olivia could take the lead. Once she was settled in the saddle, she was a decent rider, letting her body sway and rock with Brontë's gait the way she moved with mine when I fucked her.

She waited for me around the turn, where the path widened, tall and straight in the saddle as if she were queen of all she surveyed, including me.

I should have felt threatened. Instead, she lulled me into a sense of security I had to shake.

"The horse's names," she said, then waited for me to walk astride. "Is it John Keats and Emily Brontë?"

"Charlotte, actually."

"I ride corrected."

She smiled at me from her saddle, tightening a connection I'd been trying to deny. It was getting harder and harder to turn my back on the obvious.

"My mother has a degree in English lit with a focus on poetry," I said.

"And you were named for Lord Byron?"

"After Dante, my father put an end to naming children after poets. The horses weren't so lucky."

"'*I want a hero*,'" she quoted, "'*an uncommon want, when every year and month sends forth a new one.*'"

"*Don Juan* was a satire from the first line."

"Agreed," she said. "There are no heroes."

She wasn't protesting too much. She wasn't irritated by the fact or crying out for change. She didn't need a hero. She didn't need to be saved. She was the champion of her own story, and she knew it. Olivia asked for nothing not because she feared she'd never get it, but because she was a master of creating her own truth.

I didn't want her or anyone. I was going to be alone the rest of my life. But she could tempt me, this magical creature who fought like a warrior and quoted poetry like an artist. This goddess who needed no one but chose me for now.

I trusted her not to love me, but I was too trusting of myself. The ocean-scented air blew strands of gold from her ponytail and over her cheeks. With the *trop-tropping* of hooves and the lope and rock of the animals under us, I was lulled into flexibility. My thoughts came unbridled in loose, curling strands of gilded light. They were so absorbing I left the vault door open, forgot to check the lock on my heart.

That moment was when my feelings of tenderness grew from my lust, but I was equally convinced the tenderness had been lying in wait. Like a seed with the potential for the entire tree inside it, it was always there, waiting for the water of her laughter and the sunlight in her eyes.

"'She walks in beauty,'" I said. "'Like the night. Of cloudless climes starry skies; And all that's best of dark and bright, Meet in her aspect and her eyes; Thus mellowed to the tender light, Which heaven to gaudy day denies.'"

"You've impressed me." She smiled, swaying with Brontë. "But it's still satire."

"You obviously haven't met you."

She raised an eyebrow at me as if I'd lost my mind.

Maybe I had.

"Over here," I said, pointing toward a little picnic area surrounded by a log fence with piles to tie the horses. Colton had carved the words DEAD MEN TIE HERE with hacked triangulations where curves should have been.

We kept the area grassy and clean, with a teak table and chairs in the center, next to a hundred-year-old ficus that kept the space in shade.

I got off Keats, tied him, and tried to help her down, but she'd already slid off her saddle with competent grace, so I unpacked the leather saddlebags Nellie had filled with our lunch. Together, we laid out the crackers, cheese, and meats. Olivia cracked a little jar of jam and raised it to her nose.

"Is this fig?" she asked.

"No clue."

"I love fig jam."

She sat, and I straddled the bench facing her.

"Let's see." I prepared her a cracker with brie and jam, then held it up.

She took it in her mouth and rolled her eyes with a deep *mmm*. "It's fig all right."

"Chalk another one up for the Crownes."

She laughed, snapping a piece of French bread in two.

"I like your parents," she said, wedging a slice of hard cheese between the crusts. "They're nicer than I thought they'd be."

"How did you think they'd be?"

"Aloof. Guarded, maybe." I must have been easy to read, because she explained before I could ask. "My mom used to take me to these parties sometimes. She wanted me to meet people who could help me in my life, but they knew I wasn't one of them. One of your crowd. So, it was a lot of them testing me. Like Bianca Papillion." She held up her water with her pinkie in the air. "'Darling, if you want to ski, it's Zermatt or nothing.'"

I laughed in recognition.

"Maybe I'm exaggerating," she added. "But not that much."

"You don't really see it until you start working with people who need their jobs." I fed her another cracker with brie and fig jam. Doing that little bit for her was a fleeting pleasure.

"Are you happy?" she asked. "Is this what you hoped, inviting me here? If I could see you with your people, I'd be happy to raise a child with them around?"

"Yes." I looked away from the sharp edges of her blue eyes. "These people, as you say? They're better than me."

I wasn't baiting her. I didn't want her to throw back an exhortation about my value, and to my relief, she didn't.

"You're one of them."

"I haven't been in a while."

The statement was made in a moment of weakness, and I instantly regretted opening the door to questions and stories.

"Your mother told me you found Samantha."

"She must like you," I said. "Do you like camembert?"

"I do." She popped a cornichon in her mouth, and I thought we'd passed the danger zone. But no. Olivia twisted the padlock as if she were a safecracker. "I'm sorry that happened."

Happened. Like a hurricane or an icy patch in the road that you didn't see no matter how careful you were. As if my back had been turned just long enough to kill someone.

My insides seized like wet concrete the instant it turned solid.

What was I doing? Why was I looking at this woman with golden-haired beauty as if she was safe for me? This wasn't allowed. She was strong, but she was human. If I let her in, loved her and asked her to love me back, she'd expose herself, and that would be the end of her.

If I thought highly of her, the only thing to do was make sure she was protected from me.

"Well, I'll tell you a secret." I cut a thick slice of meat as if its length offended me, then I ate it with a crust of bread, chewing as my mind searched for the coldest part of my heart. "I wanted out of that engagement. The whole thing was a trap, and she let me out of it. I wish I could repay her for the favor, but oh well."

"You can't mean that."

Had I offended her? Shocked her? Made her take a step back? "Why shouldn't I?"

"It's heartless." Disgust framed her words. Perfect.

She was perfect. I hadn't realized how much. Leading her to judgment was intentional. All I had to do was nail it into place.

"Good," I said. "It won't change your opinion of me. You're the only one who knows better than to give me any credit. Hold on to that. I don't want to lose any respect I have for you."

I assumed she'd pull away in aversion. Who wouldn't?

And all that's best of dark and bright, Meet in her aspect and her eyes.

Olivia didn't run from fear. She sped to meet it.

"Why this?" The wind blew a leaf into her hair. It stuck there, an imperfection in part that served to emphasize the perfection of the whole. "Why do you need me to hate you?"

My hand rose to remove the flicking leaf, but I caught myself. "It's better that way."

"You weren't always like this." She twisted to put her knee on the bench, denying me her profile and gifting me her full attention.

"Like what? Honest?"

"Mean. Broken. Self-loathing. No, this isn't you. I saw the pictures from your childhood. You were a happy kid. I bet your mother doesn't own a picture of you where you're not smiling. And I'm not saying it matters to me one way or the other, because we're not a permanent couple, but it's a little frustrating watching you put on this performance."

"I'm not a performance. You're seeing more of me than most people ever see."

"What changed?"

"People don't change. They get real."

"Nope." She popped her P, daring me to argue my case.

She could go to hell. I was trying to help her. I didn't have to convince her of anything.

Then I did anyway.

"Look, sure, I was happy." I shrugged. "I had a painless childhood. Everything I wanted. You know what that does to a person? It makes them too weak to handle the real world and too oblivious to know it. There's nothing more precarious than being a snail without a shell."

"And now you have a shell?"

All I had to do was nail her doubt over the places I was split, and it would all be fine. "So do you. Your shell's thicker than mine, and it suits you. I'm glad you have yours. Now be glad I have mine."

Her mouth tightened, and her shoulders dropped. I'd hammered the last nail perfectly.

"You're a confusing person." She folded a piece of wax paper over the camembert, then stood to clean up the rest of the food. "Just when I think I can know you, you push me away."

I grabbed her wrist. She stopped. Her forehead was tense and jaw was set.

"They're the same thing."

"Yeah." She pulled her hand away and gathered bits of food as if the existence of an unwrapped lunch offended her. "You're some unknowable entity. All alone forever. Boo-fucking-hoo."

She had it wrong. I didn't want pity.

"It's not—"

"Why do you want this child? Is it just another temporary obsession? You want to possess it until you get bored? The way you want to possess me?"

"It's different."

"How?" she asked the canopy with her paper-filled fists banging the table. "What's the difference?"

"Just… trust me. It's different."

"No. You tell me. Now."

"Olivia. It's just my problem, not yours."

She scoffed, and when she finally looked at me, her eyes were floodlights of defiance. "I can make this not your problem very easily."

The threat was unstated but clearly made. She had the baby, and she could do with it whatever she wanted. She had authority over me. The ultimate power.

"Is this your game?" My question came out in a growl. "You're going to hold that over my head?"

"You bet I am." She crunched empty paper into a ball and stuffed everything into the bag. "You're the one playing a game. But for me, this is everything. It's my *life,* and I will not trade it for an unknown. If I can't sort out your motives? Motives I believe?" She flipped the top of the bag closed. "I will not hesitate to cut you out."

Snapping up the last of our lunch, she went to the horses with her hips swaying and her ponytail in tatters. The leaf that had stuck in her hair came loose and floated behind her.

How much to tell? I asked myself as I chased after her.

What does she need to hear? I asked as I grabbed her elbow.

What do I need? I asked myself as she jerked away, so angry I thought she'd spit in my face.

"I can't love you," I said. "If that's what you're worried about."

"Samantha was the last?"

What was the proper response to that?

I looked for doubt in her face, but there was none. Just cold, gray stone.

"You want to know my last words to her?" I asked, erecting my own wall from the tiny bits of rubble she'd left me. "I told her I loved her."

Olivia's eye twitched with a question she wanted to ask but wouldn't.

I answered it anyway. "She didn't believe me."

She only offered a slight nod that made words redundant.

Her nod said, *I don't blame her.*

That hurt. She'd aimed her arrow and hit the bullseye.

"When I first saw you," I said, "I wanted you. That's the truth, but it wasn't a big deal. I knew I'd have you. But up on the hill, when I found you jogging…and yes, I admit I looked for you because…"

How much to tell?

What do I need?

All of it.

"I wanted you, and seducing you would have made it harder for you to get in my way. I could soften you. Fuck you into a mistake. At the very least, you'd have to withdraw."

"So that was all fake?"

"I warned you. At the Stock Hotel, I warned you."

"Let me repeat you back to you," she said. "You lured me into sex with a total disregard for my feelings. You thought I was so weak you could fuck me into a mistake. You thought the fact that you gave me some vague warning at a party absolved you of guilt, and now you're telling me this? Why? So I'll forgive you?"

"Yes, but… listen." I felt as if I was chasing a leaf around a windy courtyard. "On Runyon. Talking to you. Just talking… I felt like I could listen to you forever, and it was dangerous. I shouldn't want to talk to you. You're the enemy. My job was to fuck you to destruction and leave you there."

"I wouldn't have minded that." She swung herself over the saddle, suddenly seven feet tall with the sun spotting through the ficus leaves behind her.

"I couldn't. We weren't even done, and I was finding reasons to see you again. To be with you. Give you your abatement or whatever. I didn't care. When you said you were dead—"

"It was a joke."

"I know." I laid a hand on her thigh and the other on Brontë's neck to steady her. "I can't get involved. I can't. I'm not safe for you."

"But for a child, you are?"

"Yes."

"What happened with Samantha?"

The question was precision-timed to her calculation. She was fitting the pieces of my behavior to the scraps of my story.

What does she need to hear?

What do I need?

"I was cruel," I said. "I was cold. I treated her as if she didn't matter. She was fragile, and I thought I could make her strong. But I didn't. I never did, but I kept trying. We had a fight. She cursed me and called me a monster. I thought… if she was coming back at me, that meant she was getting tougher. I slept like a man content with a job well done. I slept so well that night I didn't hear anything."

She waited as if she knew there was more.

When it was clear I didn't have the strength for another word, she finally spoke. "I don't know whether to be sorry for you or frightened of you."

"Fear is your friend."

She took the reins. "We should get back."

She tugged the strap and turned Brontë away from me, walking in beauty. Like the night.

WE RODE BACK in a silence I was grateful for. At the stables, we spoke in practicalities. Where to put the horses. Which stable hand would manage the brush-down.

Lyric had gone back to Los Angeles with her friends. Logan made enough small talk to soften the hard edges we pointed at each other. My mother fussed over Olivia's dinner preferences while my father made drinks she wouldn't touch.

The pressure of the passing hours increased over dinner, and the night signaled the inevitable rise of morning. It was unbearable. She felt it too. After my parents went to bed and my brother went to the office to prove he was worthy of his inheritance, Olivia went to the back patio and leaned her elbows on the railing, leaning into the black stretch of the invisible sea.

She walks in beauty.

"Beautywalker." I stood beside her with a white paper bag in my hand.

She smiled. "Lord Byron? What brings ye?"

"I'm sorry."

"It's all right. I get it. I mean, it was an asshole plan."

"I like to think it was an excuse to see you."

"Doesn't matter really. I have to either forgive it or not. I'm not going to be your conscience. It's not my job to needle you or nag you. I'm not getting any more information than what I have now. Either you're going to run your life in a way that makes you a good example for the kid or not."

"I will be." I fidgeted with the paper bag as if I could test whether or not I'd allow myself to drop it in the ravine. "I wish I could be more for you."

"I don't know what I wish."

"I do. You said you could take a test tomorrow morning?"

"I'll do it when I get back on Monday." She shrugged. "It can wait."

I handed her the bag.

She opened it and peeked in, sighing before she crunched the top closed. "This is the most thoughtful gift ever."

"Figured you'd enjoy pissing on something I gave you."

She smiled, and though I'd caused it, I didn't own it. Its light was directed inside her.

"If this is positive…" She let the thought hang and started a new one. "Once I make a decision, I'm sticking to it."

"What if it's negative?" I asked.

"You can breathe a sigh of relief, and... for me?" She slapped my chest with the box. "I guess it's just another month gone by."

"That what you want?"

She thought for a moment, gaze cast to where the bag with the pregnancy test rested against my chest. "I have feelings I can't explain to myself. But we... you and I... we're too complicated."

"We are."

"I'm glad you agree."

"We only have until Monday morning," I said. "Want to make the most of it?"

She turned to face the canyon, letting the bag dangle from her fingers. "Visit me across the hall later."

CHAPTER 14

OLIVIA

The ocean was half a mile away and a thousand feet below, but that night, with the back patio empty and all the goodnights said, the arrhythmic crashing of the waves ground down the edges of my anxiety.

I was smooth and empty. I thought nothing. Not about the morning. Not about the piss stick on the vanity, nor the hum of it, nor the bleach-bright light it cast. Calling it an elephant in the room was an insult to its size, so I called it nothing. A plastic piece of nothing.

One line is failure.

Two is success.

In a long T-shirt and underwear, I crawled under the fluffy duvet and closed my eyes to wait for Byron's visit.

If we hadn't tied our relationship in knots by going from opponents to casual fuckbuddies directly to maybe-baby, what would we be? How would I feel about it?

Bitter, maybe? Annoyed, probably. Resentful of my weakness with him. My submission to his commands would have eaten at me on one hand, and on the other, driven me into his bed as many times as I could bear. I hadn't bedded that many men but enough to know no one could twist me into a pretzel and make me beg for more the way Byron did.

He'd cut off the sex before I was done with him. He'd get bored or end it before his affection turned into a promise he couldn't keep. I was sure of it. He would have done it to win the game and to ensure his heart remained locked tight against me.

I'd know he was right. I would have been better off spending years trying to stop that ridiculous house, living my life, picking at him like a scab that forgot the source of its wound.

One line is disappointment.

Two lines is hope.

I didn't understand him, and I never would, but he was a complex taste I needed on my tongue again before it faded away. There was more to him than one mouthful could savor. His guilt was a bitter bite of humanity, and his poetry was a sweet aftertaste of expressive ambition.

He hadn't been acting, but I didn't fool myself into thinking it mattered. We were incompatible. I had to stop turning it over in my head.

Tomorrow.

One line, you're free.

Two lines, he's yours.

Tomorrow, no matter what, I'd shut down this nonsense.

But for that night, I'd succumb to every fantasy of us. The one where he was emotionally available and I was capable of giving up a piece of my sovereignty to a partner.

Half-asleep, a rock worn smooth by the currents and the sand, I was unmoved by the cycles of life and death, inert and passive, until I was picked up and held. Gripped in a strong hand that sparked desire where there had been death, cognizance where there had been only drift, I was locked in my final form.

"Shh," he whispered in my ear. Behind me, with his chest pressed to my back and an arm under my neck, Byron held me tight. He smelled of the ocean. Salt and sand. Coconut oils and sweat. "Open your legs."

Would I ever be able to resist that command when it came from his mouth?

Not that night. After eons of being thrown around, I was worn smooth and frictionless, parting my knees at his words. His fingers gently came from behind me, stroking inside my thighs.

"Let me tell you a story." He found where I was already wet for him.

I groaned but wasn't awake enough for words. I could only listen as he pulled off my underwear.

"There once was a man whose life was a lie." He worked on my clit from behind. "He had everything he ever wanted because he never wanted enough. When it was taken away, he promised himself he'd only live the truth. Which was he wanted to fight until he had won enough of what he wanted."

He circled my clit, gently coaxing it to attention. I spread my legs wider and bent my arm behind me, around his neck.

"Then one day, a woman came to fight him, and he wanted her."

His fingers and my cunt shared the same warmth, the same rhythm. His hand was an extension of me as it flicked, circled, stretched me out as three digits entered me. My mouth opened to let out an involuntary cry, and he covered it with his free hand.

"She was enough," he said. "But he was too small to hold her."

I shook my head against his palm because he had it all wrong. He wasn't small. He was locked up. There was a difference.

"You want to come, Beauty?"

With his hand slipping between my lips, I nodded.

"Do you want me to fuck you?"

I nodded again. His fingers teased me on the edge, and he pressed his mouth against the back of my neck. I knew what to expect, anticipating his bite. The painful erotic suck between his teeth, the spreading, agonizing pleasure as he marked me.

"I have complete control of you. I can do this all night. You'll cry for me to hurt you if I'll only let you come. Right?" He moved his spit-covered hand away.

"Please," I said. "Fuck me all night but let me come now."

"You're fucking starving for it. I've never wanted to possess a woman's hunger the way I want yours." He got out from behind me and kneeled between my legs. He'd gotten into bed naked, and his cock was thick and hard in his fist. "Pull your shirt up over your tits."

The command. The confidence of it. Tits became just another word. Not lascivious. Just a part of my body he had every right to see. I pulled the shirt over my hard nipples.

"Right here." He gently took a pinch of my breast. "This is mine."

Drifting down, he took the nipple between his fingers and pulled. I didn't think I could get closer to orgasm without going over, but the pain he gave nudged me one step away, then two steps toward the edge.

"Yes," I whispered. "Take me. Please."

"How?" he teased, flicking my nipple. "Here?"

"Yes."

He drifted down my stomach and shoved my legs apart, pulling the skin between my thighs apart to open my folds. He drew his fingers over my clit and inside me. "Here?"

"Yes. Please."

Removing his wet fingers, he slid them behind, wetting the tightly closed virgin muscle. "What about here?"

He pressed just his fingertip against the entrance, and a new pleasure center opened up. I bit back a scream of overwhelming pleasure and frustration. I never had anal sex before, but I'd give it to him.

"Take it all," I groaned, clutching for his chest.

He took my hips and flipped me onto my hands and knees, then angled the head of his cock against my pussy.

"I just needed to know you would." His thumb found the same bit of breast flesh he'd claimed and pressed the bruise. "Whose is this?"

"Yours."

He entered me deeply in three strokes, burying himself. I'd expected his delicious roughness, but he kept his hips still and kissed the soft muscle of my shoulder before sucking the skin through his teeth so hard I groaned with a pained pleasure. He pushed deep inside me, bending his body over mine to bite the base of my neck again. When he reached around me and touched my clit, the pain turned deliciously excruciating.

When he pulled away, I squeaked and twisted to see him. For a moment, a line of spit connected his lower lip to where he'd marked me. He looked at the mark and groaned, gathering me in his arms. He kissed my face and neck, gently caressed my swollen nub, soothed me and surrounded me. We rolled and shifted, always connected, cocooned in a darkness far away from the consequences of our actions.

I could be with this man. The one whose body perfectly fit around mine. The one with the tender words and soft lips. The purveyor of miracles and impossibilities made true.

The man who made love to me that night lifted me up and made me capable of miracles. I could walk on water. Heal the sick. I could break physics and common sense with shattering, incredible acts that defied logic.

If I could love him, I could do anything.

One line or two, it didn't matter. Together we were more miraculous than a white, plastic stick.

I could love him.

If I could do that, anything was possible.

* * *

"BEAUTYWALKER?" he asked so softly he must have known I was half-asleep.

I would have roused myself for a fourth time. "Hm?"

"Tomorrow, if the test is positive…"

I rolled over to see him. The moon was full on his face, and his eyes were black in the shadows.

"I'll have your baby."

"And?"

"And?" I repeated.

"I can't give you anything," he said. "Nothing besides money. But I have a lot to give a child."

"I know." I caressed his cheek. "And you'd better. Daddy. I'm holding you to that."

His breath must have been holding him up, because when he exhaled in relief, he collapsed into an embrace of gratitude.

CHAPTER 15

BYRON

I reached for Olivia when she went to the bathroom, but she closed the door quietly behind her. I usually slept three hours a night, four if I'd had a woman with me the night before. But once Olivia had drifted off beside me, I listened to her breath for a while, watching her lashes flutter and her lips relax. The moonlight through the window shifted as the minutes passed, casting her face in a changing blue glow.

And all that's best of dark and bright, Meet in her aspect and her eyes; Thus mellowed to the tender light, Which heaven to gaudy day denies.

I had intended to go back to my room, but I fell asleep and stayed that way for six full hours.

We had a strategy to build the mansion in the Bel-Air hills. We were going to slash and burn every obstacle, spend every dollar, and take advantage of every loophole. The house was a statement piece meant to attract the richest of the rich from all over the world. I wouldn't be stopped for any reason.

But maybe it didn't have to be that way. Maybe there were ways to get it done without keeping me at odds with the mother of my child. The case could reach beyond her pregnancy, and she shouldn't be stressed. I had no heart to win a battle with her under these conditions. I wanted to see this over more than I wanted to see myself win.

All this had occurred to me as I'd tried to keep my eyes open to watch how her face would change in the moonlight, and in the first moments of wakefulness, the decision had been made.

What followed was a realization that it was morning.

She was in the bathroom.

I shot out of bed, still naked, and knocked gently on the door. "Olivia?"

"I'll be out in a minute."

"Did you—"

"I did."

Silence followed. She'd been in there a full two minutes already. How long did the results take?

"Beauty," I said, laying my hand on the door.

Nothing. With a gentle pressure, I pushed down the door's lever to see if it was locked. It wasn't, but I let it spring back up.

"Olivia."

Still nothing.

She heard me and was deliberately ignoring me. I should have been irritated. I should have made it clear that the silent treatment wasn't going to fly, but I couldn't work up annoyance when all I felt was a need to give her the time she wanted.

"I'm here," I said. "Right on the other side of the door. When you need me, just—"

"Come in."

The bathroom was as big as any we had in the house, but I hadn't felt its size until I saw her naked body crouched on the other side, small in the distance, knees up, back to the white tile wall, arms wrapped around her legs with her hands meeting in the middle. Between them, the white plastic stick I'd given her as a gift.

Closing the door behind me to seal us against the outside world, I kneeled beside her.

Her head was bent down, and I saw the splotchy stain of broken blood vessels and raw skin. That was me. I'd marked her in pain, and the feeling that it was for nothing stabbed me in the chest.

"Well?" I asked.

When she looked at me, her eyes were glazed with tears waiting to drop. "Have you ever wondered why there was something wrong with you?" She continued before I could say that yes, sometimes I did. "Like were you born broken? Or is there something you're choosing? Your career. Your friends. Where you live. Or is it just who you are?"

She blinked, and the tears fell in a rush. She looked at her hands. Her voice was wet and cracked. I had a compulsion to reach for her, but I knew more than I knew my own name that she didn't want me to.

"And you think, and you pray to God, telling him, promising, I'll change. I'll fix it. I'll carve that part of myself out, and I swear I'll burn it to the ground. I'll do whatever I have to if you just tell me what? What is it about me that's wrong? Where am I not worthy? But there's no answer. There's no end. It's just this…" She hitched as she tossed the plastic stick away. "This constant wave of disappointment. Time after time. Like I can't do anything right and I don't know why. It's like getting punched in the face, and I just keep going back because I don't know how to stop." She looked at me. "I don't know if I can take it anymore, Byron. I don't think I can."

She broke down into body-racking sobs and keened toward me. I took her in my arms and let our legs twine together on the cold tile floor. I kissed her head and stroked her hair. I didn't tell her it wasn't her fault. That she wasn't a failure. That she could take it because she was strong, so strong, so very strong and so very worthy. My encouragement would have been puny against her despair. All I had for her was more comfort and patience than I thought I was capable of. I'd sit on the bathroom floor with her all day if I had to.

I reached for the toilet paper, unspooling a length, gathering it into a handful, and giving her the end without ripping it away. She took the bloom of paper and wiped her face. Blew her nose. Still connected, the tube rattled on the spool when I pulled, giving her an endless supply that gathered at her feet like ocean foam.

"Oh my God. Byron." She double-hitched. "What are you doing?"

"Making sure you have enough."

"But... trees."

"I'll plant some for you. By that house we're fighting over."

She leaned her head on my shoulder. "How many?"

"How many do you want?"

"More than the legal minimum."

"I'll double it. Triple it. Big, shady trees."

"Okay." She sniffed and took a clean handful from the floor to blow into. "I guess that's fair."

"Something good can come from this."

She huffed a laugh. "You're not the 'glass half full' type."

"I'm not the 'glass half empty' type either."

"No. I guess not. You're more the type to drink the water while the rest of us argue."

"Only if I'm thirsty." I kissed her head.

The pregnancy test lay against the base of the sink, displaying its single pink line. She shouldn't have to see that again. I let her go so I could toss it in the trash. I missed, and it clattered to the floor, lines down and out of sight.

"Fuck that thing," I said when I returned to her side.

She sat straight against the wall, stringing toilet paper as if she were turning the pages of an old book. "Yeah. I'm done."

Was she done crying or done trying?

"We can try again," I suggested without thinking about the consequences. Only getting back to the hope I'd had a few hours ago. "I'm more fun than a turkey baster."

"I want…" She took my wrist, turning it to see my watch before letting it drop. "When can I go home?"

We were supposed to have another night together and leave Monday morning. But she didn't ask me when we planned on leaving. She asked when she could.

"Yusup can be here in a few hours."

"How many hours?"

Too many. Her mind was elsewhere, and no matter what I said, it would be too many.

"I can have our helicopter here in an hour."

"That would be great." She got her legs under her and stood naked over me. "I should shower."

Reaching up, I took her hand. "Shower after I take you to bed again."

"That's a great offer." She squeezed my hand and let it go. "But no. I can't."

I stood and moved to kiss her. She turned, and my lips landed on her cheek.

"I'll see you downstairs," she said.

Like an obedient puppy who only wanted to please his master, I nodded in acquiescence and left, closing the door.

I'd wanted to prove I was worthy, but I had no clue what I'd actually done.

CHAPTER 16

OLIVIA

Hope was a disease. Hope was a veil that distorted how you saw reality. Hope was a wrecking ball smashing your control to bits. Hope was a siren singing from a faraway rock, calling you from safe shores to brave swelling seas and unbeatable foes only to disappear once you reached it.

Hope was cruel. Hope laughed as you stood on the lonely rock, wounded from battle, starving, staring at nothing... only to start singing her invitation again from the same shore you left.

I'd gone to Santa Barbara because of a broken condom. A mistake. An accident. I was sitting next to a man I'd forgotten to detest on a helicopter home because I'd let myself hope that bargains could be made from mishaps and that my deals with chance had the power of tort law behind them. As if the universe obeyed *habeus corpus* and not *lorem ipsum*.

Life would go on. I was wiser. Older. I'd looked in the face of my utter idiocy, fallen for the idea that good sex was a miracle that made sense of the impossible, and woken up with a hard slap to the face. So what if I *could* love him? Why wasn't I asking if it was what I wanted? Why wasn't I asking if I *should*?

Byron was no less beautiful with his voice drowned out by the pounding blades. His blue-and-gold eyes weren't cutting or monstrous anymore. He hadn't changed. I knew that. I'd let the veil of hope come between myself and his reality. I'd let it change what I saw, but I was onto that game. I was smarter than that. I knew when I was being lied to, and hope was—if nothing else—a liar.

When I got home, I could reassess what I wanted and whether or not I could get it. Coldly. Without distraction.

All I had to do was get there. Hold my breath, my thoughts, and my emotions until I was home and alone.

Over the California coast and the line of traffic on the 101, Byron reached for my hands. They were clutching the headset controls. He switched the channel, then switched his own to match.

"The pilots can't hear us." His voice was in my head.

"Yeah."

"Are you all right?"

"I'm fine." I smiled at him and turned back to the coastline below.

"Beauty?"

"You don't have to call me that anymore." I watched the jagged lines of ocean foam write their endless story onto the beachfront.

"I want to see you again."

Byron wanted something. Bully for him and the veil he'd put over my eyes.

"You'll see me. In court."

I'd thought he was going to leave me alone, but he was only pausing long enough to lull me into thinking he'd heard me.

"I think we're better together."

Byron Crowne wants, and Byron Crowne thinks. Gold star for Byron Crowne.

"Let the judge decide."

"Olivia. Look at me."

I didn't have to turn around just because he asked. I had my own mind. It was a jumbled mess of shattered, mismatched pieces, but it was mine.

"Please," he said, crawling through the spaces between confusion and determination.

I turned my head but left my body shifted toward the window. The sunlight chased every shadow from his face as if nothing was hidden.

"Yes?"

"I'm serious. I want you."

His declaration echoed in the hollow tin cavity of my heart and died into silence as if it had never been uttered.

"I know."

I turned away and said nothing more.

CHAPTER 17

BYRON

The negative test had shut her down. Or maybe breaking in front of me had done it. I couldn't begin to fathom why she'd gone so cold so quickly. I was never a student of human nature and had never cared to be. But as she offered me her cheek when we parted, I wished I was.

If I knew why she felt this way, I could fix it. If I could fix it, I could have her.

But either she didn't want it fixed, or she didn't want me to help her.

My impotence over the situation curled around itself into a hot ball of rage. It didn't have a name, but I recognized it. It was the frustration I'd felt with Samantha when someone pushed her around and she let them. Her sister, who plied her for money and favors. Her mother, who told her to get a bigger diamond on the engagement ring she loved. I never knew if she threw it in the toilet as a message to me or her family, and that pissed me off too.

If I'd listened, maybe I'd know. If I hadn't failed at knowing her, the whole thing could have been avoided. Then she was gone, and it was too late.

Helpless anger turned inward. That was the name of the heat in my heart. Reasonable thought could barely get past it, but a thread got through. A single question.

Why do you care?

Olivia wasn't supposed to get pregnant with my child in the first place. Why did it matter if she wasn't? I didn't need to start a family. It wasn't an immediate goal or even a long-term consideration.

So, why did I care?

Naked and shaking in the penthouse of the Waldorf Astoria, with my thick seed dripping down her leg, she'd pointed at me and told me she was on fertility meds.

Something had changed with those words. Why had it changed? Why had I gone from no to yes to need in the blink of an eye? How did I get from living an organized life to this fucking mess of unexplainable, confused cravings?

Hope. It had been a crazy hope that my failures could be made right. That I could have the things I'd denied myself for years, and she was the only woman I'd trust to get me there.

She was clarity and desire and the only one with the strength to change me. The only one I wanted to make happy.

She was hope.

The day darkened, and I knew the mark I'd left on the base of her neck was fading. She'd be clear of me when it did. Nothing would connect us. Nothing would remind her that she was mine. I'd be invisible to her except for one thing—the conflict that had brought her into my orbit in the first place.

I wanted to own her, and that was going to take subtle work. I had to give her what she didn't know she wanted…and exactly what she'd asked for.

On Tuesday, I went into my office gunning for a fight. If Olivia needed a struggle, she was going to get it, because I needed to be present in her life. Even as an opponent. Even as a thorn in her side.

Her case against me was all I had, and if it ended, win or lose, without her at my side, I'd know it was truly hopeless. I'd go on as before, but somehow chastened like a dog trying to get the food on the counter one too many times.

"Set up an appointment with Janet," I told my assistant, Clarissa. "Today. We're going into offense on the Bel-Air house."

"Yes, sir." She made a note in her iPad, long, red fingernails clicking on the glass.

"Tell her we're filing motions challenging the EPF's standing."

"Anything else?"

"Bellini. Get her or Jonson in here with the drawings. We're adding another floor. A fucking tower."

Click, click, click. "Got it. You have an appointment with Logan in ten minutes."

"I'll meet him in the conference room."

By the time I got there, Logan was already sitting at the head of the table as if he was in his own damn office.

"Nice of you to show," he said.

I looked at my watch as I sat. Sixty seconds late. Nothing like getting scolded by your younger brother when you already felt as if you'd been through a wood chipper. "We could have met at Crownestead."

"Didn't want you mixing business with pleasure."

"So, what is it?"

"Right." He straightened his posture and put his elbows on the table, hands folded as if he wasn't always businesslike. "About the One Big Thing. Dad has some concerns."

"Of course he does."

"Have you and Olivia disclosed her contacts with you without counsel present?"

"I initiated them."

"How cute you think that matters. Her name's on the pleadings, dumbass. And you're riding down to Dead Man like... what the fuck? How stupid are you? How bad does she want to beat you?"

"She's taking a risk."

"So are you! She can claim sexual harassment after they fucking disbar her. What are you thinking?"

I tapped my finger on the shiny surface of the wood, leaving a matte oval behind. Disclosing the truth was more difficult than any disclosure filing.

"There is no relationship." I flicked away an unidentifiable speck.

"Says who?"

"Olivia."

"Because she doesn't want her license?"

"No. Because she doesn't want *me*. Anything else you want to pry into? Time and place of the last time I jerked off?"

"No, no."

"I was fifteen. In Como. Natalia Vinerelli took her top off, and I ran to the pool house."

"Byron. Stop. What happened?"

"It's complicated."

"Personally or professionally?"

"Yes."

He sighed and sat back with his hands on his knees. "Here's what it is: Dad's ready to write the check, and you know it comes with no questions asked. Wipe your ass with it. He doesn't care. But he... We want you to be sure this is the best use of it. If the build's in trouble and there are conflicts, it could take decades to sort out. You've waited this long for your OBT. Why not use it for a sure thing?"

"This is a sure thing."

"Okay, then."

"Good."

I was about to stand when my little brother opened his mouth again. Jesus, this kid was drunk with power.

"Why is it complicated?" he asked.

"I'll have Clarissa write you a memo."

"Can you forget all this?" He waved at the office, the stretch of the city out the window, the sky and the stars behind it. "Tell me as your brother?"

"No," I said. "I can't forget any of it. It's hanging over me. Everything. And I couldn't figure out how to shake it loose until her. The problem is me. I'm what's hanging over me."

His fingers tapped a rhythm on his knee. This was all too vague and abstract for him. If he couldn't read it as if it was an entry in a profit and loss statement, it didn't count.

"We had a night together," I said. "We thought she might be pregnant."

He stopped tapping.

"Turns out she's not," I continued. "So, she's done with me."

"And you? You done with her?"

"No."

"No. Okay." He looked out the window as if Los Angeles had the answers. Maybe it did, because he turned back to me resolutely. "Be careful. Just be careful. You have a way of battering down a door when you could just knock."

CHAPTER 18

OLIVIA

The Tuesday morning after I returned from Santa Barbara, I got a last-minute appointment to see Dr. Galang. I didn't know what I wanted to express to him because neither my disappointment nor Byron's derailing of the medical process was in his purview, but I promised to keep it short.

After the mandatory blood and urine degradations, I was sent to the little room where he met patients. The early-morning light was unforgiving. Everything seemed more worn at the edges. I noticed chips in the wood stain of the side tables. The pilling in the upholstery where the doctor sat. The tissue box on the center table had a fluffed white flower of paper jutting from the top slit, indicating a military-grade readiness to absorb sadness. The box was different. Blue last time. Brown now. Someone had done a lot of crying in here.

My legs were crossed, and my shoe dangled from a toe.

Byron had slid my shoe back on at some event eons ago. His hands had lingered on my ankle. He'd turned my bad habit into tenderness.

"Don't," I whispered to the empty room and jammed my heel into the shoe.

When I moved, the bruise at the back of my neck protested. The muscles had broken down under Byron's attention. Before my mind got rid of him, my body had to flush him away.

He'd be gone with the pounding of the ticking clock.

The door opened, and Dr. Galang appeared with his wire-framed reading glasses on his bald head. He smelled more heavily of aftershave than in the afternoons, and his eyes were—as usual—bright with hope.

I used to hang on to his positive energy. Now it was a reminder that I'd been fooled into believing the impossible.

He sat in his usual spot and put my file on the table. "Ms. Monroe, how are you feeling?"

"Fine, I guess."

"You took my advice." He pointed at me with a smile. "Did you go away for the long weekend? You've been relaxing. I can see it."

Though he was right about the weekend, I wouldn't have called myself calm. "I did go away."

He spread his legs and opened my file, flipping through pages with tiny print and tight, illegible notes in blue ballpoint. "Nice time?"

"Yes. I wanted to discuss how we're proceeding."

"Ah!" He jabbed a slip of paper the size of a supermarket receipt stapled to a larger printout. "This." He tapped it again even harder. "We did a different panel this time and dingaling! You have an irregularity in your blood. Very unexpected but not unheard of. The hormones. The hormones are everything."

He acted as if he'd made some kind of breakthrough, and I was huddled so deep in a corner I wondered if he was talking about someone else.

"Dr. Galang. I came to tell you I don't want to anymore."

He looked at me over his wire frames. "No? You don't want a baby?"

"No, I want... I still want a baby. But this disappointment every month? It's hard on me. I need a break."

A deep-throated hum came from his closed lips. "Yes. Understandable."

"I used to be excited every time I took a test, and now? I dread it."

"Well," he put his hands on his knees. "It's your decision. There's one more packet with us, and you have up to a year to implant."

"Thank you." I uncrossed my legs and put my bag in my lap.

"You'll have to restart the fertility drugs from the beginning."

"Yeah."

"But at least we'll know which drugs." He closed the folder.

"Wait. What?"

"We'll give you a different protocol."

"Why?"

"You have a hormone in your blood usually found in women who have been nursing. Because you never bore children, we didn't test for it. This was my mistake."

"And the hormone? What does it do?"

"Keeps you from having babies too close together."

"You mean... it prevented me from getting pregnant?"

"Yes."

"And... you can fix it?"

"There's a drug that will correct it prior to implantation. I'll write it up for you, if you want? Take them or don't. Just let us know."

"Yeah," I said. "Okay. Do that."

Time was a zero-sum game.

There were no extra resources of time. No surprise seconds hiding in the couch cushions. No accrued interest. Investments of time didn't pay returns in more time. When the clock stopped ticking, time hadn't stopped or folded. It wasn't a gift. The battery had died.

I could admit I liked Byron. I desired him. He wanted me. I had no problem with my feelings. I wasn't even ashamed of them. I knew things about him no one else did. The more I understood him, the more beautiful I found him, and no one else had to like it. But understanding him meant I knew what kind of time suck he was.

After I left the doctor's office, I drove on the 101 with the top down, doing the math in my head for the hundredth time.

I was almost thirty-three.

Assume success with Byron.

Give him a year to remove his head from his ass.

Almost thirty-four.

Give us a year to get married, if we were speedy.

Almost thirty-five.

Assume we tried for a family right away.

Give us a year to get me knocked up.

Almost thirty-six.

Nine months of pregnancy.

Second child, with decent spacing.

Probably thirty-nine.

An astronomical number of things had to go right to give me two children before forty.

But what if he didn't come around? What if he wasn't temporarily emotionally unavailable but permanently closed off? What if it wasn't that he couldn't love anyone but that he couldn't love me?

I was almost thirty-three.

Assume failure with Byron.

It would take a year—minimum—to realize he was never going to commit.

Almost thirty-four.

Get back to Dr. Galang. Luck hadn't factored in in the past and shouldn't be added as a variable in the future.

So, calculate a year of attempts.

Almost thirty-five.

Nine months of pregnancy.

At the outside, with padding, thirty-six.

Second child, with decent spacing.

Again, thirty-nine.

It was a wash. Just looking at the math, failure with Byron was preferable.

Time didn't rush forward, nor was it a horror movie door at the end of a hall stretching out like temporal taffy. Time was a steady march forward, and my calculations were a prayer I recited to a god I couldn't control.

* * *

"So, I might be back to plan A, maybe," I shouted over the banging pots and chattering chefs as I followed Emilio along the length of the kitchen. The opening was in eight days, and the full staff worked to perfect the process and the food.

"I can't believe Byron's swimmers couldn't make it just out of ambition or spite."

"Turns out I was slippery. They have enough for one more try with yours. I might use it. Or maybe not. Is that okay?"

"*Mi* spunk *es su* spunk," he said, leaning over a woman with blond bangs peeking from her red bandana so he could dip a spoon into a pot of boiling bouillabaisse. "Do what you want. When I come in a cup for a girl, it's out of respect for her decisions." He held up the spoon. "Taste."

I took the stew, rolling it around my mouth. "It's a little flat on the back."

"That is *not* what she said," Emilio responded before sharing solutions with the chef. "Come."

He pulled me into his office and closed the door. The room was smaller than a Hollywood closet. The chair had been rolled in from someone's curbside trash. The desk had only fit after he'd sawed six inches off one end. Invoices and business cards were tacked to a corkboard with multicolored pushpins. An ineffective air conditioner droned in the only window, which had looked out onto the dumpsters before it had been covered with cardboard and the cracks sealed around the unit with gray goop.

I sat on his desk, and he lowered himself onto his creaky rescued chair.

"I've been busy," he said. "And I've been neglecting my supertaster."

"Your supertaster doesn't need upkeep. I see you in here, running around, and I think, 'He's getting his dreams.' I'll never begrudge you."

"But your dreams?"

The concrete floor was cracked in the shape of Ohio.

"They're a little busted up, but they'll get over it."

"You need me to give you more of what I got?"

"I don't know if I want to put you through that."

"I'm going to jerk off anyway. Might as well be for a good cause."

"I don't know what I want right now."

"That's not like you." There was a light rap on the door. "What?"

A muffled voice came from the other side. "Floor staff wants you to look at the table setting."

"Five!" he shouted before addressing me more gently. "I want to spend five minutes not talking about this opening. I make a hundred decisions a day, and I can't tell if they're good anymore. People are going to show up to the opening, and I'm going to be running around with googly eyes and my tongue lolling out. I'm leaving here in a straitjacket if I don't get five. Fucking. Minutes."

"You should…" I stopped myself from saying *relax* or adding the usuals.

Meditate.

Try yoga.

Get your mind off it.

I was becoming that person.

"I hear not thinking about problems solves them," I said snidely. "You could take a bath."

"I don't like getting prune fingers." He took an envelope from his desk drawer and rapped it on the heel of his hand. "Tell me about not knowing what you want for five minutes. Please."

"I had this idea that it would all be so easy if there was a man. A daddy. A husband even. We could order a family, three kids and a dog, like it was on GrubHub or something. And when I knew the guy part was never going to happen, I figured, okay, so I don't get to do it the easy way. I still need to eat… and I can figure it out. It's still not impossible."

"Like ordering for pickup."

"Or making it my damn self. Right? But I keep burning dinner, and I'm at the end of my rope when Byron shows up. He's handsome and terrible, and he's got this soft underside that's really appealing. He wants kids, and when I was over the shock of the condom breaking… a voice inside me said, 'Maybe I'll get a shot at the easy way.' I pretended I didn't hear it, but it was there." I shook my head, looking at my palms in my lap "I hate admitting I thought that."

"It's normal to want things to be easy."

"And now, I feel shitty that I'm not pregnant, but add to it that I feel like I got dumped."

His brows twisted into a knot at the top of his nose. "What did he say to you?"

"He wants me."

"Why do you have a puss on? I thought you liked him."

"I do. I did. I don't know. He just hit us with a ton of motions and new drawings. Now I think I couldn't tell up from down when it was wall-to-wall baby junk. He's the same. I'm the same. I should just leave it like it should have been in the first place."

"You just have to stop thinking about it," he joked.

I laughed a little at the impossibility and ubiquity of the advice.

Emilio gave me the envelope. The restaurant logo was embossed on the back with pinkish gold leaf. My name was written on the front with quill and India ink.

"You know I'm coming," I said without opening the invitation.

"But you don't know what I wrote in yours."

"Fine." I peeled back the seal and slid out the white card. A thin slice of camphor wood with foil lettering detailed the event. It was beautifully designed, sparse, thoughtful, and modern. "How much did these cost?"

"More than the menus."

"Worth it."

On the top flap of the paper card, Emilio had written a note in felt-tip pen.

SUPERTASTER,

I'LL NEVER FORGET *those nights I blindfolded you and made you taste different pear hybrids.*

Or the times you brought me lunch at La Ragazza Bella because I couldn't stand eating my own food.

Or when you got your mother to front me ten grand for that food truck.

Never forget that you're my best friend and muse. You've got the Einstein of palates.

I've never been alone, even when we didn't hang out for months... You were always there. Everything that's ever gone right for me has been because you helped me.

—Chef Emilio Spaghetti-O

PS: If our baby has your talent, I'm hiring them before kindergarten ruins their taste buds with cheese sticks and bagged carrots.

"You earned everything you're getting," I said, closing the card.

"You—"

A knock on the door interrupted. "Emilio?"

"All right!" He stood and took my chin in his tapered fingers. "No matter what happens, you're not alone."

"Thank you." I was cut off by insistent knocking.

"I'm coming already!" he shouted.

"Try to relax," I said, knowing it was dumb advice he didn't know how to take any more than I did.

"Sure." He opened the door. "If you can't take a bath for you, take one for me."

CHAPTER 19

BYRON

I wouldn't insult Olivia by pulling punches. That would imply she couldn't handle my best effort or didn't want to. It was no better than letting a child win a game of chess because they were too fragile to lose, and she wasn't fragile. Not even a little. She needed the fight.

Had she smiled at the slew of offenses I'd lobbed? Nodded in recognition? Was she angry? And did that make her wet?

It was late. The office was quiet. I was going through the architectural drawings, looking for ways to make the Bel-Air house even more ambitious, when Clarissa rapped softly on the doorjamb.

"Mr. Crowne?"

"You're here late."

"I had to take care of some invoicing. This came for you."

She handed me a small manila envelope with my name written below the seal. I recognized the handwriting.

"Thank you. You should go home. The invoices can wait."

"I will. You should go home too."

"Close the door behind you." I went behind my desk.

She nodded and left, clicking the glass door closed. When she disappeared down the hall, I opened my father's envelope, pressed the sides, and slid the contents onto my glass desk.

The check. My inheritance. The One Big Thing every Crowne heir was entitled to.

It came with a note.

DEAR BYRON,

WIRING THIS SEEMED IMPERSONAL. *I wanted you to have something you could hold in your hands.*

Logan has already expressed my concerns to you. In case he waxed dramatic about my thoughts, my apprehension is minor. You've made your own way. You've built a solid, separate business. I trust you know what you need.

I understand the six of you call my gift the OBT. One Big Thing.

The fact that you are only the second of the six to call in this chit makes me think OBT stands for Offer Blocked Today. Your mother thinks it speaks to your ability to discern a need from a want. Optimism Bides Time is what she calls it.

Frost wrote about two roads diverging and the choice between them. By waiting, you choose the road less taken. I am proud of you for this and a long list of things. Enumerating them will embarrass you, so I won't, but suffice to say your boldness with this project takes up a space, and the way you've handled yourself after Samantha is another.

I STOPPED READING FOR A MOMENT. He had no idea how I'd handled myself. I hadn't told him or anyone except Olivia about my guilt or my fear that I'd push someone to suicide again. He and Mom had seen an appropriate measure of grief. They'd seen Samantha's mother blame me and had countered it so stridently I had to pretend I believed them.

W*HICH BRINGS* me to the next embarrassing point of pride on the list. Thank you for bringing Olivia around this past weekend.

T*HAT EXPLAINED IT.* He was proud that I was moving on.

Was I? And was I moving on with Olivia? We'd been cornered, so we'd made the best of it for the weekend. Until the sun shone through her hair as we rode to Dead Man's Grove, she had been a practical consideration.

Grief and guilt were mine. One fed the other. Letting go of grief made the guilt scream over my inhuman ability to do so. Forgiving myself made grief remind me, steadily and quietly, that I was a dangerous man who could hurt someone again.

I*T WAS* good to see you interested in someone, especially someone so lovely. She reminded me of your mother when we first met. I had her completely charmed—in the bag, if we're talking man-to-man. But she made it clear she wasn't taking any of my shit. A rare combination not every man wants. A partner like that is worth it. Trust me. My marriage was the kindest decision your mother ever made.

I *WISH* you the very best, son.

—Dad

. . .

Dropping the note, I picked up the check. Eight figures. Enough to build a palace. I was pouring the foundation of a fortune with my name on it. Something of my own to leave for my children.

I laughed softly at myself and dropped into my chair.

The office was too quiet this late. No one was buzzing me with a distraction. Only the breathy hum of the air conditioning kept me company.

Two roads diverged in a wood... And I'd tried to pave a new one down the middle.

It had all seemed so easy. Have a child without the lie of a wife I couldn't love. That ripped condom had been a gift. All I'd had to do was convince Olivia that my lucky break was hers too.

Why couldn't a lucky break be planned?

We liked fucking each other. Why not save her the humiliation of the turkey-baster treatments?

The air conditioner shut down, exhaling for a few seconds before falling to silence. I couldn't move. If I got up, something precious would break. Something I'd earned. A gift I hadn't asked for, hidden inside a modest box and wrapped in a satin bow.

What was it? If I moved, what would I lose but a moment of peace? The singular contentment of a path cut down the center?

All I needed was Olivia to walk the road with me, which meant breaking through the wall between us. What if I took my brother's advice and knocked on the door?

The calm of the room shifted around me and formed itself into action.

I called her from the office phone.

"Hello?" she answered with a question as if she didn't know who it was.

"It's Byron."

Her breath. Water dripping. The air whipping around the chasm between us.

"I didn't recognize the number," she said.

"I'm calling from my office."

"Nice play."

"It wasn't a play. It was just the closest phone."

"I believe you."

"Would you have picked up if you'd known it was me?"

"I don't know."

"I can hang up and call again from my cell. You'll see my name and decide yes or no."

"No, it's okay." The sound of rippling water came through. "We'll pretend I decided yes."

That made me unreasonably, disproportionately happy. "Are you taking a bath?"

"Yeah. It's supposed to be relaxing, but—"

"But then I called?"

I gave her an opportunity to tell me to fuck off. I had to know if she'd answered my knock or if she was looking through the peephole before she chased me away.

"But it's never as relaxing as it is wet and boring," she said.

Didn't express regret that I'd reached out to her. She didn't take the bait. She'd opened the door when I'd knocked, but there was another door behind it.

Might as well knock on that one too.

"You know what I hear is relaxing?" I said.

"Meditation?"

"Me driving over there and making you come until you collapse."

"For a guy named after a poet, you have an unpoetic way with words."

"It's modernist verse."

She laughed. "I'm sorry about how I acted. I think I put a lot into that pregnancy, and it was like…" She sighed. Water sloshed when she moved. "It was like pin the tail on the donkey. They blindfold you and spin you around, and you're so disoriented and dizzy you pin the tail on the birthday cake."

"That really happened, didn't it?" I put my feet on the desk.

"Totally. It was a mess."

"How old were you?"

"Eight. I was convinced I was going to nail it. But I had chocolate frosting up to my elbow. Anthony Rubino said I looked like I'd had my arm up the dog's butt. Everyone laughed. I was so mad I cried. And we didn't even have a dog."

"I'm trying hard not to laugh."

"You're doing a shitty job. I can hear your brain."

"At least I know what to expect. If you're disoriented now, next step is you'll be angry enough to cry."

"I did that already," she said softly, falling into a heavy pause.

She had. On the bathroom floor at my parents' house, she'd expelled more tears than I'd thought the human body could hold. I let her own the silence.

"What do you need, Olivia?"

"I just… I need some time to be normal. Like, doing what I know how to do. The usual. Eating. Sleeping. Accessorizing. Taking on assholes like you."

"You don't know how to take on an asshole like me."

"You definitely are an original," she replied. "You made me stay in here until I got pruney." The water lapped on the sides of the tub, protesting her perfection stepping out of it. "I must like you."

"It's taking every effort in my body to stay in this chair."

"Don't chase. Please."

I heard the bar rattle as she removed the towel, then the rustle of terrycloth running over every inch of her skin. My dick swelled thinking about it.

"I don't want to chase you," I said. "I want to catch you. There's a difference."

"If you caught me, what would you do with me?"

"Get you pregnant." I waited for the suggestion to land.

"You're a scary guy sometimes," she replied finally.

"What scares you? That you're naked right now and I have a hard-on?"

"No, that you might actually be a devoted person." The bed creaked. "With a really big, hot hard-on."

"You're on the bed."

"You." She elongated the last vowel as if she needed a moment to think. "You're at the office."

"You're on your back."

She paused, then the mattress springs squeaked as if she'd rolled onto her back.

Was compliance consent?

"Olivia?"

"Go ahead. I just… I may be confused about what I want, but my body isn't."

"No?"

"It wants you, and it won't shut up about it."

Lazily, I pulled my belt from the loop. "You pull your knees up and wide, exposing your pretty cunt."

"Oh."

"What?"

"Yes. You pull your dick out. It's huge, Byron. It's so hard you can barely get it free."

Getting it free was the easy part. Keeping it from exploding was a different matter. "You pinch your nipple."

"There's a drop on your tip. You rub it off."

Using my precum as lubricant, I rubbed the head.

"You're touching yourself," I said, giving her a moment before continuing. "You're wet and swollen. Two fingers slide right inside you. You pull them out because you want to add another. Three fingers. Deep, Beauty. You can't get them deep enough, but you try."

She groaned.

"Put me on speaker," I commanded. The sound changed. Her obedience increased the throb in my dick. I almost came in my hand. "Crouch. Get on the balls of your feet. God, I want to be there. I'm so hard for you."

"You're here. Between my feet."

She had me talking right up to her cunt.

"Three fingers. Fuck yourself with them. Hard. Like I'm pounding you. Bury me in you. Let me see your dirty fucking soul."

"God, Byron. I—" Her sentence disappeared into a grunt.

"Push deep and use your thumb on your clit." I slowed down before I unloaded. "Do you want to come?"

"Yes."

"You want things to be normal. Fucking you is what I want to be normal. My cock deep inside your throat, your cunt, your ass. Your screams when you beg me to stop because you can't take coming anymore. My mark all over your body. Inside and out."

"Can I come?"

I didn't answer. The thought of writing on her inside and out nearly pushed me over the edge, and she must have heard it.

"Byron," she said. "Lord Byron. Come in me. Stain me."

"With me now…" was all the permission I could get out.

I knew from her groans that we came together. I was so focused on the aural connection I didn't realize my eyes had been closed until I opened them.

"Hey?" she said. "You there?"

"Still here." I snapped a couple of tissues out of the box and cleaned up.

"What are we doing?"

We were having phone sex, but I knew what she meant.

"I have a proposal." I went into the bathroom to wash my hands. The mirror was kind. Handsome enough guy. Well put together. Business. I could do some business here.

"Go on."

"I think we're sexually compatible."

"What clued you in?"

I smiled as I dried my hands. She was all right. "I'd like to keep fucking you. Generally, I'm not interested in getting attached. Romantically."

"You mentioned that."

"We're friends," I said. "You still want a baby. Let me give you one."

I stood in the middle of my office bathroom. Everything stopped but my watch, ticking away as my mind shuffled my feelings like a deck of cards.

"So, I stop the insemination."

"Yes."

"And we're friends who are trying to have a baby together."

"What do you say?"

Her sheets rustled, and her breath came in a sigh. "I think I need to think about it."

"It's a good offer. But you'll have to stop hating me."

"Also workable. I think I'm starting to kind of like you."

I knew she liked me, but hearing it made all the difference.

CHAPTER 20

OLIVIA

We'd talked through his ride home. The last thing I remembered before I fell asleep was him taking off his shoes.

I told him about Isabelle and how much my sister loved being taken to parties with our mother. How beautiful she was. How she'd lit up the screen when she acted as a child. How she met her husband at a Getty Gala and gave it all up when she had her first difficult pregnancy. How I adored her children.

He told me about his battles with Logan to take over the business and how he let go of the idea after Samantha died. He'd needed to cut weight or sink. I respected his ability to see what he needed to do for his own mental health, and I perceived how much it hurt him.

I didn't remember hanging up. The phone lay on the pillow next to me with a dead battery. All the things we'd said to each other were latent in there, but the effects of them were alive in me. The depth of Byron's regrets hadn't surprised me or sowed doubt about his truthfulness. In itself, that was astonishing.

Two months earlier, I wouldn't have believed he cared about anything but money and power.

Now I could add family to the list, and that changed everything.

Hope was a liar, but its stories were too sexy to ignore.

Byron instead of Emilio. A more precise round of fertility meds and a more enjoyable insemination method made the trade off a no-brainer.

The only hang-up was that Byron wanted to be involved with the baby but not with me. If he got bored of me while I developed feelings for him, I would get hurt.

So, I wouldn't develop feelings.

Except that it was too late for that, wasn't it?

Rubbing shampoo into my scalp didn't loosen the knot of questions surrounding my emotional vulnerability. Neither did eating, accessorizing, or getting out the door to take on Assholes of America, Inc.

I still didn't know what to do about Byron Crowne, but I knew two things:

What he wasn't and how I felt about him.

One. He was not one hundred percent asshole.

Two. I was falling for him.

I added one.

Three. I was going to get hurt.

The obvious next step was to tell him there was no deal. It was the only way to protect my heart.

Or I could demand a real relationship, and he'd say no.

And if he said yes, I'd disclose to Kimberly and the judge and everyone would wonder if I'd lost my fucking mind. Then he'd break my heart.

So, the deal was on.

My heart for a baby.

My mother had bought the house high in the Hollywood Hills when it was possible to do so for a few hundred thousand dollars you might not ever make again. She'd been pregnant and wise, putting her and Francois's Los Angeles residence under her name for tax purposes while he bought their apartment in Paris. When he left her, the house's value had doubled, but the deed was already in her name.

The house was up a curved single-lane road so poorly maintained my little convertible rocked as it rolled. I turned onto the short drive next to a small house no one would have looked twice at, parking behind a Nissan crossover with a yellow "Baby on Board" sign suction-cupped to the back window.

This would be fine. I felt a happy tug just knowing the kids were around.

Grabbing two bags of toys guaranteed to piss off my sister, I got out of the car as Mom opened the front door, wearing a hot-pink muumuu with a gold belt and a necklace made of rocks. Whenever I went too long without seeing her, I had to catch myself for a moment. She was somehow transcendent. Her smile was a perfectly symmetrical crescent under a patrician nose thousands of women wasted good money trying to emulate. Her neck was long and thin, accentuating a square jawbone that would have been too masculine on another woman's head.

"Oliveeeahhh!" She came to me with her arms out, gray-streaked blond hair flying, crossing the front yard in three steps. She was almost six feet tall, and when she hugged me, she was thread and I was a spool.

"Do you know what I found out on Google?" she asked as we walked to the front door. Her feet were bare, and though she'd found time to coordinate her outfit, she hadn't bothered with makeup.

"Anything you wanted?"

"You live five miles away as the crow flies."

"I try to visit—"

"No, no. I mean I should visit more. I get so isolated up here. I've been thinking—"

"Auntie Livie!" Ronnie dropped a Lifesaver-shaped cookie and pattered across the living room in a more-or-less-straight line, a foodish substance matted on the bulldozer printed on his shirt.

I picked him up. "Hey, Ronron!"

"What you bring me?"

"Bring you?" I pretended I didn't know what he was talking about.

"How many?"

"Well, how old are you?"

"Four and half! I get four and half things."

"No halves." I held up two bags by the handles. "Yellow one is yours."

He took it, and I let him go before I scanned the room for his eight-year-old sister. The trick of the house was its modesty on the street side. The back side crawled down the hillside, leaving verandas on all three stories with clear views of the horizon and the pool jutting out into empty space.

I was taking too long to find Sarah, and she let me know by clearing her throat before dodging behind the couch. She giggled.

"Where's Sarah?" I asked, looking everywhere but at where she was.

She cackled as I passed her and squealed when I spun around and scooped her up. Her body was small for her age, but her personality was as massive as her will. She wiggled out of my arms almost immediately.

"She doesn't hug anymore," her mother's voice came from behind me. My sister was wiping out a bowl with a dish towel. "It's undignified. Like hiding when someone comes in."

"No." Sarah crossed her arms and shook her head so hard her straight, brown hair fanned. "Hiding is funny."

"Nice to see you." I hugged Isabelle.

Ronnie had dumped the four Matchbox cars on the floor and was making short work of the packaging.

"You didn't bring her any slime, did you?" Isabelle pointed at the purple bag I had left, wrinkling her nose. "It gets in the carpet."

"Keychains," I whispered.

"Okay."

I crouched and held the bag out to Sarah. "This is for you, missy." She took it. "Thank you."

"You're welcome." I hung back while my niece peeked in the bag at the eight sparkly, shiny blinking-light gewgaws.

She pulled out a rainbow-maned unicorn bedazzled with plastic stones, letting the rest of the bag drop. "Esme has this one on her backpack!"

Before I could ask who Esme was or what was so special about her bag, Sarah ran into me, wrapping her arms around my neck and bouncing with the joyful ferocity of a jackhammer. She smelled like playtime sweat and carrot sticks dipped in hummus, and her gratitude for a simple thing created the torque that spun the earth around the sun.

I was the thread, and she was the spool.

I wanted this.

More than anything, I still wanted this.

* * *

"So, he's home studying. I lost that one." Isabelle flipped the burger container closed. "But I kind of won it."

The sun was setting. The takeout was mostly eaten. The children were playing in the shallow end of the pool.

"I never understood this decision," I said. "Overall, it's crazy to me. Nothing against Leo."

"Bullshit," Isabelle muttered into her drink.

"Seriously. I mean it. He's fine. I'm looking at you."

"You have that tone, Olivia," Mom scolded. "This isn't a courtroom."

"You quit acting to have kids," I said. "And now that they're both in school and you can make an audition once in a while, he decides to change careers and you just say, 'Okay, whatever you want, honey. I didn't want my own life anyway'?"

"Ugh." She threw back her head. "Why are you like this?"

"Not a doormat?"

"Hey!" Isabelle snapped straight. "Not cool."

"Let's clean up first." Mom led by example, balling up napkins and gathering containers.

I decided not to follow her lead. I wasn't letting my sister off the hook. "We just keep letting men do this shit."

"He's doing what's best for everyone."

"I get that," I said. "I get architecture's more stable than acting. That's why I'm not riding him. I'm riding you. You need to take care of yourself. What you need is important."

"Sorry." Isabelle took a chunk of ice in her teeth and tucked it in her cheek. "We can't all be self-propelled power bitches on a mission." She crunched the ice and tried to stare me down.

"Mom," I said when the screen door opened, "tell her what you gave up for Francois."

"She's heard the same stories you have."

"She's doing the same thing."

Mom sighed and collected more stuff.

"Same. Thing." Twice, I pressed my finger to the table until the first knuckle bent.

"So?" My sister's monosyllabic defiance was a shadow of what she was likely to get from her daughter in a few years.

"So, why would you repeat Mom's misery?"

Isabelle was working on an answer when our mother's voice cut in.

"I wouldn't say I was miserable."

"Yes," I said. "Yes, you were."

"No. Actually..." She gave up on cleaning and sat across from us. "Actually, I was relieved."

Next to me, ice clicked down the length of a paper cup as Isabelle loaded it into her mouth.

"Relieved how?" I asked.

"Acting was harder than it looked."

"You were good, Ma. Your audition reel—"

"Oh, I had talent. But your father always said an artist needs two of three things to be successful." She counted on her thin fingers. "Talent. Opportunity. Drive."

"You had talent and opportunity."

"But not drive," she added.

"Talent and opportunity. That's two out of three."

Next to me, ice was crushed between my sister's teeth.

"Your father was wrong. He was a first-class chauvinist pig, and he was dead wrong most of the time. There's no acting without drive. I needed that time with him to figure out what to replace it with."

"Badass," Isabelle said, then tipped the rest of the ice into her mouth.

"You spent all that time with him knowing you'd leave him?"

"Our past paid for my future."

"Bang." My sister plopped down the cup. "Future first."

"No," I waved my hands as if mosquitoes filled the air. "No, you're both insane. Dad was terrible! And you!" I pointed at Isabelle. "You love Leo!"

"I do. The math is the same."

"But you're giving up your future."

"Are you joking? Olivia. Wake up. I'm too old already. It's over."

Balloons blew up inside my ears, muffling her words in the pressure, as if I was taking a supersonic elevator to the four-hundredth floor.

"Stop," I said, barely hearing myself. "I can't."

"Those kids are the future," my sister said from the other side of the balloon.

My bag was on the couch. Shoes by the door. Car in the driveway. Full tank of gas.

"I have to go."

But Isabelle wasn't done. "What do you think it is when you have a baby?"

"You don't become a nonperson!" My shout popped the pressure in my head. "You're a beautiful, talented woman with drive. And if you continue like this, you're setting a shitty example for her!" My arm shot straight out toward her daughter, who was jaw-dropped and wide-eyed at her potty-mouthed aunt.

"Oopsie," Sarah said.

"I think that's just about enough," Mom said.

"Forget it, baby," Isabelle said. "Aunt Livie's not feeling good."

"I'm feeling fine. Just sick of this. Sick of how we play by the rules and they bend them and find loopholes. And we're supposed to smile and bend and twist to keep up until we don't even recognize ourselves anymore. Then suddenly, when our asses are in our faces, they pull a single lawful move and we snap. But they point to page 456 of the rulebook and say, 'Well, it's right here, ma'am. You woulda won if you'd played fair.'"

"Are we still talking about my husband?"

"No. Yes. I'm just… I'm frustrated. With him. With you." I pointed at Mom. "With you too. I mean, you won that thing with Dad, but you're acting like setting it up was a cakewalk. So now this one," I moved my pointing finger to my sister. "She's thinking she can pull off giving up her career for her kids and be happy with the guy."

"I will."

"She won't," Mom contradicted.

"What?" Isabelle cried.

"Told you."

"Hush!" One syllable from Mom turned me into a child. "Both of you."

Now we were both in time-out.

"I have an announcement." She crossed her legs. Her sandal dangled from her toe. "I'm selling this house."

"What?" my sister and I said in the same way, at the same time.

"It's worth five million dollars." Mom braced her hands on the arms of her chair. "And I won't have to update a thing."

"Where are you going to go?" I asked. The idea of my mother living anywhere besides that house was surreal.

"I'm just one person." She swung the sandal, then let it slide back down onto her foot. "I don't need four thousand square feet I can't be bothered keeping up. I'm going to get an apartment and travel. The market's right to sell. Then I can give you girls a… sum."

"What kind of sum?" Isabelle asked.

"Hopefully a million each. It's Los Angeles, so you're not rich, but…" She tipped her chin toward Isabelle. "If you play your cards right and cut out the vacations, you should be able to pursue acting before the Rolex boys decide you're dried up."

"Wow, Ma," she said.

"I don't want it," I cut in. "Give mine to Isabelle."

"You'll take it, Olivia," Mom said.

"This is your house."

I said it was her house, but I meant it was my house. And by "my house," I meant my home. My unique childhood. My nine-year-old self falling asleep in the broom closet so I could hear a late-night dinner conversation between a diplomat and a duchess. My time being photographed by the best in the world not because I was beautiful, but because I was interesting. I had only been a kid, but Mom never treated us like kids. We were part of her life and her community. She kept us safe and let us do the rest.

I'd never found that again. I'd been adrift since, and now she was taking it away.

Isabelle sat motionless with one knee on her seat, ice chewed away, her expression locked in the middle distance as if she was calculating either how far the money would get her or whether it was worth it to take it as the price of accepting the loss.

"No," I said. "I won't let you."

"Let it go, sweetie."

"I can't bear someone else living here."

"I wouldn't worry about that."

"I'll buy it," I continued as if I had that kind of money. "I'll figure it out."

"Come on, Olivia. You can't compete with the developers who want it."

"I... what?"

"I haven't renovated a thing since I bought it in 1989. They'll pay full value just for the land."

I was horrified. "You can't sell to a developer."

"Why not? My realtor says they'll offer cash. They just have to sort out some new erosion control requirements."

"No. No. Sell to someone. Sell to a *person*. Don't sell to those backstabbing, slimy cretins. They'll tear it down and build a crackerbox corner to corner. They're disgusting, awful... They'll hurt you. Do you understand? They hurt everything they touch, and they lie. They'll lie to get what they want, and you can't give them this house."

"I'm not giving—"

"This is not fair!" I slammed my hand on the table. I hadn't realized how noisy the kids' playing was until they went silent.

"Olivia?" Isabelle said timidly.

My phone went off like an alarm.

"Nothing," I said, turning the glass up to see Emilio's name. "It's nothing. Give me a minute."

Answering the phone, I went inside.

"Hi," I said, closing the door so I could pace across the living room without being heard.

"Oh my God, what happened?" By the background noise of shouts and clangs, I knew he was in the kitchen.

I stepped on something that crunched. Half a Lifesaver-shaped cookie exploded into crumbs. "Nothing. Why?"

"You stuck on the 405 or something?"

"I'm at my mother's house." I ripped a paper towel off the roll. "She's selling it. I'm annoyed at her. Not you."

On the way to the crumb pile, I kicked a Matchbox car. It spun out and smacked against the far wall, near where—at some point—a crack in the paint that I'd always imagined looked like a lightning bolt had turned into a fissure.

When I was little, I'd put my dollhouse against that wall and pretended the family inside was safe during a thunderstorm. The family lived, but time had broken the lightning.

"I have to ask you something," Emilio said, snapping me out of the imaginary rain. "Russell's PR got some Instagram influencers on the invite list. Including but not limited to Lyric Crowne. Four million followers. She posted about Bistro Bungalow, and it went wild. So…"

"I met her." I gathered the crumbs in the paper towel, which was physically impossible to do efficiently. "She seems like a normal person? I don't have any deeper intel."

"Okay, fine. Good. Okay." A pot banged behind him.

"You're going to be fine." I stuffed the paper towel and crumbs in the trash. "I'm serious."

"I know. But she put up a shot of the Bistro Bungalow burger, and that's what went crazy. I don't know if I should put a burger on the menu. Maybe a special for the night?"

He was a wreck. He needed to relax, and the last thing he needed to hear was that he needed to relax.

"Emilio Spaghetti-O," I said. "Listen to me. Listen to every word. You know who you are and what you want. You know how to get it. Stay on track. Between now and the opening, you're going to focus on what you can control. You're going to keep your eyes on the work, put one foot in front of the other, and move forward. You're not going to borrow trouble. Do you hear?"

"I hear you."

"What are you going to do?"

"Stop worrying."

"The work, Emilio. Stay with the work."

"I knew I called you for a reason. Okay. I have to go."

"Go. Bye."

I hung up. My family was on the other side of the sliding glass doors. The kids were playing again, and Mom and Isabelle were talking. I was in the kitchen, the sun angling into the house with the day's last gasps of light.

Stay with the work.

The house was a part of me, but it wasn't my work. It was my mother's.

If I was going to take my own advice, I'd have to do what needed doing and stop letting my heart borrow trouble.

CHAPTER 21

BYRON

The OBT check was on my dresser, folded into four sections like a receipt I'd forgotten to give to my bookkeeper.

It was supposed to go to my accounts manager. Why had I placed my father's note in a wooden box and let the check sit in limbo? I'd wanted the money—needed it to do things that would attract buyers who could afford the most luxurious house in Bel-Air.

And yet, there it sat while I plowed through my own investment, making the thing bigger.

When it had been assumed I would take over Crowne Industries, my entitlement to the One Big Thing was tied to that. It was an ace waiting to be played, and I was eager to show it. I sought out acquisitions, but none of them was the exact right size or shape for the company I was learning to run. There was no point in asking for it if I wasn't going to make the most of it.

Samantha had talked about that money as if it was for spending. A house. A boat. How far it would go before it ran out.

Old money wasn't always deep money. Old money got lazy, and

though it might take a few generations for it to catch up to the times, finite was finite. I hadn't known the Bettencourts were broke, but once her father told me, I knew why and how it had remained a secret. The family lived for their image and brand presentation.

My fiancée hadn't been like that. Not completely. She'd never bought it as reality, but she'd craved harmony, so she played along while it all tore her apart. Keeping up. Presenting the best face. Lying to her friends. Making sure she was photographed at the most exclusive events because it kept her parents from fighting.

She hadn't cared for it. Had hated it. Felt used and objectified. But she kept on, the little trouper. When she took it out on me, I didn't care. I loved her, and I was strong enough to take whatever she needed to give me because she wasn't strong enough to direct it where it belonged.

So, on the days it was my fault, she accused me of stalling the wedding. She wanted to get married now. Tomorrow. Yesterday. City Hall. Elope. Just get it done so she wouldn't have to worry anymore. I could save her from her mother, who was planning to divest assets for a huge wedding on a yacht they couldn't pay off.

Sometimes, in the quiet parts of the night, I looked for ways I'd failed her.

I wondered if asking for my family's gift would have saved her life or postponed the inevitable. I tried to remember what I was feeling or thinking when I'd uttered the last words I'd ever say to her. How stricken she'd looked. Face drained of blood. Mouth open.

Eyes afire, she'd asked me why I was marrying her.

As I emptied my pockets on my dresser, I bounced the question back to her.

Why do you think?

Wallet. Car key fob. Handkerchief.

Answer me, Byron!

I'd been doing the same thing. Emptying the day from my pockets.

I'd sighed. Maybe it was the sigh that did it. I'd just gotten back from a trip to Saudi. I was tired and as lazy as old money. If I told her I loved her in twenty-five words or more, she'd be soothed. That was what she wanted. Some form of overblown bad poetry so she'd know that between us, it wasn't all for show.

Knowing what she wanted wasn't good enough anymore.

I didn't know what she needed.

I gave her the truth, which was short, direct, and to the point.

Because I love you.

She'd acted as if I'd slapped her.

I should have used more words. I shouldn't have acted bored or placed the punctuation where it would sound like an accusation.

She left the room. When I didn't see her for the rest of the night, I was relieved. In the morning, after sleeping off the jet lag, I'd deal with my beloved.

Which I did.

And I swore I'd never tell another woman I loved them, because I was a monster and my love had killed her.

Knowing my logic was faulty did nothing to change it. Everyone was safe as long as I remained on the other side of my reasoning. The words were on lockdown, and that was that.

I opened the check. Everything over that number. Or nothing over that number.

I'd never know. But some phase of my life was ending, and another was beginning. If the check had four or six fewer zeroes, it would still have lifted a weight off me.

After propping the check like a tower on its folded corners, I opened the drawer under it and tipped it in, imagining a pillar of blocks falling.

On top of my things sat Olivia's stretched underwear from our night at the Waldorf. The night she'd stormed out with my seed dripping between her legs, terrified that I'd be the father of a child she wanted so badly.

I balled them in my fist and sniffed them like the filthy pig Samantha had thought I was. Then I sniffed again. Pure fucking *Eau de Pussy d'Olivia*. The cotton was dry but soaked through with the smell of her. That was mine. I'd made her this wet, and I'd do it again.

I put the underwear in my pocket and went to the kitchen. My refrigerator opened on two sides. A vertical glass window between them exhibited everything my sommelier had left to chill in case of guests.

The Dom Perignon popped and fizzed in the crystal flute. It was cold and bubbly in my throat, and I didn't give a shit that I was alone. I drained the flute and pushed it away, taking the bottle by the neck so I could drink right from the source.

"I love you" was out, but you know what wasn't?

Share this bottle with me.

Come to me.

I'm obsessed with you.

I trust you.

I own you.

Be with me.

Don't get pregnant without me.

Another gulp of champagne turned into three. Flavia had left dinner, but I didn't want it. She could take it home to her kids. I took a swig and texted Olivia.

—*You never answered me*—
—*It's been a week*—

—*I'm sorry. I needed to think.*—

A hand coursed through the miasma I'd created for myself and slapped sense into me. These things needed to be said in person by a man who was stable and sober.

But still… the monumental strength it had taken to leave her alone to think was being dissolved in champagne. Now I had her on the other side. I could influence her across distance. Soak another pair of underwear.

—And?—

—*And we should talk in person*—

—Where are you?—

—*Work, no thanks to you*—

For better or worse, she was thinking about me.

—What time are you getting off?—

She called, and I picked up.

"I'll come get you," I said, dispensing with the greetings. "Whatever time."

"Late. I don't know."

"I'll wait."

Her answer was a sigh of resignation.

"Please." I was begging. I was a pathetic beggar, but I didn't know what else to do.

"Don't come here," she said. "Meet me at the Broken Stem. On Olympic."

"When?"

"Ten."

I looked at my watch. I could get sober enough to drive in four hours, but I'd never be sober enough to hear her say no. "Done."

"See you there. I have to go."

We hung up. The screen flipped back to our texts. I typed out a string of filth that would keep me on her mind, but it wasn't going to convince her of anything except that I was a pushy asshole. I put the phone down next to her stretched ball of dried-juice underwear. My mind hiccupped on what she was wearing and what was under it. How sexy it would be if she stripped down to something that would reveal the marks I'd left on her.

I opened my laptop and searched for something to ruin.

I PARKED in the back and entered through a door with *Broken Stem* stenciled in white. The back hall had bathrooms, a closed office door, and an ajar door that said EMPLOYEES ONLY. She had me meet her in a dump. Did that mean yes or no? Was it a sign of what I could expect?

Past a black velvet curtain, I entered the bar. The place was dark, with candles every two inches across the bar, making it look as if a coven of witches had decorated for a ceremony. The logo made it clear that *Broken Stem* referred to a wine glass, because all the glasses were tulip-shaped and stemless with divots for thumbs. Mine was filled with club soda.

It wasn't crowded, so I had a direct visual line to the front door. When she came in, the fan above blasted to control the temperature, blowing her hair everywhere. It calmed, falling over her shoulders when she stepped out of the squall, which was the moment she saw me.

"Hey." She slid onto the stool next to mine. Her black skirt matched her jacket, and her blouse was a silver satin thin enough to mold around hard nipples.

"Thank you for meeting me."

"Only fair. I can't keep you in suspense forever."

When the bartender approached, she ordered a ginger ale, then crossed her legs and faced me. Her skirt slid above her knee, and her shoe dangled off her toes.

"So, you decided," I said as the soda gun hissed.

"I have."

She waited until her ginger ale landed in front of her and the bartender left. In the eternity of those seconds—and not for the first time, I considered what I'd do if she declined. I got my pitch together as if she was a recalcitrant architect or a buyer who hemmed and hawed over another ten thousand square feet.

"I'm listening." Over her calf and down to the heel, I stroked the silk of her stockings.

"When you say you can't love me, I believe you. You don't want a commitment. I believe that too."

"Good." I pushed her shoe back onto her foot.

"But I'm afraid." She drank a bit of her ginger ale and put it back carefully in the same crescent of condensation. "I know you think I'm too strong to break. But I do have a heart. I can love someone. That means I can get hurt."

I watched my hand as it ran over her heel and up her calf. "I don't want to hurt you."

"It doesn't matter what you want. I can love you. I can try not to, but I'm pretty sure I'm already halfway there."

I tore my eyes away from her leg and looked at her face. Flickering candles changed the light, but her expression was steady.

"I'm not worth it," I said.

"Women love unworthy men all the time."

"True."

"And you're worthy. If we're doing this, you have to stop saying stuff like that."

Abruptly, my hands stopped moving. "Are we—"

"Yes." She slid her hand into mine and uncrossed her legs, leaning forward so she could speak quietly and still fill my world. "I think no matter what, even if I'm hurt, I can maintain a friendship. But I want you to understand what a gamble this is for me. Long game? It's worth the potential upside. But in the short term, it's a big risk."

She said it as if it was a challenge. She was daring me to keep her from falling in love and daring me to hurt her at the same time.

Neither would happen. I couldn't see the future, but she had a limited count of possibilities.

"When do we start?" I pushed my hand between her knees and up until I was blocked at the spot where her thighs met like an inverted fork in the road.

"I'm ovulating in thirteen days, give or take."

"What if you want to fuck tonight?"

The idea of getting inside her without a condom, skin to skin, truly joined, was a drug I had to take again.

"My period's finishing up. I won't get pregnant."

"You want to, then."

"I know."

"Relax your legs."

She did it, letting my hand travel another few inches. My lips brushed her throat, and her breath came in damp gasps. I was urgently hard for her. A glass broke somewhere outside the dome of our attention.

We were in public. There were more than emotional risks between us.

"Let's get out of here," I whispered. "We'll seal this deal quick."

When I felt her nod, I got up, straightened my jacket, and walked out the way I came in. I was thinking of taking her in the car, but on the way, I found a closet door still ajar.

Olivia came through the curtain, all poise and leg, blond hair pushed off her shoulders, a golden idol ready to worship.

When I pulled her into the darkness of the closet and snapped the lock, she started to say something. I took her mouth with mine, pushing her hard against the wall. She gasped, and something clattered.

"You and me," I said, pulling up her tight skirt. "Nothing between us."

"Yes."

I felt her reach for my fly in the dark.

"Now." I was growling like an animal.

"Now." She squeaked like a wheel.

I pushed her hands off my zipper so I could shred her stockings and underpants. Owning her mouth with my tongue and shoving my fingers inside her, I filled her wherever I could reach until my cock felt as if it would break from envy.

"You ready?" I asked, releasing my erection. "Skin to skin."

She hitched one leg over my hip, and I held it there, under the knee so I could line the bare head of my dick against her.

"Go," she said. "Do it now."

She was soaked. Ready. I pushed inside her. Two strokes deep. Three to the balls. She was fucking silk wrapping around me. This was it. This was exactly what I wanted. Fucking her. Pinning her down. Taking her fully. Feeling the pulse of her cunt when she was close to coming for me.

"Say my name," I demanded.

"Lord Byron."

"Say it." I laid my hand on her throat to feel how it sounded.

"Lord Byron, I'm going to—"

I put my mouth on hers, pushing against her nub with the base of my cock, feeling the rumble of her throat as she came and the tremble of her lips on mine.

When she was done, I pulled back. "I'm going to come inside you."

"Yes. Come inside me."

"You're mine, Olivia. After I come in you. You're mine."

I exploded, writing my name so deeply inside her she'd never erase it. I etched myself there so completely she'd never forget me, even after my cold heart forgot her or her warm heart decided it had no room for me.

CHAPTER 22

OLIVIA

After taking me against a broom closet wall, Byron reluctantly took me to my car. He wanted to keep me up all night, and if my sex drive had been in charge, I would have let him.

But thankfully my brain was driving the bus. We'd agreed to create a life without falling in love. By maintaining some control, I was keeping the second part of the deal. I had to draw the lines between us, or he would tear me apart.

His full-frontal attack on the environment kept me working late. I trudged up my front steps, sick and tired of trying to figure out his strategy without telling my team I knew more about him than they'd be comfortable with.

A night of making small talk at Emilio's opening was just what I needed.

I picked up my mail. Garbage mostly. One padded manila envelope with something soft inside had been wedged behind the screen door. Figuring it was a dress I'd ordered, I tucked the package under my arm with the letters and went inside.

Junk, junk. I opened and scanned a bill, leaving the dress unopened. I checked the clock. I had to get moving.

But maybe I'd wear the dress.

I opened the manila envelope and shouldn't have been shocked that there was no dress inside. I laid the clear plastic bags on the kitchen counter. One had a white envelope inside. I opened that first. The lace underwear I'd worn to the Eclipse show fell out.

"Oh, fuck you, Byron."

The envelope had *Olivia* written on it in script. A blue foil crown was embossed at the point of the back flap. Ripping it open as if I wanted to shred the entire thing, I pulled out a card of expensive stock with the same blue crown in the center, as if that was all anyone would need to know who it was from.

The fact that it really was all I needed annoyed me. I poured another glass of wine before I read his tight cursive while standing at the kitchen counter.

DEAR OLIVIA,

YOU LEFT *these at the Waldorf.*

THEY'RE QUITE STRETCHED. *Though I'm sure they would look stunning tying your wrists behind your back, they're now unworthy of you. I took it upon myself to choose something satin to replace them. I'm afraid my imagination got carried away. I had to get you the entire set. Please accept it as an apology for ruining your lace pair.*

. . .

I know we had a limited-time arrangement. I think, based on subsequent conversations, we both agree the original deal has now proven to be wholly inadequate. I need to touch you again. I need to taste your sweet cunt and get inside you. I need to claim a part of your body.

Soon, Beauty.

Byron

Oh, my poor underpants. Not the ones on the counter, but the ones I was wearing. They were soaked, damn him. The flow had started as I read about his touch and increased to a flood with him claiming my body.

I ripped open the bag and poured the contents onto the counter.

He'd said they were satin, and they definitely were, but the black silk was sewn into half-inch-wide straps with gold fittings. I separated the black stockings and pulled the rest apart, laying it out so I could puzzle over how it worked.

It didn't take long.

The neck strap connected to three others that went under the rib cage, supporting the cups in a way that looked uncomfortable and very hot. The panties were a triangle of satin with straps around the hips that could be removed by unsnapping the gold clasps that matched the garter.

He hadn't sent underwear he'd imagined me wearing. He'd sent gear to fuck me in, and my pussy was clenching to use it when he texted.

—Did you get my gift?—

—Is it for me or you?—

*—I'll send Yusup for you now,
and we can find out tonight—*

—I can't. I have a thing—

My phone rang. Byron, of course.

"What thing?" he asked.

"Emilio's opening his restaurant tonight."

A pause as he fingered through the files in his mind. "Is he the one who was trying to get you pregnant?"

"He's a dear friend. And yes. I can't miss this." I stopped myself. I was about to offer something I hadn't thought about hard enough.

There were no fast answers, and my body was making urgent, immediate demands.

"I'll be ready for you next week." That seemed ages away. "When I'm ovulating. I'll wear it then."

"No. You wear it for me tonight."

"Byron." I fingered the gold clasp between the bra cups. "I can't skip this."

"Don't skip it. Go. Wear it underneath. I'll know you're thinking of me."

"Maybe."

"Your dress should be modest. Cover everything."

This was new but not unexpected. He was jealous of men's eyes, and I had to put my foot down before that got out of hand.

"I'll wear what I want, Lord Byron." My nickname didn't soften my scolding.

"You will. Always. But for tonight… imagine this…" His voice dropped as if we were naked together. "What you present to the world tonight is chaste and businesslike. Underneath it, I'm touching you, and you can't show it. No one can tell how turned on that makes you. No one knows I'm wrapped around your cunt."

"You're filthy," I said like the compliment it was.

"I'll take that in the spirit you meant it."

"Okay," I said, scooping up the lingerie. "I'll play. But this can't turn into you telling me how to dress."

"Have fun tonight."

I could practically hear his smile over the phone, and rather than feeling as if I'd acquiesced, pleasing him felt like a win.

WHEN I'D BEEN to Amelia's before, the house lights had been on and the room had been populated with construction workers and staff. The music had been boomboxed Spanish-language standards that echoed off the exposed brick walls.

The Uber stopped in front of a completely different place. The glass doors facing the street were open, and the bar crowd spilled out. Waitstaff bustled around candlelit tables surrounded by people in comfortable chairs.

"This it?" the driver asked.

"Yup."

"Looks like a happening place."

"Fingers crossed."

I got out, balancing on my favorite pair of black stilettos. Byron's lingerie would have shown through anything tight or flimsy, so I'd chosen a sleeveless sweater dress with a high neck and a flowing skirt that landed right above my knees. The garter hid well above the hemline, and the straps under my ribcage were invisibly tight. The sex under my dress was a secret between Byron and me, and—besides the thought of his touch—it was the most arousing thing imaginable.

He had a talent for the filthy, and he knew exactly how to use it.

I showed my invitation to the maître d' and went to the bar. It was crowded with people wanting to try the food and wanting to be seen.

Linda was at the bar, chatting with a man in his twenties. I hung back, watching her listen attentively, scanning his face for subtle clues and contradictions, then smiling so genuinely I couldn't imagine anyone holding back. I'd seen her work before. It was always a sight.

When she caught sight of me, she held her arm for me and excused herself.

"You came!" I kissed her cheek, and she turned into the woman I knew. No less charming but ten times more real.

"Dad asked me to watch everyone who got coffee. Make sure they like it so he can micromanage in the back."

"I'm glad you're here. I love this." I indicated her shiny, pale-blue trench dress with a plunging neckline. "It's not black."

"I'm nervous," she said in a low voice. "There's red wine everywhere, and I almost bumped into a food tray."

"I'll keep my eye out."

The actor-handsome bartender recognized me and started pouring red wine.

I held my hand for him to stop. "Chardonnay, please. The Alexander."

He nodded and switched.

"Everyone's here," Linda said, nudging her chin toward a dark-haired young woman in a shape-skimming yellow satin dress. "Mandy Bettencourt flew in from the Paris shows."

Samantha Bettencourt's younger sister was a fashion designer. Her clothes were bank-breakingly expensive, critically loved, and hard to find.

"That's very yellow," I murmured into my glass.

"Yeah, hey, I have to tell you something."

"Yeah?"

"There's gossip."

Linda didn't gossip idly. She didn't tell me anything that I didn't need to know.

"About?" I asked.

"You."

"Me?"

She leaned up to whisper in my ear, "And Byron Crowne."

The lingerie seemed to tighten around me to squeeze all the blood to my face. "Who said?"

Not that it mattered. People knew. I was in bed with a man known as dishonest and cruelly arrogant. One I'd pledged to take down. It shouldn't have mattered, but it did, and my heart fell into my garter.

"Carolyn Harkness. She's been trying to get set up with him for a year."

"How…"

A man in a black suit bumped Linda, and she gasped, holding her wine away from her dress.

"So sorry," he said.

"Alan!" I exclaimed, thankful for the change in subject.

"Olivia!" We double-kissed. "That's twice in a month. People are going to start talking."

People were always talking. Maybe this was a good way to dissemble.

I introduced him to Linda, laying my hand on his shoulder as we chatted about nothing. The art deco brass plates. The flower arrangements. I talked up my favorite dishes, and Alan laid his hand on my back to get me out of the way of a rushing waiter.

When I tucked my clutch under my arm, I felt my phone buzzing inside it.

I checked.

Byron. His third call.

Stepping back, I answered with my finger pressing my other ear closed against the noise. "What?"

"Olivia." He was on the street somewhere. I could hear the whoosh of cars passing and brakes squeaking.

"It's a bad time."

"Is it?"

I found a spot by the front windows. "It's loud, and I'm in the middle of a conversation."

"Are you wearing it?"

"Yes."

"Prove it."

"I'm not texting pictures of myself in a bathroom mirror."

"Pull up your dress so I can see the tops of the garter belt."

I looked around the room. Tall men. Men in suits and sweatshirts. Men with short hair and long. None of them were Byron.

"Where are you?" An ambulance screeched through traffic at the corner.

"Where I can see you in the middle of a conversation."

Through the phone, the same ambulance made him hard to hear. I faced the window again and found him standing across the street, in the middle of the sidewalk, with his phone to his ear.

He was the still point inside a whirl of pedestrians. They moved around him as if he was the north side of a magnet, and he attracted me as if I was south. Without thinking, I put my hand on the glass.

"Now," he said. "Prove it. Show me that you're wearing what I sent you."

"No."

"I think, down deep where your hunger meets your heart, you want to be dominated. You want to submit your pleasure to me. So… show me."

The flash of sensation tingled between my thighs with such power my eyelids fluttered. His voice was a sparking fuse that ended between my legs.

"I hate you," I whispered.

"I know."

I took my hand off the glass as if it had gotten too hot. "You're not supposed to be here."

"My sister couldn't make it. She gave me her invitation. Out of respect for you, I'm standing across the street."

"And telling me what to do."

"I'm going to come in there and lay my hand on your back. I'm going to kiss your face twice and tell you how nice you look tonight."

"No!"

"I won't be talking about your dress. But what's under it."

"It's not appropriate. I'm lead counsel in a case against you. And people know, Byron. I don't know how, but they're talking."

That gave him pause. He got into the driver's side of a black Jaguar that was parked in front of him. The background noise from his side cut out.

"Stay there," he said, starting the car.

"Stop!"

But he was gone.

What was he thinking? Was he going to come to the most important night of Emilio's life and demand answers?

No. He wasn't. Not if I could help it.

I went outside calmly, as if I needed a little air, and strode to the corner opposite of the one Byron had stood on. The voices and music faded into the distance, and I slowed my step.

"I told you to stay there," Byron said. "You're a moving target."

How had he known I was moving?

"Olivia!" Alan's voice came from behind me.

I turned. He was three steps away, and the Jaguar was rolling slowly at his back.

"Alan, hey." I hung up and waited for him.

"Are you all right?" he asked as he caught up.

"Yeah, I'm… just getting a little air."

"You turned and left so quickly I thought I'd missed talking to you."

"No, I—"

"I just figured I could get a redo on eleventh grade."

The Jaguar stopped right behind him.

"I'm sorry?"

"I wanted another chance to ask you out. On a date. Coffee, maybe. Or dinner's better, but whatever you want."

Alan, with his sweet smile and humble manner, would never hurt me if he could help it. He'd always keep me seventy to seventy-five percent satisfied, and that just wasn't enough anymore.

"I can't." I smiled to soften my words.

Alan's self-effacing charms would have been what I found most attractive about him, but on that night, he played a distant second to the commanding, filthy, arrogant asshole waiting for me.

"Oh," he said. "Okay. Uh. It's me? Or a bad time?"

"I'm seeing someone."

"Huh." He put his hands in his pockets. "I heard that, but I didn't believe it. Not that you'd be seeing *someone* but specifically that it was—"

"So, you know him?"

"By reputation. Anyway, I thought there was no way you'd be with a guy like Crowne."

The Jaguar was still waiting. Inside it sat a man I was about to deny by my silence and whom I wanted to join in that car. His body was ecstasy, and a warm glow showed under the locked door of his heart.

"We should get back," I said, taking my eyes from the Jag.

Alan offered me his arm. I turned so we could head back to the restaurant. I glanced over my shoulder for the Jaguar, but it was gone.

There were plenty of desirable things about Byron, but if he was angry about me talking to Alan, I would have to draw another line.

CHAPTER 23

BYRON

Alan Barton.

I knew him from around. He was from eastside circles. Studio City and Pasadena private schools. Fewer generations of wealth. More dependent on the Hollywood system. They didn't come to LA for the weather, and they didn't stay because they wanted to.

I was pushing through the foot traffic across the street from Amelia's when I saw her in the restaurant. Alan put his hand on Olivia's back.

It was only a moment, and knowing he didn't know she was mine did nothing to smother the screaming rage in my guts. Her relaxed chatter. Her smile. Her comfort in the space she occupied calmed me.

I didn't know him well, but I knew he was safe. He wouldn't press himself on her. He wouldn't touch what was mine unless she invited him to, because what was mine to own was really hers to give.

She wouldn't. She was trustworthy.

I'd come to the opening to surprise her. Maybe get under her dress to see myself strapped to her body. I hadn't come expecting to make decisions about trust or commitments, but I had to turn on a dime as if I'd been handed a rival take-it-or-leave-it cash offer half an hour before the deal closed.

Handling such an offer would have been easier than processing my trust through clogged emotional pipes. My throat backed up with the difference between what I felt and what I knew. Who I was and who she was. What I wanted and what I needed.

The smartest thing I ever did was leave before she saw me.

It was also the hardest.

I pulled my car out of the lot, intending to go home, but I couldn't. I was stuck on a restaurant-lined street with a thousand others. She was within reach, and I trusted her, but I couldn't drive away. She had me.

I parked on the corner and got out. Started across the street, walked back to the car. Paced on a sidewalk crowded with people on date nights and dinner outings. Felt comfort for a moment that she wore my gift against her body, then dismissed the comfort in favor of a demand.

I called her until she picked up.

"What?"

Impatient. Yet the sound of her voice was comforting.

"Olivia." I saw the top of her head through the crowd, and when it shifted, parts of her body were visible.

"It's a bad time."

"Is it?"

She came to the front windows where I could see her.

"It's loud, and I'm in the middle of a conversation."

"Are you wearing it?"

"Yes."

Thank God. An irrational, unexplainable relief flooded me, and with it, a need for visual confirmation broke the dam. "Prove it."

"I'm not texting pictures of myself in a bathroom mirror."

"Pull up your dress so I can see the tops of the garter belt."

An ambulance whipped by me and passed the restaurant. She'd hear it. My cover was blown. She spotted me, eyes meeting across the night.

She put her hand on the glass, and I felt our bond in that moment.

"Show me that you're wearing what I sent you," I said.

"No."

No. Flat no. Her refusal didn't piss me off, but I wanted to punish her in a way we'd both find pleasurable. Because she'd want me to. I'd ask, of course. I'd lay out the rules. We'd discuss. And in the end, I was sure she'd learn strategic refusals and I'd give her tactical, consented consequences.

You can get that anywhere.

I could. I had been. But Olivia was different.

What if she loves you? What if she wants you to say it?

She wouldn't love me. She hated me.

"I think," I said, "down deep where your hunger meets your heart, you want to be dominated. You want to submit your pleasure to me. So... show me."

"I hate you," she murmured.

"I know."

She took her hand off the glass, but the connection wasn't broken.

We wrangled a little about where I belonged and whether or not she would show me what she was wearing underneath the dress. I was going to let her go with a reminder that we'd see each other soon, and when we did, she was going to come at my discretion. Her eyelids would flutter, and her cheeks would get hot. Under her dress, she'd soak the panties I'd bought her.

Instead, she told me that people knew.

I didn't care, but she did. Her voice broke a little when she told me. She cared about secrecy for reasons I understood but, at that moment, didn't care about.

As I got in the car to get her, all I could think about was how she felt and how I could fix it. She'd told me to stop, but she'd walked out to meet me on the opposite corner where we wouldn't be seen. She wanted my help. Needed it.

Then, Boy Scout Barton.

The car windows were up, leaving Olivia and Alan darkened by tinted glass.

He caught up to her. They spoke. I hung back and waited like a fucking ghoul, getting pissed that I had to wait for her to finish talking to a man who was neither a threat to me nor a danger to her.

It was the anger that tipped me off.

Because why?

Why?

Olivia was talking to an old friend, and I was an uninvited interloper hanging around them.

For what? So she could soothe me?

Jesus Christ, was I a baby?

This wasn't the action of a man who'd just tried to prove he was worthy of being a father.

As I put the car in drive, Olivia looked at me with a longing that matched my own. Her expression stayed with me as I turned the corner. And another. And a third, until I was back in front of the restaurant.

I'd stay still for three minutes. If she wanted me, she'd look for me, and if she looked, she'd find me. Let her decide to come to me if she wanted.

If she didn't come out, I'd go home and nurse the bruised ego she hated me for.

CHAPTER 24

OLIVIA

Emilio exited the kitchen, showing his face for the first time, fifteen minutes after Alan and I returned from the street. The chime of silverware hitting glasses filled the air, and he got on a chair.

"I want to thank you all so much for coming!" Emilio said. "Sharing my grandmother's recipes with you is a dream come true for me."

My back was to the front windows, but something made me look around. A deep pull of not just my gaze, but my heart.

"I have so many people to thank! So, first, the man with the money..."

The Jaguar was idling at the curb as everyone clapped for Russell. When I turned back around, all eyes were on Emilio.

"Somehow, I attracted the most professional staff in Los Angeles and..."

The car sat there. No one was looking. Emilio was going to mention me, and when he did, everyone would turn around. If he mentioned me last, everyone would look at me, and my opportunity to slip out without being seen would be gone.

"...but there's one person I don't do anything without. One person with a secret talent I'm about to disclose. She's mine, people, so..."

I backed out the door and dashed into the street, where I got in the passenger side of the Jag. When I shut the door, I ducked before everyone at the opening could look for me.

The car coasted away, and I erupted in a belly laugh of relief. All my nerves spilled out, and when Byron laughed too, all my worries about him followed. We laughed for blocks until he stopped the car and I sat up straight.

In Los Angeles, it wasn't uncommon to start in a fancy restaurant district Downtown and, with a few turns, end up on a dark street lined with closed warehouses. But without seeing the slight transitions, it was a little jarring.

Byron shut off the car and put his hands at the base of the wheel.

"Did you bring me here to murder me?" I asked.

"Destroying you was my intention."

I wanted to be destroyed. The underwear pressed against my pussy, and the harder I breathed, the tighter the straps around my rib cage felt.

"But?" I continued his thought for him.

"But." He draped his arm over the back of the seat, facing me. "I owe you an apology."

I let my expression ask why. Casually, he drew his fingertips over the curve of my ear.

"I came here because I wanted to. It's not a risk for me, but it was for you. I wasn't thinking about you or what you wanted." He moved his hand back to the seat as if he didn't want to distract me with his touch. "I'm sorry."

He seemed honestly regretful. I was sure he was capable of guilt. That had been clear in Santa Barbara. But his regret in the car wasn't tinged with anger or self-loathing.

Was this Byron? Or some sort of impostor?

"Why the change of heart?"

He shrugged, wiping an imagined smudge from the steering wheel. "This and that."

"Start with either one."

He balled his hand into a fist and tapped the wheel with it. "Alan. Fucking Alan Barton talking to you." He gestured in a circle as if *blah-blahing* the whole thing. "And I got mad and jealous and wanted to write my name all over you in ballpoint pen." He looked out the window, then down at my lap. "Then he caught up to you on the street… and he was concerned. I could see it on his face, and we all know Alan's a Boy Scout. Right? And I'm thinking of ways to kill him because he's considering you first, but then…" He shot out a little laugh at his own thoughts. "Then I thought, 'How come I'm not concerned?' and like this…" He snapped his fingers. "I realized he wasn't the problem. You aren't the problem. The only problem on that street corner was me. You said you were going out without me, but I showed up anyway."

"Man." I put my elbow on the door and held my head up with two fingers. "This is…" I rubbed my eyes. "What am I supposed to do now?"

He stroked the back of my neck. "Forgive and fuck. In that order."

I scoffed, dropping my hands into my lap.

"No. I mean, you just… What are we doing? You and me. What the fuck are we doing?" I twisted to face him. "We're going to get involved. We are getting involved, right here. Right now. And this is the worst time for me to start a thing. The worst. We're making the riskiest decisions two people can make, and we're making them like we're plastic pieces on a board. Like it's win or lose and nothing in between. And you're impossible. You keep…" I balled my fists. "You keep pushing me and pushing me."

"Into what?"

"Into loving you!"

Shit.

"Forget it," I said. "I don't mean it. I'm on these new fertility drugs, and they're making me emotional."

I played it off, and I read him like a book as he made a conscious decision to believe me. Thank God.

"I am pushing you. But not into that," he said.

"Into what?"

"This case, unjustified as it is…"

"Totally justified."

"It's not going to go on forever."

What was he implying? If he'd stopped throwing up baseless motions and new drawings, it could have been closed in a week, but strategic adjustments based on a personal relationship weren't on the table.

"We can't discuss that here," I said. "You play to win. I play to win. No side deals."

"No side deals except the deal to get you pregnant."

"We shouldn't see each other unless I'm dropping eggs. We're complicated enough. I can't commit, and you won't. But," I took his hand and squeezed it, "here I am, letting you push me."

He stroked the side of my hand with his thumb. The skin crackled and hummed. "You need me to do what, then?"

I needed him to stop being a better man than I gave him credit for. I needed him to be a hateful partner and a good father. That was too much to ask of anyone. It was too specific, and it would be asking him to be inauthentic.

"I'm trying to keep you at arm's length," I said. "I wish that wasn't so hard."

"It's easy. You don't want someone telling you what to do. You want complete independence. I'd limit that. Any partner would. Even little Alan would. That's the way it works. The only way out of it for you is what we agreed to."

"This underwear wasn't on the list."

He laid one hand on the back of my neck, leaning in put the other inside my knee. "We're making the most of it." He slid his hand under my skirt, and I gasped as my body melted into his touch. "Because I'm not a medical instrument in a doctor's office. Your whole body is with me. You're receptive. It relaxes you to know I'm there. Deny it and I'll jerk off into a cup for you."

"That's not the point." Even as I tried to force my mind away from the way he touched me, my legs relaxed to allow him farther up my skirt.

"It is the point. It's exactly the point. Your body wants to take me. When I touch you, everything inside you reacts, and all I can think about is driving myself deeper than any plastic tube can go."

"That wears off," I told myself more than I told him. Because he knew it. He was right. This heat would wear off, and we'd hopefully be colleagues in parenting.

"Exactly. Now. Spread your legs." When I did it, he pushed deeper, just barely touching the damp fabric of the underwear he'd bought me. "Good girl."

My throat let out a hum of satisfaction.

"Pull up your dress for me."

I exposed my legs and the satin-covered triangle joining them. When he saw the black satin and the gold clasp that released the crotch of the panties, he sucked in a breath.

This was the confirmation he'd asked for. My legs opened even farther because I knew it would please him.

"It's going to be hard to be friends," he said, lightly brushing his fingernails against the fabric covering me where I was wet and vulnerable. The taunting sensation was deliciously unbearable. "What do you think that's going to be like?"

"Not like this."

He undid the clasp, exposing my wet folds to him. "Or this." He slid two fingers inside me, and my hips rose to meet them. "Friends don't fingerfuck their friends."

"No, they..." He rubbed my clit with his thumb, and my sentence broke down into a meaningless vowel.

"What did you say?" he purred into my ear and pulled the neck of my dress aside.

"They don't."

"Don't what?" His thumb was making me tighten around his fingers. His lips found the base of my neck.

"Fingerfuck in the... car. God, Byron. Lord Byron."

"Friends don't call each other Lord. They don't spread their legs to come in their friend's hand." He nipped the base of my neck. "Friends don't mark friends."

"We're not friends. Not yet."

"Good."

"Yes."

"Come, Beauty."

As I exploded in a clenched, twisting mass of pleasure, he bit my neck, sucking to a pain that tied itself to the orgasm, stretching its limits so thin I thought I would lose consciousness.

He let the neck of my dress go before removing his fingers.

"Thank you," I said between gasps.

He smiled and unlooped his belt. "Now..."

My phone rang.

"... you're going to..."

Riiing

"... leave some of that lipstick..."

Riiing

"... on my cock. That is really distracting."

"Hang on." I opened my bag to shut off my phone. It was Linda. I could call her back later.

But when I declined the call, the home screen was covered with her texts.

—Olivia—
—Where are you?—
—I'm in the bathroom. Can u come?—
—Please Olivia where are you I'm stuck in the ladies room and there are o nly two stalls where are you there's a stain on my dress and I need you to get the spare—
—Olivia???—

Byron was looking over my shoulder, pulling back my dress to run circles around the mark on my neck. "What's going on?"

"I'm sorry, but..." I held up the phone. "I have to go back."

He didn't hesitate long. Just enough time to put my neckline back in place and drape my skirt over my thighs.

"I'm sorry," I repeated, texting Linda back.

"Don't be." He started the car. "That's what friends are for."

His smirk and the twitch in his eyebrows should have shaken me like a thunderclap on a clear day.

He was being genuine.

Sincerity was the last thing I'd ever expected from him.

CHAPTER 25

BYRON

I suggested we park around the corner from Amelia's so we wouldn't be seen, but she didn't care.

"She's upset, and the more upset she gets, the more she won't let anyone help her. Park there!"

I swung into the spot and let the car idle.

"You have to come in with me."

"But—"

"Just do it!" She got out and slammed the door.

I shut off the engine and caught up to her in the middle of the street. Cars stopped for us, but it was close.

"There's a crosswalk right there," I objected, jogging to catch up.

"This is faster." The restaurant was just around a corner. "She has a thing with food and stains and people seeing. Especially her father, who's in the back. So, I'm going to stay with her while you get her change of clothes." She turned to face me. "She's a very functional person otherwise."

The block was lined with crowded open-front restaurants, and it was dinnertime. We either blended in or made a spectacle. There was no way to know.

"Olivia, you didn't want anyone to see us together."

"I know." For a moment, she seemed tormented, scanning the street for prying eyes. It was probably too late. "It's just... You're right. I don't know what to do. The only other person she trusts is Emilio, and I'm not ruining his night. But I need someone to go to her car."

"Go around back," I suggested. "I'll meet you outside the bathroom."

"Yes. Okay. Yes. Thank you."

She strode in the opposite direction, as if she knew exactly where she was going, and disappeared around a corner into a narrow alley. My blood was flooded with the pull to follow her and make sure she was safe. The area had turned upscale, but Downtown was still Downtown. The seedy underbelly lived and breathed.

Don't. Just do what you said you would.

Dinnertime on Restaurant Row. There were people everywhere. Employees and staff would be in the alley and the kitchens.

I swallowed my instinct and went into Amelia's. The crowd had thinned, but I still had to push through without making eye contact. As I got to a short, carpeted hall with two doors, she entered from the other side.

"Stay here," she said before disappearing behind the ladies' room door.

I waited, standing in an empty hallway like an attendant after she'd spoken to me in a way no one else dared... without a question mark at the end or the possibility that I wouldn't obey. I could have gotten riled about disrespect. Made plans to punish her insolence. Instead, I found myself pleased.

She trusted me.

Being liked was fine. Being desired wasn't unusual.

But being trusted by her was something new between us.

I'd planted my flag at the top of the tallest mountain, overlooking the landscape of our relationship, way out to the farthest horizon, and from that most distant place, where the future met the present, a sliver of our last conversation called to me.

You keep pushing me and pushing me.

Into what?

Into loving you!

On that mountain peak, where trust was a height I'd never expected to reach, I squinted for the sight of friendship at the horizon—and it was there and everywhere in between. It was the fields and the fog. The welcoming clouds and the scribbles of green getting smaller in the distance. It was part of the landscape, not a goal. Not as far as she was concerned.

I'd sworn off love because I'd botched it so spectacularly that my failure had destroyed the object of it.

The ladies' room door opened, and Samantha came out in a long, yellow dress, snapping into my thoughts like a puzzle piece.

"Byron," she said with her hand out.

It wasn't Samantha. It was her sister. Mandy. Right.

I shook the shit out of my head before I took her hand and kissed her cheek.

"I didn't know you were here," she said.

What God had declined to give my fiancée in shallow social confidence he gave to her sister twice.

"I came late. How have you been?"

"Very well. I released the new collection in Paris, and it's been simply explosive."

"Congratulations."

"You should come around more." She tapped my chest with her clutch. "I miss that serious face."

"Thank you." I said, surprised. The Bettencourts had made a public show of amnesty and a private show of rage and vilification toward me. "I'll try."

"I don't blame you for not." She lowered her voice. "My mother was an utter bitch. But, Sam... I loved her so much."

"So did I."

"She was so sensitive. A raw nerve, you know?"

"Yes."

"It wasn't your fault." She laughed at herself. "Of course, you know that. I'm sorry. My therapist had to tell me that for six months before it got through."

"Why would you blame yourself?"

"Oh my God." Mandy rolled her eyes. "That day? Nightmare. She borrowed a pair of jeans that were too big for me, and they were small on her. She freaked out about being a size ten, and I said, 'So lose weight,' like it was nothing and then... well. It was terrible. You know how she was." She waved it away, then delicately rubbed the inside of her eye before the tear fell.

"I do."

"I know it wasn't my fault but..." She cleared her throat. "Anyway. I heard about your new project! In Bel-Air? Sounds so exciting!"

She wanted—needed—to talk about superficial things. My pitch was on the tip of my tongue when Olivia came out of the bathroom. I expected her to pass us so she could deny we were connected, but she came right up to us.

"Olivia," I said, "this is Mandy Bettencourt."

"Nice to meet you," Olivia said.

"Pleasure." Mandy directed her attention to me. "I should get back."

"Sure," I said, but when she turned away, I had one more thing to say. "Mandy? Thank you."

"Don't be a stranger." She gave me a wave and a smile.

Then I gave Olivia my full attention. "What do you need?"

She pressed a key into my hand. "Her car's parked in front of LA Bistro. Black Mini Cooper. License plate ends in 349. Brown leather bag in the trunk. Text me when you're here."

"I'll be right back."

"One more thing." She bit her lip. "I have to stay with her. It's fine. She'll be fine, but I need to drive her home, and I might stay with her. So, I can't... I need you to get the bag and go."

"Not a problem."

"I'm sorry."

I took her chin in my fingers and tilted her head up to see the outline of the distant horizon in her eyes. "Don't be."

She kissed my lips quickly and disappeared behind the door.

I could love this woman. I just didn't know how to tell her.

CHAPTER 26

OLIVIA

Once Linda had on her spare outfit, the anxiety attack subsided. By the time I drove her to her apartment, she seemed back to her old self, but she asked if I'd stay. The fear of another attack could make her nervous enough to bring on another.

Her spotless one-bedroom was in a U-shaped stucco complex with parking underneath. She'd pulled up the carpets and laid seamless linoleum flooring because it scrubbed easier, and she left the table surfaces free of knickknacks because having them placed perfectly was one less thing to think about.

"Esther's going to have a field day," she said, taking off her shoes as she invoked her therapist.

"She's got to earn her keep." I put my bag under the hall table and kicked off my shoes, lining them up next to Linda's.

"Do you think anyone saw?" She pulled out the trench dress and looked at the tiny spot of wine someone near her had spilled next to the chest pocket. "The stain?"

"No way." I actually had no way of knowing, but being anything short of completely definitive wasn't what she needed.

"I don't know what made me wear this color."

"It's pretty."

"Such an idiot." She balled it up and stuffed it deep in the garbage.

"We can hold a crucifixion tomorrow."

"Shut up."

"At noon." I sat on the couch while she went into the open kitchen.

"Fine, just don't get blood on my shirt. Do you want water or something? I have ginger ale."

"That would be nice."

"Thank Byron for going to get my bag," she said with her head in the fridge.

"I will."

"Did you tell him why?" She came out with two green cans. "Ice?"

"I kind of had to. And yes, please."

She pulled out an ice tray and twisted it. "I hate that." She plucked out cubes and dropped them into two glasses. "I get anxious, then I'm ashamed of that, then I'm ashamed of my shame. Which is shameful. It's a funhouse mirror of humiliation."

"Yeah."

"My therapist says all I have to do is break one link in the chain." She cracked a can. "Find the weakest one and break it. Like it's so easy."

"You're not embarrassed in front of me. Maybe that's your link?"

Linda poured the ginger ale, waited for the fizz to die in both glasses, then topped them up without answering, as if she needed to take that time to think.

"Esther's wondered that too." She handed me a glass and sat on a chair. "Like, why you?"

"Why me?"

"You weren't around when the thing happened."

The thing was in sixth grade at her strict Catholic school. Linda had gotten her period early and unexpectedly during church service. She wasn't allowed to leave until mass was over. So, she'd had to sit in a constant flow for half an hour before methodically lining up with everyone else to go out.

The teachers had been cruel. The kids took cues from them.

"You'll figure it—"

"Esther asked if you have shame too," Linda interrupted, staring into her glass. "She thinks I can sense it and that's why I respond to you."

"Huh. That's—"

"She thinks if I ask you, it might be a link, but—"

"Wait—"

"I don't want to, and I told her that, because I wouldn't want anyone asking me. So, forget it. Just forget it. Do you want more ice? I have plenty."

"No ice, and yes," I said, shutting down a desire to tell her that shame was the human condition. First, because she didn't need to hear that, and second, because it was a platitude I didn't really believe.

"Really?"

I sighed, reaching for a coaster.

Looking this in the face was something I'd avoided and brushed aside. Linda couldn't do that for herself, and she needed me to.

"My thing's not as clear-cut as yours." I placed my glass in the exact center of the cork coaster. "And I'm not sure it even makes sense, but if it'll help you to talk about it…"

"You don't have to, but—"

"Okay." I slapped my knees. "So. Alviro. The musician."

"The asshole you dated for five minutes?"

"Right." God. What was I about to say? "Well. It was more like five months. But I didn't tell you because… he had a reputation. Asshole. Like you said. But he had this thing he did when we were in bed, which was…" I cleared my throat. "Assholeish. He was rough, and…"

"Oh—"

"And I liked it."

"Ah."

"And so… you know my father was a terrible person to my mother. And I always told myself I wouldn't let anyone treat me like that, ever. But there I was, doing the thing with Alviro. So, I told him I wanted us to be secret so it wouldn't disrupt study group. Which was eighty percent bullshit." The ginger ale steadily bubbled, releasing its fizz into the air. "But every day I'd think people knew I was with a man as bad as my father. I was convinced they were looking at me and laughing, and it made me… I made me… I humiliated myself. Like I was going to repeat what had happened to my mother and I should be ashamed of repeating the cycle." A drop of condensation dripped down the glass and darkened the cork underneath. "So, I thought the only way to beat it was to stick with passive-aggressive guys like Shane. Which didn't work because I have no patience for it and what I wanted was still there, and I was… I am… I'm still ashamed of it."

I picked up my glass and sat back. Linda's feet were curled under her.

"And so, Byron's passive-aggressive?"

"Nope. Just aggressive."

She drank her ginger ale and put it on her coaster. "And that's okay?"

"Yes. No. But yes. Maybe. Anyway. It's not a long-term thing, so it doesn't have to be okay. But I… We're trying to get me pregnant."

"Really?"

"Might work better than the doctor visits."

There was no way Linda could have missed the way my face came alive with prickly heat, and like a gift to me, she said the exact right thing. "I hope it works."

"Me too."

We sat in silence with our cold drinks. I didn't know what Linda was thinking, but my mind was cleansed and acerbic. I could be myself and break the cycle with my children. Lacing together my history and fixations with words had sharpened the lines between what my mind knew and what my heart wanted.

King of the Assholes.

Surprisingly decent yet an emotionally unavailable and complex human. Byron Crowne.

He wasn't the king of anything except me.

* * *

BYRON CALLED THAT MORNING, but I texted back that I couldn't talk.

My better self always knew I shouldn't care what people thought of me, but the fact had never seeped into my convictions until the night before, when I'd made them porous by being seen with him.

I didn't have a map for what had changed inside me or what hadn't changed about Byron. There was no chart for all the ways this could go.

Maybe he'd just been a catalyst in my life. Maybe he was there to teach me a lesson and move on.

But when I imagined giving him up, my heart tightened into a fist.

"Kimberly needs you," Amara said when I passed the copy room.

"What do they want?"

"They didn't say except I'm not invited. It's just you."

She raised a penciled black eyebrow, layering the request with meaning I could read like my own shorthand. Amara went everywhere with me as a witness and second set of ears. To disinvite her made the meeting utterly confidential.

I stood next to her, watching the sliver of light under the feeder move back and forth.

"Are these the Romaneski briefs?" I asked over the *hiss-click* of the machine, then lowered my voice to drown the question in the din so only Amara could hear. "Did they say why you have to sit out?"

"No idea. They've been on the phone all morning, but that's whatever."

"All right. Thanks."

When I got to Kimberly's office, they pointed at the couches in the corner as their call finished. I sat, gazing out the window. I had to make the right decision about Byron. Whatever this was, I'd deal with it, then call him. He'd want to meet. I'd have to refuse unless I wanted to end up in bed with him. Which I did, but I didn't.

Kimberly hung up and stood, buttoning their jacket. "So," they said, walking over. "A Crowne-sized donation to the judge's campaign fund means our motion to stay construction's going to be rejected."

"You're joking."

"Nope." They sat across from me. "A cartoonishly bold move but not a joke."

"What about an emergency writ?"

"For what emergency? But in other news, I just tipped the *LA Times*."

"Great idea."

"And that means you need to withdraw and pray there's no ethics complaint outta the judge."

"What?" My spine went straight, and I shifted to the edge of the seat. "Why?"

"Why," Kimberly replied without a question. "Let's see. You're having a relationship with the developer we're suing?"

I had to bite my lips to keep from speaking before I processed what was just said and what wasn't.

They said you're fucking Byron Crowne.

Did Kimberly know? Or was it a guess? Was my boss trying to tease out an admission or waiting until I lied to drop proof? And how did they find out? When? Was it one of the staff in Santa Barbara? The elevator guy at the Waldorf?

Who had seen us last night, besides everyone?

Too many seconds had passed cataloguing moments Byron and I were in public.

"It's nothing," I said.

Nothing if you didn't count the baby that wasn't, the half promises, or the contingency plans. The days we'd planned to screw until we shook hands and relegated ourselves to platonic parenthood.

"Okay, so let me get this straight. You contacted an opposing party who was repeatedly represented by counsel. Which on its own could get you sanctioned. You went to bed with him while the case was pending, but you didn't disclose it to me or opposing counsel. Now I'm supposed to let you talk to reporters? Whose job it is to dig up whatever they can about whomever, and when they find out, are under no ethical or legal obligations to pretend they don't know. Sure. I'll let them jump down your throat and rearrange your internal organs. You're right. It's fine. Not like it's my job to protect you or anything."

"I don't need protection."

"Yes, Olivia, it's all about you."

My goose was cooked, as the saying went. I'd lost a battle I hadn't even known I was fighting but one I should have seen coming.

"I should have told you," I said.

"That is correct. And I can tell you now, like I got a looking glass right to the future, that you're never going to hold back a meeting—casual, accidental, or otherwise—that can hurt this organization again."

They were right. Shamefully, I'd been so focused on myself I'd lost sight of the bigger picture. In more ways than one, I didn't know who I was anymore.

"Right." I stood. "I withdraw. But I need to stay on as a consultant."

"Why?"

They'd asked a simple, one-word question that had a million answers. I wanted to see what happened in real time. I wanted to finish what I'd started. I wanted to be there the moment one of us lost the lawsuit and won our choice to be together or not.

"This case relates to *Haldor v. City of LA*, which I litigated. I can be of use."

"Fine." Kimberly went behind her desk. "But you are not to advise in strategic decisions. Contact with the team assigned to this case goes through me. You will have no contact with opposing counsel. Not a paralegal. Not the bathroom lady at any of their gyms. Don't make me fire you."

That was it. We were done here except for the one important thing Kimberly might tell me now and never again.

"Who told you? Was it the Bettencourts?"

"No. Crowne's people brought it in yesterday afternoon. I waited for you to come clean, and you didn't. Then the *LA Times* started sniffing around. So…" They spread their hands in defenselessness. "Here we are."

Here we were. The mark on my neck throbbed from betrayal. "Thank you."

I left the office, taking confident steps to the bathroom, where I locked myself in a stall with my back to the wall.

That. Fucking. Asshole.

For a silver-spoon-fed rich boy raised in an ivory tower, Crowne was a scrappy fighter. He hadn't beaten me with dirty backroom dealing, but with upfront, ethical behavior I should have exhibited.

The ringer on my phone echoed on the tile walls.

Byron.

Maybe he wasn't the shitty one. Maybe I was.

He'd exposed how alike we were, and I despised him for it.

I stared the screen, where his name boiled a bitterness on the back of my tongue.

Now was my chance to tell him to fuck off. He wasn't worthy. He was shit.

My finger hovered over the green button that would accept his call.

I couldn't do it. He'd have an explanation. I needed a piece of my anger to turn outward, or I'd burn myself so hard I'd turn to carbon. I'd humiliated myself in front of him, and now I was humiliated in front of my colleagues because of him.

This is on you.

You didn't walk away.

You let yourself be seen last night.

I was enraged at myself, but he'd betrayed me.

I hung on to that and rejected his call.

CHAPTER 27

BYRON

I had a fraught relationship with patience. With building permits, legal actions, and architects, I had infinite amounts of it.

With Olivia's habit of rejecting my calls... less so.

"Mr. Crowne?" Clarissa peeked into my office. "Logan on two."

"Thanks." I picked up the phone. "I'm busy."

"Heads up," Logan said. "PR got a call from the *LA Times* about some campaign contributions."

"They're trying to do a rectal. Don't spread your cheeks open."

"Thanks for the image." Street noise rose from his side, and a car door was closed. "And you're welcome."

"For?"

"For plugging your ass."

He'd entered a building. Echoes. Marble. Must have been Crowne HQ.

"How?"

"We'd already disclosed your relationship with Olivia. She's been removed from the case."

I rubbed my eyes so hard I saw stars. "You inch-dicked little shitstain."

"Truth is the best protection. When—not if, but when—the *LA Times* finds out… you won't have to explain anything, and neither will Olivia. So. Done. All good. You can bring her around anytime now."

All good. Olivia wasn't fighting me anymore, which took the air right out of the balloon.

"Is that it, Logan? Or is there more I should kill you over?"

"Not before lunch."

He beat me to hanging up.

What now? What the fuck now?

My palatial office was a tiny prison, and my suit was a straitjacket.

She'd think I'd disclosed and hadn't told her last night.

I had to move. Stretch. My thoughts came in questions with the *rat-a-tat* speed of a machine gun, and I made my feet on the stairs match their cadence.

She didn't answer when I called the first time.

Did she think I'd push a disclosure without telling her first?

I knew what a colossal asshole I could be, but she didn't.

Or maybe she did.

How much had I hung on her opinion of me?

She didn't answer when I called the second time. Or the tenth.

This I didn't know how to manage. Samantha hadn't iced me out. She'd breathed hot fire and put me out with her tears. I had her down to a science. She'd never turned her back on me like this. Not until her last hours, leaving me upstairs while she…

Why wasn't she picking up?

At least… just to yell, berate, argue, or apologize.

Nothing. As if this was all nothing.

Fuck my chest for hurting. It was something.

And if it was nothing, then fuck her.

Unless that was her strategy?

To float facedown in the swimming pool so I'd try to resuscitate her? So I'd nearly dive in to my death before realizing the lights were out? So I'd panic in the ten seconds it took to find the circuit breakers, then in the next minute when I didn't know if the electrical current had killed her or rendered her unconscious enough to drown her?

Was she laughing at the kisses I thought would save her? Or the wet pajama pants sticking to my balls while I held her?

Did none of that prove I loved her?

Did this mean I was supposed to prove something?

Was she waiting for me to act? Put my open mouth on hers to breathe in life that was gone?

Take the chance that this time it was different?

The panic grew from the same place as my denials, my lust for penance, and my hopes. The only thing that would quiet it was seeing her. Talking to her. Asking what the fuck she was thinking by not talking to me.

The stoplight turned green, and I had no clear recollection of deciding to get in my car.

A horn honked behind me. I passed through the intersection.

No, I remembered. It was fine. I was fine.

Her block was so quiet an ambulance was audible from half a mile away. Her car was in the driveway, and on the second floor, a light was on.

She was home. Good. All I had to do was get out and demand answers. But knowing she was all right, alive, and just angry at me had quelled the visions of that morning when I found Samantha. They hadn't been that insistent in a long time, and never had they been so real.

I was losing my mind.

The upstairs light went out, and another window on the side of the house lit up.

Boundaries were important to her. Maybe I needed to draw some.

—Don't answer this now—
—If I don't hear from you in three hours, I'll assume it's off—

I put the phone down and drove home.

CHAPTER 28

OLIVIA

My plan to call Byron and talk honestly went right out the window. So mature of me. Straight-Shootin' Monroe tripped on her spurs and wound up all akimbo in the center of town.

Over the next three hours, I went from mad he didn't tell me what he'd done, to vengeful, all the way to grief-stricken over the pregnancy that wasn't, and back again multiple times a minute.

I tried to tell myself everything was fine, but I wasn't used to being outmaneuvered so succinctly. I felt like a different person. Every time one of my coworkers looked at me, I was sure they saw someone different than they had before Byron. I didn't assume they pitied me. Nor did I think they'd succumbed to schadenfreude. But I'd gone from royalty to commoner in a snap of Byron Crowne's fingers, changing all my good work to hollow gestures.

I couldn't sleep, thinking about how I'd submitted to him. How he'd dominated me in ways I hadn't seen coming. I could barely eat, knowing I'd let him own me, how much I'd wanted to give myself to him, and how much I wanted to do it again.

Every day, a sticky bitterness grew in my chest, transformed from disappointment in myself to anger at him to something cold and brittle I couldn't define or ignore.

Home alone, I'd stepped into sweats and socks as if it wasn't now or never. He'd drawn the line at three hours, and as little as I thought of him, I couldn't ignore the fairness of the timeline.

The sun was going to set soon.

Tick tock. Time was doing its thing with or without me.

I texted him.

—I'm here—

No dots. No answer. I threw the phone on the couch and went to the kitchen for water, drank it, rinsed the glass, and came back to a screen full of nothing.

My house was too quiet. Too small and empty. The world outside seemed intent on driving me out and right to the source of my frustration. The apartment building to the north was gearing up for a party. A car alarm from the building's lot to the south made me jump out of my skin. It was as if the ground under me had shifted and I couldn't get my balance back.

Then he texted.

—I'm home waiting for you—

I tapped out a strict aphorism of disgust, then a missive about emotional treachery.

Then I erased it.

Then I checked myself in the mirror, put on my shoes, and got in my car with a sense of relief that even though I didn't know what I was doing, I would by morning.

On the way to Byron's house, one thing became clear.

This was a mistake. A life-fucking, humiliating, regret-inducing mistake.

And I knew another thing too.

I couldn't wait to make it. I'd wanted this fuckup for days.

With the top down and fully visible to every security camera, I drove up to the gate of Byron Crowne's estate, ready to lash into him. I buzzed the keypad and looked right into the camera, daring the person on the other end to recognize me. My tight-lipped face showed up on the little screen, no less cold for the warm light of sunset.

Nothing happened.

I buzzed again, and before I had my finger off the button, the gate clacked and rumbled open. At the end of a long, tree-lined driveway was a one-story ranch with windows for walls. I could see through the front to the back, where a patio overlooked the valley.

He stood just outside the front door with his hands in his pockets as though he owned the world and had plans for the universe.

The gate clapped shut behind me. No backing out now.

I took my sweet time on the full length of the driveway so he could fucking wait for me to get there. When I stopped the car, he didn't move, and I didn't rush to turn off the engine. Tugging the emergency brake. Checking my lipstick. Picking up my bag. Getting out. Walking up to him until I could smell his cologne.

His house, as I could see through the window behind him, was spotless and impeccably modern. The piano had pictures standing on the cover like rectangular soldiers. The concrete-floored front patio roof was held by white plaster pillars. The burgundy couch was indented where a man would sit as a habit, and the table in front of it was worn where he'd put his feet up.

"Welcome," Byron said, green eyes blazing in the setting sun.

"You won."

"I did?"

Was he being serious? Did he think I didn't know?

"I recused myself, thanks to you. The fight goes on, but you beat me." I clapped once, then again, slowly applauding his tactical mastery. I continued as he took a step closer.

"That's enough," he said. Sex dripped off him. He stank of orgasms and risk.

Clap. "Not until I get an encore." *Clap.* "Again." *Clap.* "Beat me again." *Clap.* "Show me what a man you are." *Clap.*

He took my wrists so quickly I gasped, and a wave of arousal I didn't have time to resist shot down my spine.

"You want to play," he hissed. "But you don't know how to lose."

"You don't know how to win."

"Obviously I do."

I shoved him away with all my strength, and though he let go, he stayed close enough to stick his fucking finger in my face.

"If you'd picked up the goddamn phone, you'd know it wasn't me. It was Logan. He disclosed to protect both of us. But you shut me out. You. Shut. Me. Out."

I slapped his accusing finger away. "Take a fucking hint, Byron."

"You're here. In front of my house. Is that a hint?"

His face was like a movie screen replaying every moment of our nights together. Every slap on my ass and every tug on my hair. He was remembering the moments he'd owned me and comparing them to the tricked and disgraced woman standing in front of him.

"Yeah. What are you going to do about it?"

"You have five seconds to turn your ass around and get back in that car."

This fucker was the worst human being I had ever met, and though my mind was defiant, my body was turning white-hot and pliable under his gaze. "Or what?"

"Or you're getting what you came here for."

"Which is?"

"Five."

"Oh, you mean you think we're going to fuck?"

"I'm going to punish you."

He saw it. He saw it all. He read my horror and my arousal. My dare and my fear. It all said yes. I was a Rosetta stone of emotional languages.

"What?" I tried to confirm, but he'd said all he was going to.

"Four."

"You're full of it." I crossed my arms.

His pecs were twitching, and his neck was tight. He was a coil of pent-up rage twisted around a shaft of potential ecstasy. He was angry bones and hungry flesh. "Three. Drive away, Olivia."

He was all those things, and I was the uncomfortable, twisting hand that tightened the coil. I was the constricting tendons pulling anger and lust together. I didn't wonder why I wanted him or whether it was good for me. I just did.

"Make me."

"Two."

"Do it." My lips moved, but my voice failed.

"If I say one, I'm taking that as a yes."

We stared each other down. I'd come to tell him I knew he'd betrayed me, and his actions were over the line. I never wanted to see him again. He was wrong for me. Wrong in spirit and mind. He was everything I hated. I was going to say all those things and yet…

"Did you forget how to count?" I challenged him.

…yet, not yet.

"Don't test me."

"Say. One." I swallowed. "Lord. Byron."

My hips were made of raw, molten heat. When his lips moved, my knees went weak with anticipation.

"One."

I didn't make a move toward the car. If the top had been down and the skies opened to buckets of rain, I wouldn't have even looked at it.

He took me by the throat and pushed me against the pillar that supported the roof over the patio, holding me in place without cutting off air. Like a rattlesnake striking, he kissed me with raw savagery. Not a kiss of tenderness or even passion, but ownership, running along the deepest places of a mouth that was his property, corner to corner, crevice to crevice. He was tasting what was his, and I gave myself fully because the gentleman was the source of my doubts but the animal was the supplier of my lust. Between them, I was pulled apart. Exposed as human, failing, broken, and weak, I let him do what he wanted with what he found. His tongue stole my regrets and dealt them back to my desire at a profit.

"You should have withdrawn weeks ago," he said through his teeth, yanking my pants down with his free hand.

"Yes."

"Why didn't you?" My pants were halfway down my thighs when he pulled my shirt and bra up to expose my pebble-hard nipples.

"I'm bad." The words dropped out of me, carrying armloads of anxiety. "So bad."

At the setting of the sun, the lights flicked on.

"Why didn't you?" He tightened his grip on my neck ever so slightly, and though I wanted him to hurt me with that hand, I needed to tell him.

"I was ashamed."

"Of fucking someone you were suing?"

Unable to lie and unable to speak the truth, I shook my head as much as I could in his grip.

"Ashamed of what, Beauty?" he asked through his teeth, making a curse of his nickname.

"Of you."

His face softened into tenderness. I wasn't ready for that. It wasn't what he'd promised.

I clamped my jaw and pushed him.

His expression went hard again, but with a devilish approval. He yanked me forward and turned me to bend me over the railing around the patio with my ass up and my breasts hanging on the other side. I looked over my shoulder to see him towering above me, running a hand over my body with dominant satisfaction. Seeing me watching, he grabbed a handful of my hair and made me face forward.

Front yard. His hand on my back. Rosebushes. Between my thighs. Darkening sky.

He slapped my ass so hard it burned. My legs kicked in the confines of the half-down pants, and my hands clutched the rail.

"Fuck you," I gasped.

He pulled my hair back and leaned down to growl close to my face. "Shut up and take it."

He hit me again, then on the other cheek again and again before sliding his hand between, and I squeaked when I nearly came.

"Little wet here."

"So?"

He chuckled and pulled my pants all the way down, then took them off with my shoes. When he stood, he kicked my legs open. "You want another chance to leave? Walk back to your car and drive home?"

"Why? Is that all you have?"

"No." When he stroked my bottom, it hurt like hell and flooded my body with heaven. "We're not done. On the couch."

By my hair, he threw me onto my back and bent my legs to either side.

He slapped the backs and insides of my thighs over and over, punctuating every few with probing fingers that made me bend my pussy into him before he started again. The sting was maddening, and the humiliation was infuriating as I took the gradually more painful blows.

I was beyond words. In tears. Aroused beyond measure. Just a fleshy mass of obedience, looking up at the painted wood slats of his patio roof.

"Relax," he said, stroking inside my thighs… and I did.

I let it all go. The stress. The grudges. The fight. Whatever it was, I tucked it into bed, turned out the light, and closed the door.

I relaxed.

He slapped my pussy twice, so fast it created a single sky-breaking orgasm. Pleasure transformed from the pain, and I went outside myself. I'd given it all up. My very self.

"Beautywalker?" he said from another galaxy.

"Lord Byron." My lips were spitty, and my tongue was thick.

A moth bounced against the light for the temporary satisfaction of feeling its heat.

My hands went for his waist, curling into the space between his pants and his skin, and pushed down.

"Give me this," I said, reaching down to the damp heat of his cock.

"You sure? It's been a lot."

He'd won, and it made me want him more. I wanted to rip the price tag off myself and give my body for free, without reservation, in a state of utter submission, as if I had no needs or desires outside his. As if I was a toy he owned.

"I'll beg," I said.

He didn't make me beg. He didn't make me do anything. I was in a state of looseness, emptiness, and yet somehow unsatisfied. When he kneeled between my legs and put my hand on his cock so I could feel how bare it was, the dissatisfaction became a need with a name. When he slowly entered me, I said that name.

"Lord Byron."

He filled me, and I understood the inadequacy of the orgasm I'd had seconds ago. It had been an overture. A store sample in a little paper cup. A movie trailer that seemed to tell the whole story but didn't come close to the depth of the film.

I lost myself in the swirl of him, lifted into the mindless heights of ecstasy.

"Say my name," he growled.

"Byron. Lord Byron. My Lord."

"Fuck. Yes."

"My..." Words left me.

"This is... mine." He jammed himself deep, shuddering inside me.

We lay panting together as I became slowly more aware of my senses. The crickets. The breeze. A rustle in the rosebushes. The moth's *slap-slap* as it chased a frustrating, inborn desire that would be thwarted until it burned alive. I opened my eyes to watch it chase the uncatchable.

There were two moths now.

At least they had company.

CHAPTER 29

BYRON

Behind a hedge, set back two hundred feet, with the staff gone for the night, I'd forgotten we were outside until the breeze cooled the sweat on my back everywhere except where she'd scratched me.

When I picked up my head, she was watching the moths batter themselves against the porch light.

"I need to get you inside." I pulled myself off her, but she didn't move. Her limbs were flaccid, and I could feel the effort it took her to keep her eyes open.

"Were you always like that?" she asked.

"Like what?"

The bump in her throat moved as she swallowed, then she smiled a little as if she'd told herself a good joke. "Lord of precise pain."

"No." I sat up and thought better of my answer. "Yes, but no."

"Explain." Her request was no more than a breath of submission.

"Let me get you inside first." I wedged my arms under her and lifted her.

When she rested her head on my shoulder, I wasn't her conqueror.

I wasn't victorious. Her surrender wasn't the prize for a game well played.

She was heavy. Not her body, which was but wasn't.

The gift she'd given me didn't shine like a trophy. I didn't feel like a better, bigger man when she let me possess her. I was insignificant against the weight of it. I was a man on a string, and she was a pin I'd tied myself to. I'd fight it. That I knew. I could circle and circle, but she'd be the center point until she set me loose and I spun away into nothingness.

I laid her on my bed and turned on the lamp.

"My clothes are outside," she said.

"Don't worry about it." I sat on the edge of the mattress. "Turn over so I can see what I did here."

With a sigh, she rolled over. I put a pillow under her belly and inspected the bright pink of her ass.

"How does it feel?" I asked.

"Burns." She hugged a pillow under her cheek, her gaze glinting through a fall of hair.

"Have you been spanked like that before?" I pushed her hair away from her eyes.

"Someone tried once."

"Did he live?" My hand ran over the length of her back. I couldn't stop touching her.

"I asked him to do it. But he didn't want to really. So, it was just me wishing I hadn't asked."

"I wanted to," I said.

"I got that."

"Stay here."

"Yes, Lord." She smirked.

I hesitated, enjoying the nickname but unsure of exactly what she meant, then I got aloe gel from the bathroom cabinet. Sitting on the edge of the mattress, I squeezed a pile into my palm, then flattened it between my hands to warm it.

"I used to think it was anger. You know, this urge to hit someone? What else could it be? I was in therapy for my 'unexpressed rage.' It was useless."

She hummed some sort of agreement or sympathy. I spread the aloe on her bottom. It tightened in protest.

"Relax," I whispered. "Breathe."

She inhaled deeply. Her muscles loosened.

"After Samantha died…" My hand stopped moving for a moment. Why was I still lying? "After she took her own life, I knew what real anger was. I was a monster. I was mad at myself, at her, everything. Therapy was a bust… so I found an outlet."

"Random women in Silver Lake," she said with the side of her mouth not smashed against the pillow.

"Not random. Friends of friends who liked getting what I had to give." The aloe was gone, but I kept massaging her ass anyway, appreciating the way my fingers made divots in the raised skin. I wanted to tell her things I hadn't told anyone. Things I hadn't even thought of in years. I didn't know where to start, nor could I calculate where it would end. "This is going to sting tomorrow. Think of me when it does."

"Yes, Lord Byron."

"No one's ever called me that."

"Are you serious?"

"Very."

"The lack of imagination is shocking."

Her yawn was so relaxed I smiled with a deep satisfaction.

In the time I'd been fucking women who wanted their asses raw, I'd heard a lot about how they felt sleepy and drained after an encounter. How they needed to be cared for and tended to. But little had been said about the soreness of the dominant partner's palms or the feelings of tenderness and appreciation. They were as overwhelming as a drug I knew would wear off.

With Olivia, I was again overcome, but the attack on my senses went deeper. The doubt at the bottom of my heart had been scraped, and the wisdom of experience washed away.

With a hand slick with aloe, I teased her pussy and worked back to her ass, teasing the place that would seal my ownership of her.

We were in that bed for a single goal that tight little hole wouldn't achieve.

But I had to.

Like an animal with no sense, just needs, I had to plant myself everywhere inside her.

This was how a smart man turned stupid.

CHAPTER 30

OLIVIA

I was droopy and passive, fully awake but relaxed to the point of listlessness, letting his hands course over my raw ass and between my legs, then my ass cheeks, until he found the opening. It loosened for him, and I groaned.

For a moment, he froze, then he spread my cheeks apart, exposing a place no one had seen. Still spreading me open, he ran a finger across it, then circled, stimulating the muscle and nerves.

"How does that feel?" he asked.

I looked at him over my shoulder. He didn't look back. His gaze was fixed on my most private place, and instead of being ashamed, I was aroused.

"Good."

He looked up at me before bending his face toward it. His tongue, warm and wet, ran along the awakened nerves, loosening what he teased. Blood flowed between my legs, and I came alive again, ready for his dick.

He got up on his knees.

"What if I did this?" he said, pushing the tip of his finger into my ass.

I sucked air through my teeth. "Good."

With his free hand, he squeezed a line of aloe onto me. "Or this."

He went deeper and pulled out. The sensation was unusual, enormous, stirring. When he pushed back in, he used the tips of two fingers.

"I want to fuck you here," he said.

That wouldn't get me pregnant. My asshole was outside the scope of the deal.

But everything about this was outside the scope of the deal.

"It'll hurt," I said because fuck the deal.

"Does this hurt?" He buried two fingers in me, stretching me in the most pleasurable way. I groaned and stiffened with arousal.

"No." I pushed my hips against his hand. "But your dick's huge."

"It'll only hurt for a second if I do it right." He bent over me to whisper in my ear, "And I will."

Still inside me, he turned me to my back, opening my legs. His dick was a deep-red rod, and right before he dipped his face between my legs, his expression was hunger. His tongue flicked my clit as his fingers fucked and stretched me, binding two places that hadn't been bound before.

I clutched his hair as he brought me to the edge, then he put a third finger inside. The shot of pain racked my body but was pulled back by the very beginnings of an orgasm.

"Let me take your beautiful ass," he said. "Tell me to stop if you need to. But you won't. You'll come harder than you've ever come before."

"Yes," I agreed through my teeth. "Do it."

"Good." He gave my nub a couple of flicks of reward. "You're so good."

When his fingers came out, I felt an uncomfortable openness. He squeezed more aloe on it and touched the widening circle with careful attention, then he shifted me to my side and got behind me, lifting my top leg high.

"Slow. I'll go slow. Just relax." His head pressed against my ass, slowly stretching it as he breathed against the back of my neck.

"Ow," I said when the pain pinched.

He touched my clit, and the pleasure joined the hurt in a coupling only he could make. "Push out like you're fighting."

It didn't make sense, but I obeyed him, and when I did, my ass opened for him. Inch by inch, he worked his way in, and the pain never turned to agony. It disappeared like my inhibition.

"You okay?" he asked.

"Yes."

"I'm all the way in your ass," he said. Every word was arousing.

"Fuck it," I squeaked.

He pulled out only to drive in again, pushing deep against my raw bottom while tweaking and rubbing my clit.

I'd never felt so fully owned, so defiled and worshipped. So abused and cared for. So much freedom held down in a man's arms.

The orgasm was shattering enough to break bones, stop hearts, and cause madness. My senses shut down, and my consciousness left my body. I was watching myself go rigid, hearing myself scream, feeling the pulse of his cock as he came in my ass as if I was sitting a foot away.

"Byron," I said in a gasp after he jerked his hips for the last time.

"Thank you," he replied, gently pulling out, leaving the muscle with a strange openness. "You're perfect." He kissed my shoulder.

I rolled onto my back, and he crawled on top of me to kiss my face and neck over and over. I held his face, caressing his cheeks with my thumbs, but no touch could have made me feel closer to him than I did right then.

"How was it?" he asked.

"Perfect." I wanted to learn every crease in his face. Count his eyelashes. Memorize the crest and slope of this nose. Understand how the blue-and-amber flecks in his eyes made green.

"How do you feel?" he asked with lips too beautiful to fathom.

I was so drunk on sex, so overdosed on intimacy, that I didn't hear the question as a mental and physical health check. I heard open interest in the state of my heart.

"Lord Byron," I said with sincere reverence, "I think I love you."

My mistake was immediately clear in the suddenly cold cast of his face. His reaction sobered me up like a B12 shot.

I should have just told him I was a dead woman.

CHAPTER 31

BYRON

I was trying to understand what it meant to possess a woman whose life was independent from mine.

Because I owned her. That much was true. My bones knew it with the same certainty that they knew they had to fight gravity from below. What I'd put inside her could never be erased. My ownership was written in her cells, and yet I didn't have—nor would I ever have—control over her. The facts weren't in question. Only what it all meant for me to have to ask a woman I owned how she felt because I didn't know and I needed to. What it meant to anticipate the answer. To have to sort out whether she was minimizing discomfort, then respect the fact that she wanted to for her own reasons.

Maybe in the post-orgasmic bliss, I'd assumed a permanence that wasn't there, but I was sure that given a moment or a lifetime, I could figure out how independence was possible with someone who was physically part of me. The fact that I couldn't read her mind or completely understand her heart seemed impossible when I felt so close to her.

Why did we pursue connection when the real miracle was the tenacity of separateness?

"Lord Byron." My name in her mouth was a familiar and unique song. The words that followed were a shock to my nervous system. "I think I love you."

The first time she'd said it, my first reaction had been disbelief, like seeing a cheap, plastic Halloween spider. You knew it wasn't real before your fear centers could tell you otherwise.

But in my bed, with her nakedness under me, the spider was real, and it was poisonous.

My first reaction was to remove it, but I couldn't.

She was the spider.

I was the spider.

Together, we were a deadly thing I couldn't get off. It was stuck on the cold slickness of her blue-white skin. The chlorine smell that came out of her mouth when I pumped her chest. The dead bee trapped in her hair when I held her dead body.

No.

It's nothing.

No.

"It's nothing." My thoughts thrust against me so strongly the words came out of my mouth.

Of all the things I would have chosen to reply with to deny or distract from what she'd said, "it's nothing" wasn't even on the list.

"I have to pee," she said, shoving me off her.

"I didn't mean that," I said.

"I know." Naked, proud, standing tall, she swung her hand across the space between us as if showing me how very real it was. "It's fine. I know the rules."

She closed the bathroom door behind her. I got into a pair of sweats and washed my hands in the hall bathroom. When I came out, she was looking down the length of the hall.

"Where are my clothes?"

"The patio."

"Right." She cocked her pointer finger.

"I'll get th—"

She was already headed down the stairs.

"Wait." My most commanding, calm, forceful voice didn't even slow her down.

I chased, catching her outside, where she was picking up her pants. She shook them out by the waistband until the legs were right-side out.

"Olivia, listen."

"Shut up, Byron. Don't speak." One leg in. Once she was dressed, she'd be gone.

"I have feelings for you," I said.

"My problem isn't with you. It's with me." She jammed her foot into the other pant leg as if she wanted to punish it. "You are who you are, and you told me straight out. There's nothing. Period."

"There is something." I got her shirt from under a chair as if helping her get dressed would stop the clock from ticking. "There *is*. I've never let a woman inside this house. I've never—"

"Do you understand that I'll never stay in the lines?" She snapped the shirt from me and threw it on a chair so she could retrieve her bra. "This is who I am. My mind knows the boundaries, but my heart's hell-bent on jumping fences."

She looked away as she unraveled her bra.

"I'm thirty-two years old," she said as she looped her arms through it. "I know myself and what I feel. I can't pretend otherwise. I'm in love with you, and I won't lie about it anymore."

She reached behind her back to fasten the hooks.

"Turn around." I reached for her. "Let me—"

"Don't touch me."

I was left with empty hands while she hooked herself.

"I want you." The words felt new on my lips because they were true in a different way.

She shoved her arms into her sleeves. "I know. That changes nothing."

She buttoned faster than I'd thought possible. Once her shoes were on, she was gone, and that would be it. I'd lose the chance to convince her to her face. I saw the shoes by the patio rail, one sitting upright with an open mouth, the other tipped to the side. I got between her and the shoes.

"Beautywalker."

She spotted the shoes behind me and crossed her arms. "Please, Byron."

"Listen to me. I've never met anyone like you. I was dead inside. I was chasing meaningless objects and trying to force some kind of order in my life just so I'd feel something again. But I didn't. None of it worked. I forgot why I was doing it. I forgot what it was like to feel anything. I was made of dry sticks and gunpowder. You were the spark I was waiting for. You set me on fire."

"What does that mean?"

"I was trying to possess you, but all this time, you owned me. We walked the earth as two separate people, but I was yours and you were mine."

"Do you love me?" she asked. "Can you? Ever? Do you need more time? Just tell me, is this a waste? Is it just about the baby, or can it... will it ever be more for you?"

"Come inside. Please. Let's talk."

I reached for her, but she pulled away.

"Just tell me. Yes or no?"

It was so close to what Samantha had said to me that night that I nearly choked.

And my answer had been wrong.

My answer had killed her. How could I say it again?

"Why are these words so important? Do you want me to recite it from a script? Write you a fucking note? Here. I have an idea. We'll have a lawyer draw up a contract. We'll outline the exact meaning of every word and why it changes anything."

"It changes everything."

"How? We agreed to a baby together. Period."

"You don't get it." She unfurled her arms to point at me with stiff accusation. "I love you, you shithead. I need to be loved back."

"You're mine. That's the end of it. It's more than we agreed to, and it's the end." I slashed the air at the invisible boundary.

"It's not enough. I want a family with someone who loves me. I'm sorry I changed my mind. I'm sorry if that breaks our agreement. But I sold myself short. I don't want to settle anymore. I want it all, and I want it with you."

"You can't have it all."

"Yes, I can."

"Not with me."

The finality of those three words was harder than I'd expected. Even before the last syllable left my lips, regret got in line to follow, making a little *nn* of denial at the end. But my fear held the rest back.

She pointed at my feet. "My shoes."

"Olivia, listen. Don't go."

She picked up her bag, and with bare feet on the gravel, she walked onto the driveway. After scooping up her shoes, I ran to her, catching up as she opened the car door.

"You mean something to me," I said, handing over her shoes.

"Get a puppy." She tossed them in the passenger side and got behind the wheel.

"I don't want a puppy." I was growling, and that wasn't going to work. I breathed. "I want you. All of you. Your fight. Your laugh. Your body. The moments in between that hold it all together. They're mine. They've always been mine."

She started the car. The open-door alarm beeped. "That's not love."
"So what?"
She tried to close the door, but I held it open.
"Let go," she said calmly, "before I take your fucking arm off."
I let go.
"Don't call me," she said, grasping the handle. "I mean it."
She slammed the door and clicked the locks, then drove away without looking.

CHAPTER 32

OLIVIA

When I got far enough away from Byron's house, I put the top down, thinking the wind would blow the shit out of my head. But it didn't because my mind was already as clear as the cloudless night above me.

I pulled into my driveway and sat there, looking out the windshield. When the engine clicked into silence and the headlights blinked off, I stayed under the starry sky. I was afraid to move. Afraid to tempt time into going forward, even though—with or without me—it continued its cruel march.

If I couldn't have all of Byron, I'd break under the weight of the pieces he couldn't give me. My body throbbed for him. I was sore, raw, tender, and hurt in places no one could see. He'd done this to me because I'd needed him to.

The wounds would heal, but who would open them again?

Only him.

I loved him.

He couldn't love me back. He wanted to. His pleas had been strained with his desire to give me what I needed, but he couldn't.

He'd stayed honest. I respected that. Even loved it. But I couldn't live with it.

Sitting in my car with the crickets and night birds making their mating calls, I created a new reality without Byron Crowne.

Time was a zero-sum game.

Time was heartless but consistent.

Time would never change, even if, in the course of its cruel passage, I did.

* * *

THOUGH TIME IS LINEAR, life is not. It curves, and if you let it arc long enough without reversing course, it will come full circle. For me, the ends met at a place of wisdom. I wanted the same things I'd always wanted, but this time I knew that I was settling for less than everything.

Life sucks, then you die knowing you reached for the stars but your arms were only long enough for the moon. In the end, it was what you got, and what you got had to be enough.

In the hall, on my way to meet Dr. Galang, I caught Luciana coming out of an exam room with a familiar tray.

"Olivia, nice to see you again. How are you?"

"Good. Hey." I furrowed my brow when I caught a glimpse of something sparkly on her finger. "Is that what I think it is?"

"*Si*." She held out her hand so I could see her diamond ring.

"Congratulations! Who's the lucky guy?"

"My next-door neighbor for a long time now. Name is Andy. It was so fast."

"I know. Wow."

"I always thought he was cute and nice, you know, but he said when I cut my hair, it was like *pow* for him."

"Pow, huh? Was it pow for you?"

"The next morning it was." She gave me a knowing look, and I laughed.

"Does your son like him?"

"He's said, 'Thank God, Mama. Finally.'"

"I'm so happy for you."

"Thank you. Okay, don't keep the doctor waiting. Go." She shooed me toward Dr. Galang's little couch room.

He was already there. I sat across from him.

"Sorry," I said, knowing he kept a tight clock.

"Ms. Monroe." He slapped his knees and launched right into it without the niceties. "Says here you've been consistent with your fertility boosters?"

"I have."

"And you want another insemination?"

"I do."

"Good, good. Based on the calendar, you should be back here in two days."

That was our court date in the Crowne case. I had to go. He couldn't think I was avoiding finishing this.

"I'm busy then."

"Your body sets the date. If you want to wait until next cycle, that's fine."

"No," I shot back. "No more cycles. It's good."

"Excellent." He waved his pen at me, smiling. "I make no guarantees, but the new hormone regimen could make the difference."

I had a feeling he was right. This one had a better chance of sticking.

Success would be as hard to deal with as failure, and seeing Byron in court right before—even from the gallery—would make it harder. But I wouldn't miss it.

I said goodbye to the doctor and went to the front to make my appointment.

CHAPTER 33

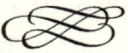

BYRON

Jan Jonson was the more talkative side of Bellini and Jonson and pitched the revisions as if he'd made earth-shattering discoveries about space when, in fact, he'd done more or less what I'd asked him to do. But I let him walk me from one end of the property to the other, along colored strings tied to wooden stakes, to compare the new boundaries to the old, until we were back at our trucks.

"Do you want us to expedite through plan check?" he asked, rolling up the drawings. The wind blew his long hair all over the place. He never buttoned his sports coat so he could show off his trendy belt. That had never annoyed me before.

"After the court date. We'll win, then we can do whatever we want."

"Cool, cool, man."

I wasn't a *cool, man* kind of guy. Either I hadn't known that about myself before, or I'd expected him to know it from the beginning. I'd hired him because he was a hot name, but that day, I was convinced they were giving out architecture licenses by mail order.

"Hey, so, if you have anything else going on…"

"Not at the moment." I held out my hand.

He took it, and we shook. With relief, I thought that was the end of it.

"Okay, hey," he said. "Wanted to mention. I got a buzz on this property up Mulholland. Sweet, sweet views. Totally in your wheelhouse."

"The Georgina tract."

"Bang!" He snapped his fingers and turned them into a pointer. "That's the one."

"I saw it." I looked at my watch as if the time mattered. "I have an appointment."

Get the fuck away from me.

He took the hint and, with another handshake and a few more *cools,* drove down the hill. When he was past the gate, I believed he was gone, and I was alone on the barren hill.

Alone was what I'd chosen. Alone was what I deserved. What I could manage. What I was built for. It was fine. Just fine. I could accept being alone. Power through missing her. Come out the other side a new man.

The wind shook the string lines of the building's footprint. I walked along them, comparing the new to the old, imagining the money and prestige that would come with making this house a reality.

Had I ever imagined anyone would actually live here?

I looked over the view into the ravine and over the next crest of hills to the fuzzy gray line of ocean and imagined a tall structure behind me.

Through all the CGI videos and 3D renderings, had any of it made me feel as if I was actually standing between a cliff and a thirty-foot wall with only five feet between them? In my passion to create the biggest house legally possible, I'd thrown proportion out the window.

We'd created a trailer with a man driving a Ferrari over a bridge to what passed for a front door. He was met by his butler, and as he passed through his palace, he passed women reading, women sunbathing, women lounging. They all looked at him as if he were a king, but he kept his eyes forward.

Was that why I was building this house? So I could be some kind of king who couldn't connect with the people around me?

The late afternoon wind whipped up dirt. A shard of pebble that would have been innocuous underfoot pelted my cheek.

I'd carefully targeted the market for the house. It was meant as a fourth or fifth property in a portfolio. It was a showpiece, not a primary residence.

Because... who would live here? Wake up in the morning? Make love at night? Have family over? Raise children?

No one. The scale of it was perfect for a guy with a two-inch dick and a colossal fear of rejection.

It's too big.

So what?

So. Fucking. What.

It'll be an empty shell.

I didn't give a shit about that or anything anymore.

I walked back to my car.

Bringing the footprint down by half would still leave me with a huge structure and room for a tennis court or ten. It would comply with the most rigid environmental standards. I could get that fucking monkey off my back.

No court date.

Avoid seeing Olivia on the opposite side of a fight.

Maybe.

I'd have to concede. I'd never be able to spin it as a win.

I shut the car door, sealing myself from the wind.

Could it work? Could I take a loss for the good of the project?

A fine layer of dirt covered the windshield, clouding everything in front of me. I was in stasis with an idea I hadn't let myself have. It had been fermenting in the back of my mind, and I hadn't dared pop the cork until I was in the front seat of my car, considering a surrender.

Olivia wasn't leading the case against me, but she'd be there, watching.

I'd known that from the beginning, of course. I knew I'd see her in court before she drove through my gate to my house that night, and I knew it when she drove away.

But I hadn't realized that when looking to the future, that date was a blinking light. I'd stuck a pin in it, and from that pin, I'd hung a measure of anticipation and every last hope. If I pulled the pin, they'd all drop.

As they should.

As she'd asked.

Cancel it all.

Give her what she needs.

Save yourself.

The sand crackled against the windows. My throat turned dry and abrasive, as if a Santa Ana wind was inside me, kicking up detritus down to the bedrock.

I wasn't the man I thought I was.

The winner. The king. The top dog.

Maybe I'd never been that guy.

It was night by the time I got to Santa Barbara, and I looked as if I'd walked the entire ninety-five miles. My tie was undone, and my jacket was in a pile in the back seat. My cuffs were open and shoved up my arms. I hadn't shaved in a day or run my fingers through my hair since the wind got control of it in Bel-Air.

"Byron!" My mother's voice greeted me as if she hadn't seen me in years. She gestured urgently and stepped aside. "Come in, come in!"

She couldn't wait to see me. She had no idea what I wanted and didn't care if I bore gifts or needed wounds tended—as long as she could be a part my life.

She loved me, and if I wasn't worth another single human's love, I was worth hers.

"Mom," I said, still outside. "I think I fucked up."

* * *

ONCE WE WERE SETTLED on the back patio with the still waters of the pool glowing blue and her favorite tea in front of us, I told my mother what had happened with Olivia. I didn't ask how she was or hold back. She loved me, and she wanted me to lean on her.

I explained the court action, the date, and my expectations. I blew through our deal to get pregnant and how it ended. I described the difference between winning and losing and asked her which she thought I should choose.

But Mom wasn't interested in winners and losers.

"Do you love her?"

I rubbed my temple, turning to the side to hide my face.

"Byron," she scolded, "did you not know that was the point?"

"Sure. But the point isn't the point."

She sipped warm tea through a straw. The medication kept her hands still enough for a teacup, but it worked better on some days than others.

"You were the one who always kept your brothers out past dinner, you know. There's a habit you boys have of blaming malfeasance on Dante and mischief on Colton. But that one, that was you. Boy number one. It was your responsibility to get the horses back and brushed. But you always tried to squeeze in one more game of whatever you were playing. You always won, but you had to keep winning until it got dark and you were all in trouble. You, my oldest baby... you were the dead man."

By incremental avoidance, my whole body faced the pool.

"And you just smiled through it all." She laughed. "You were just happy. Who could be mad at Byron? You were impossible to punish. And then... she came."

I turned to her as she laid her straw on her lower lip.

"Samantha?" I asked.

"I don't like to speak ill." She plucked the straw out of the cup and laid it aside. "She needed help, but... well, then the Bettencourts would've had to admit they weren't perfect. And that was right out, so... you just... you tried to help. She drained all the smiles out of you." Mom held up her hand before I could object. "She got the worst of it. She didn't do anything intentionally. Samantha was a good person. She did the best with what God gave her, but you haven't been the same since."

"Thanks for the talk, Mom."

The pool filter shut off. I hadn't realized it had been humming so loudly until it did and the ocean and its birds became audible.

"Do you love her?"

"Yes," I said without thinking, then reacted with surprise when I heard myself.

The pool rippled in the silence that followed, and the webs of blue light grew wider as the water stilled.

"Yes." I turned back to my mother. "I do love her."

"The tingle's never wrong."

"I love her." I said the words normal speed but rolled them around my mouth. Felt the rattle of the opening vowel, the pinch of my teeth on my tongue with the first sounds of *love*, the soft breath passing my lips for *her*.

"So," my mother said, "what are you going to do about it?"

On the tabletop, I drew an invisible five-sided shape. A house fit for a family.

I tapped the center of it.

"I'm going to win."

CHAPTER 34

BYRON

I could barely sleep. Never in my life had I ever been so eager to lose. Never had I seen the upside of a loss or anticipated surrender with such excitement. On the drive home, I drafted my concession in my head.

Your Honor, we've decided to comply with all present and pending environmental regulations. We're redrawing plans and will be submitting them for approval before continuing.

I told no one. Not my lawyers. Not my assistant. Not Logan. Not a whisper that could find Olivia's ears. I wanted to own her surprise completely.

Your Honor, my life's work has brought me no joy. I've had a rush of sanity that the shape and size of this house must conform to. I've asked counsel for a stay until I can have someone draw it with this new vision.

Olivia would be in the back benches, behind me. I wouldn't be able to see her reaction.

She'd get it. She'd understand that the size of the house was only the most obvious part of the story. The rest couldn't be said to her without embarrassing her in front of a judge and her colleagues.

Without speaking to her directly, I had to imply that there were underlying reasons why I was giving up. That I'd been putting myself into something that would never fill me the way she did. That because of her, I was ready to change. That winning her love was worth losing.

Your Honor, I've fought hard for the privilege of building the biggest house in Los Angeles and in the process... enriched half a dozen lawyers (pause for laughter). However, I've had a change of heart. Let someone else build the biggest. I'm going to build a house someone falls in love with.

Then maybe I'd look around to her. Just for a moment.

And she would be surprised.

Or smiling with her hands clenched to her chest.

Or wiping a tear.

Biting her lower lip.

Covering her mouth.

Studiously ignoring me.

I ran them all as I worked on our legal defense as if I wasn't going to sabotage it like a toddler erecting a tower of blocks so he could knock it down for the laughs.

Your Honor, I've reprioritized my goals.

And then, exactly on time, it was morning.

I put on a suit and tie, shaved, brushed my hair, and when I was at my very best for her, I went to the courthouse.

Yusup's gift was his ability to intuit traffic and avoid it, getting us Downtown at rush hour even though Gregory, one of my lawyers, had been five minutes late. Flanked by Gregory and the rest of the legal team I was about to shock, I walked across the park. The morning was perfect. Clear sky. Light breeze.

I scanned the faces walking into the courthouse with us, the people in line at security, the crowd outside the elevators. She wasn't there.

"We're not late," I murmured as the elevator rose.

"No," Gregory said. "Close though. Sorry."

"Not a problem."

I still hadn't decided exactly what to say after *Your Honor*. I needed to get my eyes on her first. Even if she flipped me the bird and sent me a note saying she hated my guts, I was making the statement. The words would change based on how she reacted but not the outcome.

I'd changed because of her, and I was committed to that evolution even if I'd lost her in the process.

The elevator doors opened, and we piled out.

At the end of the hall, a group waited outside the wooden double doors. The senior legal counsel for the Environmental Protection Fund dressed like a man but had a woman's name. Her lapdog, Mitch, was an egg-shaped man in an ill-fitting suit and an Hermès tie.

I recognized a handful of local reporters by their studious attention to everything and the spiral notebooks that made the press badges redundant.

Olivia wasn't talking to them. She wasn't anywhere to be seen.

I looked at my watch. Two minutes.

She wouldn't be late, and neither would the judge.

"Mr. Crowne," the woman in the suit said just as I remembered her name.

"Ms. Tamarin."

"Mx."

"Thank you," I said, making a mental note.

A blond woman in a suit turned the corner, heels clicking. Not Olivia, but she'd directed my attention toward the bathroom.

"Pleasure. I just want to remind you that we can still settle this without wasting time in a courtroom."

We could. In fact, I was going to do her one better, but where was Olivia? Asking would have been inappropriate.

"We're committed to following the law," Gregory said. "And…"

Gregory went on as I'd paid him to do, but I couldn't keep my eyes off the hall. If she'd been in the bathroom, she'd have been out by now. Wouldn't she? Did I have time to check?

The double wooden doors slapped open. A bailiff a couple of inches taller than me stood in the center of the doorway.

"Environmental Protection Fund vs. Crowne Properties," the bailiff said.

"At least we agree on something," Tamarin said, entering the flow of traffic into the courtroom.

I didn't know what she and Gregory agreed on, because my lawyers joined the flow, and I was expected to fall in line. I stopped right outside.

"Give me a minute," I said, gesturing down the hall.

"Forty-five seconds, Mr. Crowne." Gregory pointed at the clock above the door as if highlighting the dead-serious matter of punctuality.

I did everything but run down the hall. Big steps. No delay turning the corner. Two doors with big, blue circles and white silhouettes. I pushed the lady and peeked inside.

A woman with a rolling cart of files was washing her hands.

"Olivia!" I called.

"Sir," she said sternly, making eye contact in the mirror.

"Olivia!"

"The court doors opened." She pumped the towel dispenser. "No one's here."

I walked in, and she brushed past me with her cart behind her. I looked under stall doors.

God damn. Where was she? Where the fuck was she?

An ebony-skinned woman I recognized as Olivia's legal assistant rushed out of the last stall.

"Uh..." she said when she saw me.

"Where's Olivia?"

She hesitated, then went to a sink to wash her hands.

"Please," I said. "I mean her no harm. I just... Why isn't she here?"

"She had a doctor's appointment."

"What kind of doctor?"

She shook the water off her hands. "Back up."

I moved out of her way. She ran down the hall to make it back in time. I was right behind her without a second to spare.

The gallery was half-empty, but the chairs on the left side of the room were all taken with her colleagues. The judge was a woman in her sixties with blond, shoulder-length hair and reading glasses she could easily deliver a death glare over.

Besides her, all eyes were on me standing between the two tables as I calculated the days since our broken condom. She'd had an insemination appointment the next day.

I didn't like the number I came up with.

What was the doctor's name? She'd said it.

This was now. No time for drama.

"Your Honor," I said, "I want—"

"Can you identify yourself, sir?" she said.

Galang. His name was Galang.

"I'm Byron Crowne, the owner—"

"Your Honor." Gregory stood. "Mr. Crowne—"

"Sit down, Gregory," I said.

"You should sit with your counsel, Mr. Crowne," the judge said. "Then we can get started."

"I have something to say first."

"Wait your turn. My courtroom isn't a theater."

"Yes. I know, but..." I took a breath. "Your Honor—"

"I will hold you in contempt if you don't sit down."

They'd take me away and hold me for a few hours. By the time I paid my way out, it would be too late.

"Your Honor, I'm dropping this matter with the intention of complying fully."

Gasps from the left met groans from my lawyers on the right.

"And you need to turn my courtroom into a circus to do that?"

"Please. I have an emergency that can't wait."

She took her glasses off to get the full measure of me. "What kind of emergency?"

"Personal," I said. "It's my family."

She put her glasses back on and looked at the papers in front of her.

"Byron!" Gregory said in a cross between a shout and a whisper. "What the—"

"It's over," I said. "I'll fill you in later."

"All right," the judge said. "Counsel will confer in the jury room. We will reconvene and put the final agreements on the record."

The room burst into murmurs.

I spun around and out the doors to beat the crowd and the questions.

CHAPTER 35

OLIVIA

I'd left the house early because I had to keep moving or drown in doubt. At a table in the cheap cafe on the first floor of Dr. Galang's office building, I watched the traffic on Sunset. The building was twenty-four stories of medical offices. Tables and chairs were gathered around a fountain out front. Executives from the surrounding talent agencies scurried across the street and through the lobby for a quick coffee. The city kept moving. Only I was still.

Eight in the morning. The courtroom doors were opening.

Byron was there. He was probably looking for me. Maybe wondering where I was. Probably relieved he didn't have to look me in the eye.

I'd made the right decision. I wouldn't have been able to bear seeing him right before the insemination. He was the dream of having it all, and that had slipped through my fingers. Seeing him would have made me want to catch some part of it. In his green eyes and steady, commanding voice, I'd have lost my will to refuse to settle. I'd let the clock tick down for months, grasping for a love that was always out of my reach. I couldn't do that to myself. I didn't deserve a lifetime of disappointment.

Eight fifteen.

Motions to dismiss. Rejections of same. Opening statements. Kimberly was an absolute genius and would add some obvious-seeming twist of logic his team would scramble to meet.

Eight thirty. My coffee was cold. The traffic on Sunset was at its peak, and I was already late. I tossed my cup into the trash and took the door to the lobby.

The elevators were across the sun-drenched space. A wall of glass looked out onto the fountain in front of the building, and I took a moment to glance at it as I made my way past. A black Bentley drove up onto the sidewalk as if that was perfectly legal and slowed.

When I saw the driver, my skin tingled with recognition.

Before the car was fully stopped or I was in control of my shock, the back door flew open.

"Byron?" I whispered to myself as he bounded up the steps, unbuttoned jacket flying.

The Bentley moved off the sidewalk, and the man I couldn't bear to hope to ever see again opened the glass doors, gaze darting all over the lobby before landing on me.

The tingle had dissolved into pure energy, leaving me in a state of numb focus on the narrow space between Byron and me. I couldn't break it to go to him, nor to run away. My will to do anything at all was preoccupied with adjusting to this man coexisting in the same space.

He buttoned his jacket and closed the distance between us. My pupils tightened on him, and everything around us went dark except the light in his eyes. Just before his lips moved to speak, I remembered why I was there and what he'd refused me.

Everything.

"What are you doing here? Did you win?"

"Maybe." He paused, holding back a smile. "I took a loss."

"What?"

"I'm changing the house. For you."

The world, with its bright lights and sounds, flooded back. Was that why he was here?

"You think this was about a house?"

"No." He smiled at his own folly and opened his arm toward the café I'd left. "Can we talk? I want to start over. Just—"

"I'm late for an appointment." I tore myself away and walked toward the elevators.

"No." He got in front of me. "Listen. I know why you're going up there."

"And?"

"And don't. Please."

"Byron. What do you want out of me? I'm just trying to live the life I want."

"I know." His fingers curled with the tension of holding back one thing to say another thing he couldn't.

"You don't want to be a part of it. You can't be what I need. Okay, fine. Just get out of my way."

I went past him, but he shifted until he was blocking me again. People were watching. He was going to make a scene.

"I'm going to be late," I said through my teeth.

"Don't do this. Please. I'll go insane. I'll lose my mind. When I think of another man's child inside you, even though he's a good man, a friend to you, a great uncle—I'm not insulting him, but just... He's not me." His pleas dropped in volume and grew in intensity, and I changed my posture before some well-meaning person called security. "Someone else writing himself inside your body... Olivia, it drives me to a despair I can't fight. Not disappointment, but misery."

"You don't want what I need."

"It's not about what I want anymore. I'm a foolish, conceited man.

Whatever fate gave me, whatever the advantages, it didn't give me the sense to see my own heart. But I can't unsee it now. I can't cling to my idea about myself while you live in the world. I can't. Please. Let me look into a child's eyes and see both of us there. I'll do whatever you want. Whatever. You. Want."

"I can't…" I said before shutting down out of self-preservation. I couldn't ask for it. I couldn't reach for everything and come up short again. My face crumpled, and a tear fell onto my cheek. I wiped it with the back of my hand.

"I can." He took my biceps in his hands and bent to eye level. "I love you, Olivia."

I must have misheard him. "You what?"

"I. Love. You. I swear it. God help me, I love you so much I'm more alive. I'm happy when I'm near you. I love you selfishly, jealously… I love you so completely I can't deny it anymore. Not for another second. You've written your name inside me. Please… Olivia." He closed his eyes. "Please say you still love me."

When he opened them, I saw him through a cloud of tears, and when I blinked, they dropped like rain.

"I'd say…" I couldn't finish past the hitch in my breath. He handed me a handkerchief. "I'd say this is a game you're playing because you're a possessive, hateful asshole."

"I am."

"But you're not a liar."

"Not today."

I balled up the damp handkerchief and looked away from him to the people moving in and out, the fountain in the front, the sun crawling higher in the sky, and the clock behind the security counter, its hands moving ever forward.

Putting my eyes back on Byron, who hadn't moved in the passing seconds, I took a deep breath. "Some things change. But I love you and I always will."

The joy in his smile flashed, and for a moment, he was the happy boy in the painting.

He kissed me, and I closed my eyes to taste all the layers of his happiness, knowing that I'd see it again, over and over, for the rest of my life.

EPILOGUE 1

BYRON

She waddled.

Olivia pacing the Crownestead garden with her phone stuck to her ear was the cutest fucking thing I'd ever seen in my life. I couldn't take my eyes off the way she walked as if her hip joints were coming unglued… until a volleyball smacked my head so hard I saw stars.

"Hey!" Olivia shouted.

"I'm fine!" I said when the grass took on a normal hue and the sun didn't look like a hole in a cardboard box.

"Logan!" she shouted, pointing her phone at him like an accusing finger, undeterred by my fineness or anything else. "You did it on purpose."

She was due in a few weeks and a little… on edge.

"I did not," he said from the other side of the net.

He most certainly had done it on purpose.

"Forget it." I snapped up the ball. "I'm fine."

"Not like I hit any vital organs." Logan shrugged.

I tossed him the ball, but even pregnant, Olivia appeared out of thin air and grabbed it mid-arc and waddled back to me.

"Did he concuss you?" she asked, touching the red spot.

"There's not even a bump."

"You should lie down."

I didn't need to lie down. I needed one more point to crush the insect on the other side of the court. Except he wasn't there anymore. "Where's that little turd?"

"Talking to your father." She tilted her chin at the glass door, which was open so Ted and Logan could talk. "You win."

"Excellent." I kissed her. "You had lemonade." I kissed her again to get another snap of Nellie's ginger lemonade.

"Yes." She put her arms around my neck, and I put my hands on her waist, pressing her belly to mine.

"What did your mother say?"

"She's not cutting you a deal on the house."

"But I'm a developer with an all-cash offer."

"One of many."

I felt an urgent shift against my stomach. The baby kicking.

"He's getting impatient," I said between lemon-drop kisses. "Trying to beat the clock."

"Trying to get you to close on that monstrosity in Bel-Air."

The monstrosity didn't live up to the hype. A scant thirty-four thousand square feet with gardens, a hedge maze, and specially cordoned off where the creek's boundary fell, it was even modest.

Eleven months after changing the plans and one week left to completion, I already had offers on it. Once it was done, sold, and off my plate, Olivia and I were getting secretly and quietly married. Then we'd have our son.

"For fuck's sake," Logan cried, "she doesn't need to be resuscitated."

I ignored him to kiss her, imagining all the ways I'd own her body when it was healed. I enjoyed being gentle with her, but we both craved our old selves.

"Byron," my father's voice followed, and I pulled away from Olivia long enough to look over at him. "Come join us in my office."

"Better go," she said. "Before we start something you can't finish the way we want."

We parted, and I jogged to the house.

* * *

TED CROWNE KEPT an office at Crownestead. It was more of a sitting room overlooking the side yard, but he still oversaw Crowne Industries operations and needed to sit behind a desk sometimes.

Logan sat across from him, and I sat in the chair next to him. Outside, Olivia and Mom drank lemonade. My mother was comfortable enough around Olivia to drink through a straw as they watched the sun set.

"What's this about?" I asked. Our father hadn't called an across-the-desk meeting in years. Not since I'd abdicated my succession rights.

"Fucked if I know."

Dad shut the sliding wooden door and moved behind his desk. "Gentlemen." Dad hitched up his trousers before sitting. "So, your mother is getting worse. This was completely expected. It's a degenerative disease. You boys don't have to look like I slapped you."

"Shouldn't Dante and Colton be here?" Logan asked. "What about Lyric?"

"All of us have an interest," I added. Intentionally or not, Logan always forgot Liam.

"This is business," Dad said. "Which means it's you two."

"Then why's this guy here?" Logan jerked his thumb in my direction.

"Logan's shutting up now so you can finish."

"Thank you." Dad directed his gratitude at Logan. "She's getting the best care available. We're moving a staff in. But..." He tapped his fingertips against one another. "She needs me. More of me, more of the time. And I need her."

The energy that came off Logan could have lit up a city, but when I glanced at him, he was all business. Good for him.

"So, first things first, we're moving out of Crownestead and back down to Los Angeles."

"Why?" Logan objected. "Mom loves it here."

"She wants to be near her children, and whatever she wants, she gets. She has a property in mind. She saw the house. It's wheelchair accessible—when it comes to that. I suggest… both of you… to not try to talk her out of it."

"Fine," Logan said.

"Where is it?" I asked so I could gauge the neighborhood, the price, and the best way to make it perfect for her.

"Bel-Air," Dad said.

"Great," I said like a fucking idiot. "The neighborhood council loves me now. I need to see it sooner rather than later."

"Jesus," Logan said under his breath.

Dad leveled his gaze at me, and for a moment, I felt as if everyone knew Colton's missing Range Rover was at the bottom of the lake except for me. Again.

"You built it, son."

"Ah, Dad…"

"It's perfect."

"I didn't have you in mind when I started it."

"You didn't when you finished it either. Don't worry, we'll pay market unless we're outbid. Then we'll match it."

"No bidding, Dad. If Mom wants it, it's hers."

"Are you serious?" Logan said. "The OBT goes to some environmental fund, and now you're paying market for the house it was supposed to build?"

I hadn't needed the money to make the house smaller, nor would I ever need it. I had everything I'd ever wanted.

"What's the difference?" Dad asked.

"We're not negotiating? Just, 'Here… Take it'? It should go to Crowne for cost."

"Mind your business, twerp."

"Exactly." Logan jammed his finger in my direction. "It's business. This business. Which is my business. Dad—"

"And there's something else," Dad said. "If you two can get your thumbs out of each other's eyes for a minute, I'll tell you."

We took a breath.

"Logan." Dad looked at his second son. "Your mother and I talked about this… God, if I could count the hours we talked. We've watched you work yourself ragged to prove you can manage an international company the size of Crowne. But every time I ask you what you want out of your life—just a month ago was the last time—you say you want what your mother and I have."

"I do. You guys are perfect. So?"

"How are you going to get it like this? Twenty-two-hour days. Constant travel. The last time you socialized, it was to practice Cantonese."

"You managed."

"We were stupid. We got married at eighteen, before Uncle Jerry died. Before I knew it would be mine. You're running into a lonely life like a starving man chasing a sandwich."

"You're telling me to date? Dad. Come on."

"I'm telling you to get married."

"What?" Logan sat straight up with his hands leveraged against the arm rests as if he were preparing to launch.

"Dad?" I said incredulously. "Are you serious?"

Our father laid his hands flat on the blotter. "Your mother and I don't care how much money you make in a lifetime. Or how much you grow the business. She said, and I quote, 'I will die weeping if the room dims before my babies find their happiness.' Which isn't her best bit of verse—"

"Just get married?" Logan interrupted. "Should I pick a girl off the street? Hire someone? What even is this?"

I held my hand in front of Logan's chest as if he were in the passenger seat and I was coming to a screeching halt. "Dad, is this even legal? What did Joe say?"

"The board follows my lead," Dad sat back in his chair. "And management is contingent on my approval. I don't have to put my children in charge, you know."

"What if I'm like this asshole?" Logan jerked his thumb at me. "I'll be dead before I'm married."

"He has a point," I added.

"The fact that Byron's happy has changed the whole equation for us. So, you can blame him for what I'm about to offer, but it's not negotiable."

"I don't want to hear it." But Logan didn't move. He sat at attention with his foot shaking in pent-up frustration.

Dad said, "Effective immediately, I'm resigning as CEO of Crowne Industries so I can spend more time with my ailing wife. I'll maintain a controlling interest in voting shares, but I'll otherwise take on an advisory role from my new home in Bel-Air."

"Who's running it, Dad?" Logan growled.

"Byron."

"What?" Logan snapped.

"Whoa, whoa!" I held out my hands to slow this fucking freight train down to the sound barrier.

My brother looked as baffled as I was. "Why?"

Dad leaned up and folded his hands on the desk. "Byron, you were raised to do this. You're more experienced, and with what's coming..."

He jerked his chin toward Mom and Olivia at the table outside. "You've become a serious, capable, and thoughtful man."

"I don't want it."

"That's the point. You're the only one who can do it well *and* easily give it up when Logan gets settled."

"Married," said Logan. "You mean married."

"Joe says you haven't bought another property. Correct?"

I'd lost interest in putting my name all over the city. Pissing in every corner, as Olivia would say. I'd finished the builds I had going, was managing the properties I'd decided to keep, and now I spent my days and nights enjoying her and the anticipation of our son.

"Correct."

"Will you do it?"

"If I don't?"

"Yes or no."

He was depending on me. Without my agreement, he'd either have to place someone over Logan—someone who wouldn't step down without a fight—or stay on and lose time with Mom.

"Yes," I said. "I got it."

My brother looked at the ceiling. I knew he felt betrayed by both of us.

"So. Logan." Our father leaned toward his second son. "Go out. Have fun. Meet people. Learn what you can from Byron."

"How long?" Logan's expression was pitch black.

"If you're not married by your fortieth birthday, we'll revisit." Dad put his hands on the desk and stood. "Meeting adjourned."

EPILOGUE 2

OLIVIA

In the dark and quiet of the night, I was on my back with my knees up, watching the ceiling fan rotate. Byron was curled up next to me with his hand on our son's kicking pulse, finishing a story.

"And then he stood up and said, 'Meeting adjourned,' and walked out."

"Wow."

"Logan just sat there staring straight ahead."

I faced him. "You're not going to do it, are you? Run the whole thing? I mean, you just said you would so your brother could keep the job. Right?"

He shrugged.

"Byron Crowne!"

"What? I know how." He rolled onto his back and laid his wrist on his forehead. It was his turn to watch the fan. "It's just hiring the right people and delegating. Half of that's done already."

"No, I mean you're not actually going to support this medieval requirement that he get married?"

"Is that what you meant?"

"Yes."

"So, you wouldn't mind if I did?"

"What? Run the company?"

"You've been working all this time. I've been slacking off, and I need... something."

"A life?"

"You're my life, Beauty."

"Lord Byron." I rolled onto my side and draped my arm over his chest, feeling the muscle under his T-shirt. "You are a clever, brave, and dangerously handsome individual. A man like you shouldn't be locked up. You need to do things. Take on projects. Fight hard and win big."

He stroked my arm absently, and I wove my legs in his.

"Then I just give it up when Logan turns forty or gets a wife?"

"Yep." I ran my hand over his torso. I was huge and cumbersome, but I wanted him. My body flipped like a switch as if I wasn't already pregnant.

"Surrender," he said.

"You get used to it." A trickle of moisture ran from between my legs to the back of my thigh.

"Just... here you go. Take it all..."

"Byron?"

"Yes?" He kissed my forehead.

"I think my water broke."

***

We had the obstetrician on the phone as we piled into the Bentley. He'd started out calmly telling us we could make it back to LA with hours to spare but seemed less convinced as the contractions got closer. By the time we pulled into Sequoia, he was barking out instructions as he muscled toward the car.

We held it together long enough to get to delivery.

It was all a blur after that. I was a rag doll made for poking, carrying, and feeding ice. The pain was behind the epidural, but I was tired… so tired. Pushing took so much strength. More than I had on a good day. I wept with exhaustion, and still, for the hundredth time, they made me push one more time.

And like that, through the noise of the machines and the men and women talking, there was an earth-shattering cry of frustration and rage from a set of tiny new lungs.

"Hey." Byron's face blocked the light, and his mask moved when he spoke. "You did it."

"I did it," I repeated mindlessly.

"You were amazing."

"I was…" The fugue was lifting into stark awareness. "Where is he?"

"Doctor's checking him out."

"Want to see." I took Byron by the neck of his scrubs and clenched the fabric in my fist. "Now. I want him now."

"Hang on." He moved, letting the bright light hit my face.

I opened my fist and closed my eyes. "Byron. Where are you?"

The light was blocked again, and I opened my eyes to find him there. He laid a weight on my chest, and I wrapped my arms around my son. I burst into tears again, not with exhaustion but gratitude.

This warm little baby, smelling of soft biscuits and vanilla milk, was everything I'd ever wanted, and the man standing over me with a smile under the blue mask was everything I'd been afraid to hope for.

I'd been given more than I'd ever dared to fight for.

I had it all.

Thank you for reading *Iron Crowne*.
Logan's story, *Crowne of Lies*, is FREE on Kindle Unlimited.

Get CROWNE OF LIES today!

KEEP FLIPPING to read an excerpt from Logan's story.

CROWNE OF LIES

Logan Crowne needs one year from Ella.

Twelve months living in his house, holding his hand, wearing his ring on her finger, and in exchange, she'll get her father's company in the divorce settlement.

They have one year to convince his skeptical parents that they're happily in love, and he's settled enough to run Crowne Industries.

Ella wants the company badly enough to live with a man who will never love her. She'll sleep in his room and kiss him for show.

Her heart may melt whenever he's around, and his touch may ignite a fire inside her, but surrender will break her heart.

She's sure she can last a year without giving him her body.

She's wrong.

Get CROWNE OF LIES today!

CROWNE OF LIES EXCERPT

LOGAN

"I think we should win," Byron said. "That's what I think."

The conference room we'd occupied for the past four hours still smelled of dinner, and the halls outside it were quiet. The head of supply and the VP of operations were catching my brother up on shit he would have known if he'd been around.

"There's no point to winning the contract if we overpay for it," I said.

"We can make money back," Byron said as if there was nothing more obvious. "Losing damages our reputation. Forever. You want to risk that for a few pennies on the dollar?"

This fucking guy. He couldn't read an EPS report or between the lines of an MD&A, but here he was tossing numbers around as if he were on a Mardi Gras float.

My phone rang. Mandy.

"I think we should pick this up in the morning," I said, standing.

The operations VP closed his folder.

I slid into the hall, whispering, "Well?"

"You owe me," Mandy said.

"She in?"

"Open to the idea. It's going to cost you."

"How much?" I closed the door to my office.

"A strategic buyout of her father's company."

"I need you to be more specific. This WalMart or the corner store?"

"If I tell you who she is, you're on for a meeting. Okay?"

The interior walls of my office were glass, and I watched Byron walk down the hall with the VP, talking like a man making a point. Probably selling him on spending a few more pennies on the dollar.

"Agreed," I said.

"The company is Basile Papillion."

"Ella," I said without hesitation.

"I knew you'd remember. See? It was meant to be."

Ella Papillion.

What did I remember?

Cute. Very cute, actually. Smart. Dead mother. The age difference was a joke now, but at the time, she'd seemed too young to touch.

I remembered her alongside Millie, my senior year girlfriend and director of the school theater production. Her costumer had been a sophomore, still been young enough to be called a prodigy, pins in her mouth, hunched over a sewing machine or sketching so quickly my girlfriend hardly had to finish a sentence.

Cooper Santon was supposed to be investigating the rest, but I couldn't wait. I had Mandy arrange a meeting for the next evening. Ella insisted on her place. I was already halfway across Beverly before Cooper called. I pulled over to take it.

"You have five minutes," I said when I picked up.

"You didn't give me a lot of time."

"Fast, cheap, and good, Coop. You get two out of three in life and I didn't bother with cheap. So tell me what I paid for."

"Okay. Ella Papillion. She still works at her father's company. Lives on—"

"Highland Ave. I know."

"It's not zoned for a residential lease."

"Anything else?"

"Like I said, I didn't have a lot of time."

"Yes, you said that."

"There aren't any liens against her." He rattled off the relevant facts. "No drug arrests. No mental health issues I can see. And—you said this was important, so I made sure before I called—the internet's clean. No bad publicity with her name on it."

"No drug arrests."

"Right."

"The specificity is weighing on me, Coop."

"That's what you asked about. Specifically."

"Has she broken any laws that matter?"

"She was into graffiti as a kid. Got picked up for vandalism and trespass in 2007. Pled and took the fine. Then again in 2008. Community service picking up garbage on the side of the 101."

That was after I knew her. She'd left Wildwood School a few months before I graduated, leaving Millie without spring production costumes. Must have had a few downhill years after her father got remarried.

All of that was a long time ago. I had a few hours to decide if I could live with it.

"Thanks," I said. "Do you have an opinion? A gut reaction?"

"Depends what you want with her. Would I date her? Yeah."

"Would you marry her?"

"If I loved her. Wouldn't give her my bank account numbers right off."

"Thanks, Coop."

We hung up and I pulled back onto Beverly with a few minutes to ask myself how desperate I really was. How important was getting married? How much time did I have before Byron wedged himself in so deep I couldn't get rid of him? Every day for six months, he'd gotten more comfortable. He kept his woman happy, played around on the floor with his son, and ran a multinational business with me. Every day, he proved he could handle Crowne and a personal life without breaking a sweat, and every day I wasn't married, I proved I couldn't.

My father held the keys. He was in charge of succession and wanted a Crowne to run the business. It had always been Byron, until his first fiancée committed suicide and he left to flip real estate. Then my father turned to me, and I jumped in with an exhilaration I'd never felt before, working at his side for six years until he decided I wasn't happy enough.

Byron was winning. He thought everything was about winning, but it wasn't. It was about getting in the ring and staying on your feet for every round. Beaten bloody, aching from the battle, ears ringing so loudly you could barely hear the last bell—that was the point.

Born two and a half years apart, we'd spent one season in the same Little League division, but on different teams. He hated baseball, and I figured he stayed in another year just to play against me. He pitched. I hit. And when our teams met in the playoffs, the fucker beaned me cold. Swore he didn't do it on purpose. Maybe he hadn't. But I'd be damned if I was going to let a pinch runner take that base. Damned if I wasn't going to steal a second and drag my ass up to the plate in the next inning.

I was a hitter. I knew where to put the ball. And when he sent an off-speed pitch I saw coming a mile away, I sent it right to his fat fucking head. He dodged but couldn't catch it, and I got to second.

It was the last time he let a man on base, but I stole third and made it home on a sac fly. It was the last run we needed to win, so fuck him. When we got home, he apologized and I slept like a concussed baby for fourteen hours.

For him, anything less than total domination was a loss.

I was more surgical. I wanted what I wanted. He could have the rest.

And I wanted Crowne. I didn't want to lie to get it, but I had to, and I had to lie now or let Byron take everything.

The address on Highland was in a semi-industrial zone on a block of converted warehouses built when the neighborhood was one big storage unit for Hollywood studios. Most had been turned into restaurants and furniture stores. Ella Papillion's sat between two galleries and had a billboard on the roof. The barred steel door and small window in front had been integrated into a graffiti-style mural that said BREAK SHIT.

Not a great sign.

My family would have to be convinced I'd marry into a message like that.

I turned around the corner and found the back alley. Two cars were parked behind her building. An El Camino that had been dark blue when it came off the factory floor, but was now a cool gray, and a new black Toyota Camry.

I pulled my BMW into the last available space and got out, then went up the concrete steps to the metal door, which was ajar. I pushed it open. "Hello?"

The space stretched to the front of the building. Clean white wall on one side. Fucking mess of small, stacked canvases on the other, along with shelves of paint, brushes, a slop sink, a drafting table, and a mismatched couch and chairs that looked as if they'd been dragged in from the street.

The white wall had a single, seven-foot-high, five-foot-wide blank canvas on it. The fluorescent light made it seem to glow.

A door in the back of the white side opened, and Ella stepped through. "Hey, Logan."

Not the same girl. First off, she was pierced. Nose. Ears all the way around. Her wavy black hair was pinned to the top of her head, and her eyes seemed to be a paler brown. Almost amber. The freckles I remembered from high school had paled, making her seem sexy instead of young. She wore a black choker and a sleeveless *Star Wars* T-shirt that hugged her curves. The ripped jeans sitting low on her waist were painted, patched with contrasting thread, and wide on the bottom in a way that was out of style, but somehow right with the red cowboy boots.

"Ella," I said. "Nice to see you again."

"You too."

She was looking at me the same way I looked at her. Taking stock of my face, my suit, with her thumbs hooked in her belt loops, ringed fingers tapping her hips.

Bit of a challenge, this one. Maybe I'd make a deal with her. Maybe I wouldn't. But no matter what my decision was, I wanted her to agree to the proposal. I wanted her to want it as desperately as I needed it.

I said, "You look good."

"Let's not start with bullshit, okay?"

Before I could answer, a man came from the same door. Six-three. Built. Dressed for business and looking right through me.

"Logan Crowne," Ella said. "This is my friend, Amilcar Wilton."

We shook hands and I wondered if the El Camino was his. That would be a kind of relief.

"Good to meet you," he said.

"Same."

He turned to Ella and nodded. "I'm out."

"Yeah?" she answered as if he'd said more than two innocuous words.

"Yeah." He kissed her cheek, and though she and I hadn't agreed to a damn thing, my blood ran a little hotter and my hands tightened into fists as if she was already mine.

"Okay," she said. "I'll call you later."

"See you," Amilcar said to me as he passed.

Behind me, the door closed and we were alone.

"Cool place," I said.

"Thanks. You want to sit?"

"Before I get comfortable, Mandy said you were single. That meant unattached. Completely unattached."

Outside, a car started in the back alley. It wasn't the rumble of an El Camino, but the whirr of a new Camry.

"You mean Amilcar?" she said, eyebrows raised. "No, no. He's a friend. A good friend, but you know... *just* a friend."

"Ah. Right. Just checking."

"Full disclosure. I wanted him here to meet you. He's a first impressionist. It's like a gift. One look and he knows."

Every person who knew about what I was trying to arrange was a potential leak, and if my family found out, I could kiss Crowne goodbye. I didn't know this Amilcar person well enough to trust him.

"You told him?" I asked.

"I said you and I are dating, if that's okay."

"And he gets an impression of everyone you date?"

"I wanted to make sure you're not just trying to get laid."

"I don't need to go to this much trouble to get laid."

"Or maybe you're a serial killer."

"I didn't kill Millie. We just broke up."

She laughed.

"Sit." She indicated a worn couch and two chairs around a chest that served as a coffee table. "I've got a pot of water boiling. Or soda. I have Sprite. But..." She looked me up and down again, and I squinted at her as if that would help me discern what she was seeing. "I can get you a glass of milk if you want that."

Milk?

"Whatever you're having."

I'd be fucked before I let her get milk out of the fridge just for me, because even though it didn't matter what she thought of me as a man, I cared.

Get CROWNE OF LIES today!

ALSO FREE IN KINDLE UNLIMITED

The *New York Times* bestselling Games Duet

Adam Steinbeck will give his wife a divorce on one condition. She join him in a remote cabin for 30 days, submitting to his sexual dominance.

Marriage Games / Separation Games

* * *

Monica insists she's not submissive. Jonathan Drazen is going to prove otherwise, but he might fall in love doing it.

<u>COMPLETE SUBMISSION</u>

* * *

Theresa Drazen is about to accept a proposition from the most dangerous man in Los Angeles.

<u>COMPLETE CORRUPTION</u>

* * *

Fiona Drazen has 72 hours to prove she isn't insane, just submissive. Her therapist has to get through three days without falling for her.

<u>FORBIDDEN</u>

* * *

Margie Drazen has a story and it's going to blow your mind.

THE SIN DUET

* * *

CONTEMPORARY ROMANCES

Hollywood and sports romances for the sweet and sexy romantic.

Shuttergirl | Hardball | Bombshell | Bodyguard | Only Ever You

ACKNOWLEDGMENTS

This is the space where I acknowledge my failings and apologize for any instance where you said, "Nope." I encourage you to contact me with errors you've noticed. If you have experience on the subject (you are a medical professional or patient, lawyer or developer), I will make every effort to correct the text.

I'm not a lawyer, but Jean Siska is. Her help with this book cannot be overstated. If it seems like I know what I'm talking about, it's because she does. I did contract the calendar for this sort of legal action because I needed to. If you find other inaccuracies, don't call Jean. That's me.

The timeline. Shoot. Me. Now. I'm not a fertility doctor, nor have I ever been a patient of one. Not that it matters, because if you take the Clomid through days three and seven without a trigger shot, you get your IUI on days ten to sixteen, which is staggeringly unhelpful. With a trigger shot means there's a two-day window where your eggs will drop, which is less staggering but still not helpful. I need rules. I need to fill out a calendar. But the human body isn't into accuracy, nor is the medical profession.

So, I did what I always do. I researched the hell out of the thing and fudged the text, because in weighing the emotional trajectory against factual accuracy, emotions win every time... as long as they don't take readers out of the story or put Olivia in the doctor's office *constantly*.

For those of you who have undergone these treatments, you are goddesses and paragons of patience. You have my utmost respect. This process is not for the weak.

Thank you to my Facebook fan group for keeping my head above water during a difficult year. You'll never know what you did for me and I hope I can repay you with more books in less time.

You really should preorder Logan's book right now.

Made in the USA
Las Vegas, NV
25 June 2021